Praise for
The Fangover

"Outrageously funny and romantic."   —*Night Owl Reviews*

"There is a lot of humor in this romance, and that is where the writers truly shine. *The Fangover* is the perfect story for readers looking for a more lighthearted vampire romance."   —*Romance Junkies*

"A new, hilarious romance version of *The Hangover*, with an erotic supernatural twist."   —*Fresh Fiction*

Praise for the novels of *USA Today* bestselling author

ERIN McCARTHY

"Steamy . . . Fast paced and red-hot."   —*Publishers Weekly*

"A runaway winner! Ms. McCarthy has created a fun, sexy, and hilarious story that holds you spellbound from start to finish."
          —*Fallen Angel Reviews*

"The searing passion between these two is explosive, and the action starts on page one and doesn't stop until the last page. Erin McCarthy has written a fun, sexy read."   —*Romance Reviews Today*

"This is Erin McCarthy at her best. She is fabulous with smoking-hot romances!"   —*The Romance Readers Connection*

Fangs for Nothing

ERIN McCARTHY
and
KATHY LOVE

BERKLEY SENSATION, NEW YORK

THE BERKLEY PUBLISHING GROUP
Published by the Penguin Group
Penguin Group (USA) Inc.
375 Hudson Street, New York, New York 10014, USA

USA I Canada I UK I Ireland I Australia I New Zealand I India I South Africa I China

Penguin Books Ltd., Registered Offices: 80 Strand, London WC2R 0RL, England
For more information about the Penguin Group, visit penguin.com.

This book is an original publication of The Berkley Publishing Group.

Berkley Sensation Books are published by The Berkley Publishing Group.
BERKLEY SENSATION® is a registered trademark of Penguin Group (USA) Inc.
The "B" design is a trademark of Penguin Group (USA) Inc.

Library of Congress Cataloging-in-Publication Data

McCarthy, Erin, 1971–
Fangs for nothing / Erin McCarthy and Kathy Love.—Berkley Sensation trade paperback edition.
pages cm
ISBN 978-0-425-25744-9
1. Vampires—Fiction. I. Love, Kathy. II. Title.
PS3613.C34575F38 2013
813'.6—dc23
2013007611

PUBLISHING HISTORY
Berkley Sensation trade paperback edition / July 2013

PRINTED IN THE UNITED STATES OF AMERICA

10 9 8 7 6 5 4 3 2 1

Cover photography by Claudio Marinesco.
Cover design by Rita Frangie.
Interior text design by Kristin del Rosario.

This book is dedicated to The Outfield.

Wherever you are, whatever you may be doing now,
please know that your song about trying to cheat
on Josie while she's on a vacation far away
still has people dancing every night.

On Bourbon Street anyway.

Chapter One

AGAIN? SERIOUSLY?

WHEN Johnny Malone jerked out of sleep suddenly, he became aware of three things in rapid succession. One, his bandmate Drake Hanover's butt was in a sling, literally, just a few feet away from Johnny's face, cupped in assless leather chaps, his arms slack and head back as he snored loudly. Two, Johnny realized that there was a pale, petite hand spread across his crotch comfortably, like it had been there for quite some time. Three, he had no clue where in the hell he was and his head hurt like a bitch.

Okay, so maybe that was four things, but as he shifted a little from his slumped position on the floor of who the hell knows where, all seemed equally important. The dim room didn't look familiar at all, not that he could see much with Drake blocking his view as he slept in what Johnny thought just might be a sex swing. There was a lot more of Drake dangling in front of him than he had ever wanted to see. Which made his usual stomach of steel more than a little queasy. He supposed he should be grateful he was behind Drake, not in front of him. Actually, neither was a great position to be in if you got right down to it. Struggling not to groan out loud, Johnny swallowed hard and blinked several times. He was clearly not dreaming and he was clearly hungover, which was a feeling he hadn't had in damn near a century. It all came hurtling back to him why hangovers had sucked so bad. He felt like ass.

Speaking of ass, which seemed to be a theme for the night, he wondered if he had gotten any the night before, thus explaining the female hand on his junk. Which could be damn awkward, because he couldn't remember a bleeding thing. The last thing he was aware of was enthusiastically dancing the Cupid Shuffle at his buddy Saxon's wedding, then . . . nothing. Trying not to wake whoever she was, Johnny chanced a look to his left, praying she wasn't hideous.

Oh. My. God.

She wasn't hideous. It was worse.

She was Lizette.

The uptight, paper-pushing French chick who had frozen his assets and was determined to make his life a living hell with her bureaucratic bullshit. She was a rep from the Vampire Alliance, she was beautiful, and she had all the warmth of an iceberg in Alaska during a blizzard. They had argued, he had ditched a meeting with her, and she had tracked him down at the wedding with a systematic determination that scared the shit out of him. One look from her, and his balls had shrunk.

She definitely gave a whole new meaning to the phrase freezing his assets.

He would never have had sex with her. Even if he had been crazy enough to try, she would have stamped a giant DENIED on his dick in red ink.

Yet not only was her sleeping head lying on his shoulder, her very staid and proper blouse mostly unbuttoned, but her right hand, the one that was splayed across his lap?

It was handcuffed to his left wrist.

Johnny practically swallowed his own tongue in an effort to keep his shock and horror from ringing out in the silent room.

Holy crap. This was not good.

Stretching his leg as far as he could without disturbing Lizette, he managed to get his foot on Drake's ass and give him a shove, grateful he was still wearing his boots so there was no skin-on-skin contact.

But Johnny needed some serious help from his buddy.

And metal cutters.

He kicked Drake again, harder.

48 Hours Earlier

"I am here on behalf of the Vampire Alliance to collect the re-mains of Mr. Malone and dispose of his property in accordance with the Death Code. Please allow me full access to his personal belongings at this time. Your cooperation in resolving this matter is greatly appreciated."

Johnny stared at the thin woman in front of him wearing a gray business suit, her hair in a tight bun, clipboard in hand. He listened to her speech, directed at his sister Stella, and was perhaps for the first time in his long life totally at a loss for words. "Um."

"But he's not dead," Stella said with no small amount of bewilderment in her voice.

"I'm not dead," Johnny parroted. Because he wasn't. He may be dead like a vampire was dead, but he wasn't for real dead, as in never-to-walk-the-earth-again dead.

"This is him," Stella added, pointing to his living self. "Standing right here. Next to me."

Stella had called Johnny over to the shotgun cottage on Burgundy Street in the French Quarter that she shared with his best friend, Wyatt Axelrod, because she had gotten a phone call requesting a meeting from the VA regarding Johnny's death. Not the first death, back in '28, but his second one, which he had faked six weeks earlier but had reneged on a few days later. Only it seemed the Vampire Alliance hadn't gotten the memo that it was a joke. A lousy joke, he had to admit, but a joke nonetheless. And if this chick in front of them was any indication, the Vampire Alliance didn't have much of a sense of humor.

"I am sorry, but that is not possible," the woman said, her accent French, her manner calm and professionally polite. She wore designer glasses, and her dark brown eyes behind the lenses barely swept over him. Considering no vampire had bad eyesight, they were clearly intended to make a certain impression. "Johnny Malone is on the list, and so I must proceed accordingly."

"I don't care that he's on 'The List.'" Stella made air quotes as she spoke. "He's not dead! It was just a simple misunderstanding."

Nice of Stella to put it that way. Frankly, it had been a bumble-fuck on his part. Feeling pressured by a pregnant girlfriend, though he used *that* term loosely, and knowing full well that as a vampire he was shooting blanks and could not be the father, Johnny had gotten the incredibly stupid idea that it might be a spot of fun to fake his own death to shake her loose. Okay, so maybe it had been a bit cruel to put his sister and his friends through that, and maybe he would have been super pissed if someone had done that to him, but it had been an impulse. A very bad, very stupid impulse. He hadn't thought it would result in all his friends getting shit-faced drunk at his wake and blacking out for an entire night. Nor had he thought it would result in Miss Paper Pusher showing up on Stella's doorstep.

Not wanting to stress his sister out any more than he had already in the past few months, he decided he needed to be the one to deal with this little mix-up.

"I'm sorry, what was your name again?" he asked her.

"Lizette Chastain."

It was a name for a silent film star, not this woman whose bun was wound too tight. Though she was attractive underneath the thick layer of boring, he had to admit that. She had long cheekbones and creamy skin that gave away her French heritage, and perfect, raspberry-stained lips that would form a perfect O while she was having an orgasm . . .

Whoa. Where had that thought come from? Johnny shifted, suddenly aware of his dick, which hadn't seen much action lately since the debacle with Bambi and her baby-daddy accusations. He couldn't say that he missed Bambi, but he could use a little horizontal shuffle, clearly.

"It's a pleasure to meet you," she continued, her delicate hand coming out to offer a handshake. "May I inquire as to your name?"

Johnny forgot about her bone structure and his boner and realized this was not going to be as easy to fix as he'd thought. So he said, "My name is Johnny Malone, and I'm very much alive. So why don't we head down the street, sit somewhere quiet, and discuss how we can fix your list?" He figured Stella had earned the right to be exempt from mopping up his messes.

She hesitated. "I would prefer we take care of this as soon as possible."

"We will," he assured her. "But let's do it with our butts on a barstool instead of standing in Stella's doorway. We're letting the cool air out of the house."

Her lips pursed, and then she nodded. "I would prefer a coffee shop."

Johnny shot Stella an amused look and waved to her. He indicated to Lizette that she should head out of the house in front of him. "We want to go right. We can go to a coffee shop if you'd like, but the walk will be longer. A lot longer. The closest one is on Dumaine, whereas the nearest bar is—here." He pointed to the corner, which was only one house down from them. "I don't mind walking, though, if you'd really prefer coffee."

"I have no objection to walking," she said. Right before the spiked heel of her shoe got caught in a giant, gravel-filled pockmark of a hole that characterized all the sidewalks in the Quarter.

She made a sound of distress, her ankle turning, and she would have gone down in a French fumble if he hadn't grabbed her arm and managed to keep her upright.

"Oh, *pardon!*" she said, clearly flustered, straightening her glasses and adjusting her purse on her shoulder. Smoothing her hair, she eyed the crumbling walkway with suspicion and added, "Perhaps the bar is not such a bad idea after all. It is rather warm as well, yes, especially for the evening?"

"It's hotter than a crotch," he told her as they walked the few feet to the bar and the magic of air-conditioning. "It's New Orleans in June. The only thing worse is New Orleans in July and August."

"Hotter than a what? I do not recognize that word."

Oops. Now that he had to define it, he realized that might not have been the classiest thing to say to a woman like Lizette. "Um, it refers to the area down south," he said, trying to be vague.

"Geographically? Yes, this is the South, but I still do not understand."

Geez. "I meant on your body. Below the waist. And between

your thighs." He pulled the door open and gestured for her to enter.

She nodded her thanks, clearly puzzling out his words. When understanding dawned, her head whipped back to look at him, cheeks suddenly flaming with color. "Oh! Oh, I see. Yes, well, I understand. So anyway, yes, let's see, we are discussing the demise of Johnny Malone. Do you have any information regarding how he died?"

The broad was not listening to him. He no longer felt so bad for shocking her with crotch talk. "Yes, I can tell you exactly what happened because I'm him."

As they approached the bar, he nodded to the bartender. "Hey, Nigel, what's up?"

"Hey, Johnny, good to see you. Who is your friend here?"

"This is Lizette, from the VA. Apparently Paris thinks I'm dead for real." He turned to her. "Lizette, this is Nigel, who will tell you the full story."

"Dead, huh? Sure, I'll tell you the story, Lizette," Nigel said cheerfully, a British vamp who always remembered to add an extra lime to Johnny's rum and coke. "Stella found a pile of ash and we all thought this bugger was dead. Even had a wake for him. But then he popped up the next day, unharmed and as devilishly handsome as ever. There was much rejoicing. So there you have it."

Sounded about right to Johnny. It was clear and to the point.

Lizette. "So you are saying you really are Johnny Malone?"

At what point had he *not* said that? "Yes. Precisely. I am Johnny Malone and I am alive." Just to clarify for the fifth time.

"But that is not possible. You are on the list."

Johnny wanted to take that list and cram it up a French bureaucrat's ass. "First of all, I need a drink. Nigel, my usual, please.

Lizette, would you like something?" When she shook her head, he continued. "I can understand there was some confusion, but now that you know I'm alive, just stamp 'Still Kicking' on my file and send it back and we're all good."

"I am afraid it is not that simple. You see, until an investigation is launched and the decision is made conclusively that you are in fact Johnny Malone and you are in fact alive, you cannot be removed from the list. No one has the authority to do that."

Was she for real? "Is it carved in stone? Written in blood?"

"Yes, it is written in blood, but that is only for the archival copy. Most of our files are on the computer, of course. Encrypted for privacy."

Sarcasm clearly wasn't her strong suit. Speaking of suits, Johnny marveled that she wasn't sweating in that heavy jacket. She didn't even unbutton it, nor did she look the least bit overheated, despite her comment about the weather. No dewy forehead, no shiny nose. He probably had armpit stains the size of grapefruits on his T-shirt, and he would give his left nut to dive into a swimming pool. Yet she was utterly unflappable.

"So do I have to take a blood test or something?" He honestly had no idea how the Vampire Alliance really worked. He just knew they were a bunch of uptight rule-makers whose mission it was to make sure humans didn't figure out that vampires did in fact exist. Their secondary mission seemed to be pissing him off. He didn't like the idea of just throwing around his DNA, but he didn't want the VA on his back either.

"Yes, as well as a series of interviews with you and your cohorts."

Cohorts? She knew *cohort* but not *crotch*? What the hell were they teaching those kids in Paris? "Fine, whatever you need to do, honey. I'm at your disposal." This is what he got for pretending to commit suicide. So much paperwork, he might actually wish he were dead. He drained the rum and coke Nigel had brought him in two long swallows.

"Excellent. We just need to proceed with the confiscation of your property then while you are undergoing investigation."

"*WHAT?*"

Lizette loved her job, but this was one aspect of it that she did not enjoy. It was difficult to deal with grieving friends of deceased vampires, who wanted to cling to the possessions of the departed. But in order to ensure their survival as a species and prevent detection by humans, it was VA policy that all personal belongings and property of dead vampires be obtained and disposed of appropriately. Photos and clothes were burned, along with locks of hair, furniture and draperies liquidated, and real estate quietly sold. But given that so many vampires reacted poorly to losing every last material bit of a friend, it wasn't unusual for Lizette to show up only to find a friend who claimed the death hadn't occurred at all in order to keep the goods.

Much like this gentleman next to her, consuming his alcohol far quicker than Lizette suspected was wise. He was halfway through his second drink.

Was he Johnny Malone? She did not know. Experience had taught her that he most likely was not, but she would wait and see what the facts indicated. Clearly this bartender had referred to him by the correct name and had given an explanation quite readily, but frankly, to Lizette's ears it had sounded rehearsed. It was also telling that Johnny, as she'd have to call him for now, had suggested this particular bar. Or a bar at all to discuss the matter.

"Rules are rules," she told him apologetically. "In order to ensure that nothing goes missing during the investigation phase, I need to confiscate all your belongings." Reaching into her handbag, she retrieved the list she had printed of all Johnny's possessions.

"Are the majority of these belongings in your apartment on Toulouse Street? Or have they been moved? I realize it has been six weeks since your passing."

Johnny snorted. "Nothing has been moved. I still live there."

"Excellent." Lizette inserted the paper into the clipboard she always carried for ease in going over the list with him. "Does this look like an accurate representation? I believe at this time you have $1312.48 in your bank account, which was frozen as of this morning."

"*What?*" he repeated. "You can't do that!"

"I'm afraid I can," she said, feeling genuinely bad. If he really was Johnny, this was a huge inconvenience. However, the rules were the rules. As she had told him.

He tore the list out of her clipboard, ripping the top-left corner and startling her. "I don't have a lot of stuff. I don't even have my Elvis cookie jar anymore."

"I'm sorry," she said, crossing her legs and wishing she had ordered herself a drink after all, though she never drank when she was working. "You do realize, of course, that you will not be able to enter your apartment while the investigation is ongoing."

He stopped scanning the list to stare at her. "You're fucking kidding me."

"No." Lizette strongly believed in the preservation of their secrecy, or she wouldn't be able to do this job. But after watching her very first lover being captured and tortured in the late nineteenth century, she had vowed to do whatever was necessary to keep vampires out of the reach of dangerous mortals. It might not make her a favorite person among her vampire peers, but she could live with that consequence if it might mean saving a vampire life.

"Where the hell am I supposed to stay?"

"I believe you have a sister?" That was whom the VA had authorized her to contact. "Stella Malone."

"I know who my sister is! But you can't keep me out of my apartment. I need to change my clothes. I have to work. I play in a band on Bourbon. My drum kit is in my apartment."

She gave her best look of apology. "I will try to be as quick as possible. Today is Thursday. Perhaps by next Thursday we will have our answers."

"Next Thursday? Are you insane? I can't lose a whole weekend of work, especially since you're telling me my bank account is frozen." Johnny swore, shoving his empty drink across the dull and scraped bar.

Lizette wasn't afraid, but she was disarmed. Johnny Malone, was, for lack of a better word, arresting. He was not the best-looking man she had ever seen, as his jaw was too square, his nose perhaps too short, but there was something compelling about him. He shifted from annoyed to charmed and back again with very little effort, his emotions clearly displayed on his face for all to see. There were some people who had that special something, that joie de vivre, and he was one of them. It was making it more difficult than Lizette would admit to stay on task.

"I can take a blood sample to start the analysis tonight, then tomorrow I can begin the interviews. If you'll just provide me a list of your confidants, I will be happy to make appointments with them. In the meantime, I will contact headquarters in Paris and await instruction. Can we meet tomorrow at say nine, so I may retrieve the list, and ask you some questions?"

Johnny didn't look at her, but stared morosely at his drink. "I have a wedding to go to tomorrow night. My friend Saxon is getting hitched. It will have to be earlier. Let's say seven."

"I can accommodate that."

"Well, thank you," he said sarcastically.

Lizette frowned, suddenly unsure of what to say. She was used to a belligerent response to her job, and normally she was sympathetic, but she could distance herself from taking it personally. Johnny Malone had her shifting uncomfortably on her barstool. He had a casual nonchalance that roused her ire, yet at the same time intrigued her, as did the unmistakable fact that she found him physically attractive, in spite of the fact that he wasn't traditionally handsome.

Despite what certain vampires may think, like her assistant Dieter, she did notice men. She just chose not to do anything with that acknowledgement. Johnny, if that's who he was, was a man she couldn't help but notice. He had short black hair, the front sticking up slightly with some form of hair product. His skin was cool and alabaster smooth, his eyes an arresting blue, with eyelashes that women would kill for. He was wearing a T-shirt that fit him, instead of the huge shirts a lot of men wore, and his jeans had a tear in one knee, exposing soft dark hair on his thigh. He was the kind of man who gave sly, sexy smiles and kept a woman awake long after the sun rose. And that made Lizette want to clear her throat and be done with this case, because she was not the kind of woman who had casual sexual dalliances.

Unfortunately.

"So we are all set then? Where shall we meet tomorrow?" she asked him. Her cell phone dinged on her clipboard as she spoke, and she murmured, "*Pardonnez-moi*," and glanced at the screen. It was Dieter informing her that he was outside of Stella Malone's, and she quickly texted him her locale.

"So how do you know what stuff I have? Because you know, there is a whole creepy-stalker Big Brother factor to this list," Johnny said, running his finger down the itemization of the contents of his apartment.

"We have our ways," she said vaguely. Ways that usually involved someone on the Retrieval team breaking and entering. Dieter had accomplished that the day before. But in these modern times, there was an element of technology to the process. "It's amazing how much of a paper trail we create without being aware of it. I was surprised that you only have a bank card, but it did allow us to trace your purchases for the last several years." He seemed to spend a large amount of his income on drumsticks and downloaded movies.

"That's invasive. Illegal. Unethical."

Lizette was not intimidated by his irritation. "It's also perhaps the only way you can prove that you are in fact Johnny Malone."

He gave her a long stare. "You're one of those logical chicks, aren't you?"

"I would say so."

His eyes moved past her to the door, and he frowned. "Who is this douchebag?"

Lizette turned. "Oh, that's Dieter, my assistant." She raised her hand in greeting.

Johnny snorted. "Dieter? Perfect name for a tool. What do you need an assistant for anyway?"

Mildly insulted by his assumption that her job was easy, Lizette felt herself frown. "He has his useful qualities. Plus it is less noteworthy for me to be traveling with a man, than as a single woman. Especially in a city full of tourists, like New Orleans. People will simply assume we are a couple."

"The two of you do not look like a couple."

Dieter reached her and immediately placed his hand on her back, something he didn't normally do, and Lizette realized the men were glaring at each other. There was some sort of alpha-male standoff going on. Dieter was larger than Johnny, his German roots giving him broad shoulders and eyes so light they sometimes appeared opaque. There was nothing personal between her and her assistant, nor had he ever indicated interest in such an arena, but at the moment it appeared the men would lock antlers in competition, if they'd had them.

It was rather bizarre, and unnerving. And yet, it was also a teeny bit arousing.

Alarmed at the thought, Lizette leapt to her feet and shifted out of Dieter's touch and away from Johnny, swiping her list out of his hand. "Excellent. I will see you tomorrow at seven then, at your apartment. It's been a pleasure. Have a good evening."

He just gave her an amused smile and a nod. "You, too."

As she walked out of the bar faster than was strictly normal or appropriate, Dieter ambled along beside her, glancing down at her from his substantial height. "How did it go?"

"Fine," she said, in a clipped tone.

"That guy was a pig, by the way. His apartment was a disaster."

"Is that so?" Lizette stared at the sidewalk as she walked, concerned her Louboutin might land in a hole again. It was none of her business really if Johnny Malone was a poor housekeeper. Yet it didn't surprise her.

"Want to go out dancing on Bourbon Street?" Dieter asked.

Lizette shot him a glance. Dieter was grinning, because he already knew her answer.

"Absolutely not. I would like to do an architectural tour of the area, then perhaps see a film."

"Then I'll see you tomorrow night. I'm going to hit the bar scene."

"Do not be conspicuous."

"Do not insult me. I know."

He did. It was their job to blend. Lizette gave him a distracted smile of apology. Dieter went off down the street, and Lizette stood for a second, getting her bearings. If she walked to Bourbon Street, she anticipated she could easily get a cab, but the distance of only two blocks seemed daunting. She would have to reconsider her footwear while on this trip. Even Paris wasn't as crumbling as New Orleans, though she would never recommend traversing Montmartre in four-inch heels. The air was so warm and humid it felt like it surrounded her, embraced her, and Lizette was curious about the city, and somewhat amazed that it was her first trip there. How was it that her work had taken her to Atlanta, Georgia, but never to New Orleans?

She planned to explore as much as possible while she was here, when she wasn't attempting to stay professional around Johnny.

Glancing back toward the bar, she realized he had come out and was standing on the street corner, watching her. When he caught her eye, he saluted.

Embarrassed to be standing around like she was uncertain, Lizette gave a half wave and strode off in the direction of Bourbon Street, head up, purse on her shoulder, determined to look professional. Only to let out a shriek when she walked over a grate and her skirt blew up, exposing her thighs and possibly another thing or two.

It was not an auspicious beginning to this case.

Chapter Two

IT'S A NICE DAY FOR A DOMME WEDDING

"**W**HO the hell would marry Saxon?" Drake shook his head in disgust as he watched the newly wedded groom chatting merrily with a man in an expensive suit.

Any idle observer would have thought the man in the suit was the groom, not the goofy-looking guy with blond hair poking out all over his head like he'd stuck his finger in a light socket earlier in the day.

"Well, he did marry a dominatrix," Cort, Drake's good friend and bandmate, pointed out, taking a sip from a plastic champagne glass filled with something that looked like it had been ladled out of some backwater bayou. Cort grimaced as if it tasted about as good, too. "Besides, is that how the best man should be talking about the groom? Saxon showed you the love. Where's the love for him, man?"

Drake snorted. "Yeah, he showed me the love all right." He gave a pointed look down at his best-man attire. Ruffles of linen and lace spilled down his chest and dripped in cascades from his wrists. "I look like Adam Ant, for Christsake."

Cort sputtered, trying to stifle his amusement, but failed. Miserably.

"I particularly like the pants . . . you can really pull off knee breeches. And shoes with buckles. Although those look a little more leprechaun than pirate," he said, barely getting the words out before dissolving into an outright chuckle.

"Laugh it up," Drake muttered, and then automatically lifted a hand to call over the bartender only to drop it back to the bar when he realized all he'd be able to order was a soft drink or some of that god-awful swamp water Cort had. "If Saxon and his whip-wielding bride are going to make me dress like a goddamn pirate, they could at least have some rum for me."

Cort actually swiped at the tears of amusement dampening his eyes, then after a few more laughs and sniffs, he managed to pull himself together.

"Besides, Saxon likes you better—why didn't he pick you?" Drake pointed out, which wasn't totally true. Cort just happened to tolerate Saxon's "alternative" outlook on the world better than Drake. Saxon didn't really play favorites. He was a bit like a not particularly bright but sweet puppy. He loved everyone.

"Well, that's simple. You two have been in the band together longer than I have. Saxon is pretty loyal."

Yep, definitely just like a puppy.

"Lucky me," Drake grumbled. "He's been in the band just as long with Johnny and Wyatt."

"But would a gangster or a cowboy really make sense for this wedding?" Cort said, looking around at the odd assembly of people as if he were making a valid point.

"Nothing at this wedding makes sense."

Cort didn't even try to argue that. "Well, anyway, you know Saxon loves pirates. And I think it's nice he wanted to take you back to your roots."

It was Drake's turn to snort, but not with amusement. "My roots? I was a lord, my friend. Not a lowly gangster like Johnny. Or a dusty, flea-bitten cowboy like Wyatt. I was Lord Hanover. Pristine bloodlines. Royalty."

"You were a pirate, too, my friend," Cort pointed out with a smirk. "Turning to a life of pillaging and plundering on the high seas? To avoid the penal colony? Because you were framed by your mistress as a thief? Ring any bells?"

Drake gave his friend a haughty look that only a true aristocrat could manage. "That is not a time I want to relive. Especially dressed like some ridiculous extra who wandered off the set of the *Pirates of the Caribbean*."

Cort laughed again.

"I think you look rather dashing," Katie, Cort's wife and eternal ray of vampiric sunshine, said as she joined them. Cort immediately pulled the petite blonde against his side and kissed her temple.

More bitterness welled up in Drake's ruffle-covered chest at the sight of their affectionate embrace.

Who needs this lovey-dovey bullshit all the time? he thought sourly. Sharing an apartment with Cort and Katie, who were also newlyweds—although Drake had long thought their "newly" status had expired months ago—and now being the best man at one of the most ludicrous weddings he'd ever been to was enough to make anyone cranky.

He tugged at his sleeve, and just when he would have ripped off the ruffles oozing from his wrist, Saxon's new wife, Zelda, approached them.

The bride should be the center of attention on her special day, but this woman was impossible to miss any day. Almost six feet tall in bare feet, she was an absolute Amazon in her six-inch, patent leather, thigh-high boots. Above the boots was an expanse of pale thighs encased in fishnets that disappeared under a micromini leather wedding dress. The skintight skirt cinched into a corseted top, which barely contained high, firm breasts that had probably cost her more than the whole wedding.

Especially given what they must have saved on alcohol, Drake thought bitterly. But he did almost admire that this woman dared to wear all white. Her hooha might be perilously close to being exposed to the whole reception, but she was going to wear virginal white.

"Hello, guys," Zelda greeted them with a smile that always made Drake a little nervous. Of course it could be the cat-o'-nine-tails that had also served as her wedding bouquet, which she now absently tapped against her outer thigh. Did Saxon really enjoy whips and chains?

Drake shuddered. That had never been his thing. At all.

Sure, Zelda was hot in a statuesque, unnaturally shapely and intimidating way, but she was definitely not Drake's style.

Out the corner of his eyes, Drake noticed a curvy brunette hurrying through the courtyard toward the cupcake buffet with a fresh tray of minicakes.

Cupcakes.

Even those irritated Drake. But the woman carrying them, on the other hand, now she was more his style—all sweet looking, with ample curves. *Natural,* ample curves. Soft and warm against him, offering him her sexy little body. Yeah, that was how he liked his women.

Not armed. He looked back to Zelda. That was so not his idea of a dream woman.

Of course, he couldn't imagine anyone finding Saxon to be her dream man. Especially not as a husband.

Something about the fact that these two—a flaky vampire keyboard player and a gigantic, silicone domme—had managed to find love, depressed Drake almost as much as the lack of liquor.

Weren't weddings supposed to be uplifting? His gaze returned to the cupcake table, but the curvy woman had disappeared.

"The wedding was beautiful," Katie told Zelda with her usual generosity.

Zelda beamed, her wide, bloodred smile, making Drake uneasy again. Of course, the bouquet/deadly weapon was still swishing idly at her side.

"I think so," Zelda said and the two women sank into conversation about decorations and dresses and wedding songs. Funny, even a Pollyanna-like Katie and a sniff-my-boots dominatrix like Zelda could find common ground discussing wedding preparations.

Cort took another sip of his bog water and perused the scene, seemingly quite content with the festivities, if the courtyard could be described as festive. The tables were decorated with bloodred roses arranged in black miniature coffins. Red candles burned everywhere, and the guests looked like a combination of undertakers, the dead, and the crazy-ass dommes who killed them with . . . with things like—Drake's gaze dropped to Zelda's bridal whip—things like that. Even the cupcakes were decorated with red frosting, black piping, and small silver handcuffs made out of fondant.

At least that part was apropos. Marriage did mean being shackled to someone else. Until death do you part . . . or until the divorce papers were signed.

Drake scanned the crowd once more, then leaned closer to Cort and muttered "You know you are at a pretty fucked-up shindig when the vampires are the cheeriest ones in attendance. And the least scary."

Cort chuckled, still looking content to be there.

Drake tried to affect the same collected air, but the lace at his throat itched. And his knee breeches tugged in all the wrong places, and one of his hose was sliding down into his big buckled shoe.

"This sucks."

"Shh," Cort hissed, and Drake saw Saxon standing at his elbow.

"Hey, bestie," the goofy blond greeted him. "Bestie man, that is. How are you digging the pah-tay?"

"I'm dressed as a pirate, where's my fuckin' rum?" Drake asked.

In typical Saxon fashion, he was unaffected by Drake's scowl, or he thought it was a joke. "Dude, I think I have some butter rum Life Savers in my backpack." He looked around, suddenly appearing very confused. "But dude, I don't know where my backpack is."

"Don't worry about it," Drake said.

Cort chuckled again.

"So have you tried one of the cupcakes yet? Zelda hired this new caterer who specializes in gourmet cupcakes, and they are supposed to be totally fab."

"We're vampires," Drake pointed out slowly. "Cupcakes aren't really part of our diet plan anymore."

"Right," Saxon nodded, his goofy expression fading to one of serious reflection. "I forgot."

Then his silly smile returned. "But they are cool to look at, too."

Drake fought the urge to roll his eyes, and managed to say in a somewhat pleasant voice, "You know, I think I will go check them out now."

"You totally should," Saxon said happily.

Drake started to wander away, when Cort snagged his ruffled wrist and stopped him.

"Come on," Cort whispered, all his earlier humor gone, "try to have fun. This isn't about you, it's about Saxon and Zelda."

Drake sighed. Cort was right, damn him. He could suck it up for one night.

He nodded to Cort and wandered toward the buffet table, which was surrounded by a motley assortment of attendees. But he was focused on locating one person, the cute woman with the serving tray. One reason, she was pretty adorable, and another, if she worked in the kitchen, maybe they had some booze in there. Hell, at this point, he'd take a few swigs of cooking sherry . . . anything to make the rest of this bizarro night tolerable.

But he'd barely reached the buffet when the woman he immediately recognized as the maid of honor approached him.

"Hey there, matey."

Shit. He had not gotten a good vibe off this chick. She'd been staring at him through the whole ceremony like she was planning on a little maid of honor/best man hookup tonight. Or in her case, more of a tie-up than a hookup. God, he hoped she didn't have hooks.

He grimaced, but then forced the look into a stiff smile. The willowy woman strode up to him, the twinkly lights decorating the courtyard glinting off her black PVC, fetish bodysuit. This woman, while still tall in her stilettos, wasn't as Amazonian as Zelda, although there was something just as unnerving about her. Then again, she, too, had a whip as an accessory. Not a cat-o'-nine-tails, just a mere riding crop, but Drake knew that would really sting, especially on bare flesh.

"How are you . . . ?" he said stiffly, drawing a complete blank on her name.

"Obsidian," she answered.

How the hell had he forgotten that?

"I'm much better now that I've found you." She smiled, glossy red lips curling back over small, sharp-looking teeth.

He shifted away from her. Why was it that he really did find the dommes far more creepy than the undead? Maybe because the undead posed no threat to him . . . chicks with implements of torture . . . that was another story. Pain was so not his thing.

He hesitated, not sure what to say, which gave her the opportunity to make her move. She stepped closer and ran her crop down the length of his arm.

"Have you ever been dominated, pirate?"

Something that felt akin to panic tightened Drake's chest, and he immediately cast a frantic look around, searching for any escape he could find. As if answering his silent entreaty, the sexy caterer rushed out of the kitchen, carrying a tray of something that looked like bleeding skewered hearts.

"Sorry," he said with a quick raise of his hand to Obsidian to halt her line of questioning, not to mention to get the riding crop away from him. Then he reached out to the curvy caterer, catching her free arm.

"Cupcake," he said sweetly. "You are working so hard. Surely you have time to steal a moment with your beloved seaman."

And before he thought better of it, he kissed the shapely stranger.

THIS WEDDING WAS in the bag. Josie Lynn Thibodaux felt confident about that. Creating a successful catering company was at least 75 percent word of mouth, and she needed this bride and groom to have nothing but complimentary things to say about her food, her service, and her staff. Okay, *staff* was a generous word. Her staff was herself and two college kids who she could only afford to pay minimum wage at the moment.

All the more reason why she needed to hustle.

So being grabbed by one of the wedding guests and kissed was not part of the professionalism she was hoping desperately to portray. Not to mention, the surprise lip-lock caused her to lose her balance on the tray of sashimi tuna sculpted in the shape of hearts and skewered with stalks of rosemary and topped with a roasted red pepper and sundried tomato puree—one of the gothic-themed appetizers she was particularly proud of.

She registered the metal tray clattering to the ground, but she was still too shocked to pull away. The lips moving over hers seemed to hold her immobile and she was powerless to break away.

But finally good sense kicked in, and she shoved at the man holding her. She looked up into a pair of intense, dark eyes and was lost again. Wow, he was good-looking. Like ridiculously good-looking.

Once more, common sense took effect when she noticed several of the guests staring in her direction. All the dazed desire clouding her thoughts disappeared, replaced by much more distinct irritation.

"What are you doing?" she demanded.

The man, who she now saw was dressed as a pirate—*damn, this is an odd wedding even by New Orleans standards*—smiled. A roguish smile that suited his attire.

"I'm sorry to catch you off guard, cupcake," he cajoled. "But I couldn't resist a quick moment with my lady."

Then he jerked his head slightly and his dark eyes shifted in the same direction.

Josie Lynn frowned. Was there something actually wrong with this guy? Maybe he wasn't quite right. Some of her anger subsided.

Then he did it again, a little more adamantly this time, and she realized he was silently gesturing to the tall, latex-clad woman next to him. So the kiss had been for this chick's benefit. Although from the sour frown on the woman's heavily made-up face, *benefit* might not be the right word. She looked pissed. And she had a crop.

Josie Lynn took a step away from her, slipping on some of the slimy sashimi.

The pirate reached out and caught her elbow to steady her, but she jerked out of his hold.

Okay, now Josie Lynn was truly pissed, too. She so did not need to be a part of this guy's drama. He could use someone else to make the plastic-encased woman jealous, or scare her away, or whatever he was doing. She didn't care. She did, however, very much care that she was now standing in the middle of over a hundred dollars' worth of sushi-grade yellowfin.

She started to open her mouth to tell him so, but caught herself. If he were just some random drunken jerk, she probably would have socked him in the gut and given him a very sharp, very pointed piece of her mind. But this wasn't just some drunken jerk; this was a guest at the wedding.

Assaulting one of the guests, physically *or* verbally, was not going to get her the stellar reviews she needed from the bride and groom. Presumably they liked this guy, since they'd asked him to be a part of their special day, and complaints from him could be the kiss of death for this job, literally. So, even though she wanted to gag on her own smile, she forced a wide, charming one toward the pirate-turned-kissing-bandit.

"You know I love our moments, too, but not while I'm working, sugar plum," she cooed, mocking the ridiculous endearment he'd used, then dropped a pointed look at the mess around her. "It makes me clumsy."

She couldn't quite keep the annoyance out of her voice, even as she continued to smile.

"I am sorry about that, cupcake," the pirate said, his dark, intense eyes twinkling with amusement. He was enjoying this.

God, she hated men.

He started to crouch down to clean up the mess, but Josie Lynn placed a hand on his arm; she noted the feeling of his bicep, bulging lean and hard, under his puffy shirt.

"No, honey bear, I'll get it," she said, annoyance clear in the tightness of her words, but this time directed more toward herself than at him. How could she be thinking about his damn muscles when profit was scattered all over the floor and stuck to the bottoms of her shoes? She might have blown this whole gig.

No, *he* might have blown it. Damn men.

But he stopped and stood, towering over her.

She dropped her hand from his arm, flexing her fingers as she did so, as if that would banish the memory of his lean strength and how much she'd liked the feeling of him. It didn't work, but she gathered herself enough to wave over Eric, one of the college kids that worked for her.

"Get a broom and dustpan," she told him, her no-nonsense demeanor somewhat returned. "And a mop."

Eric nodded, but didn't rush off quite as quickly as she would have liked. Making minimum wage only earned minimum speed.

So, even though she wanted to get away from this man as soon as possible, she had to wait, not wanting to leave the mess unattended. All she needed was someone slipping on raw fish or getting puree on their fetishwear.

She shot a glance to the woman in the shiny PVC catsuit . . . of course, the puree would wipe right off of that.

"I can wait here until he returns," the pirate said, and this time when Josie Lynn met his gaze, she saw what looked like flashes of remorse in his dark eyes. That wasn't much compensation, however.

But rather than respond to him, she remained rooted in the middle of the mess and scanned the courtyard for the bride and groom. As long as they still appeared happy, she should be okay. No harm, no foul. Aside from being out the pricey cost of the tuna. She could hardly charge them for an appetizer no one got to eat.

"I am really sorry, cupcake," the pirate said from closer beside her, his husky voice no longer dripping with the syrupy-sweet quality he'd used earlier.

Josie Lynn stopped her search of the crowd and raised an eyebrow at him, not quite believing his apology. Men like this only said they were sorry when it furthered their cause. She'd seen it a dozen times . . . the last time less than three weeks ago.

Damn, men were bastards. Especially the good-looking ones like this guy. With deep, intense stares and roguish smiles. And who kissed a woman until she was senseless. And who probably made love to a woman as if she were the only one in the world who'd ever mattered to him.

Dear, freaking God, what was she doing? Imagining how this man made love? She needed to get a grip. A very serious grip.

Fortunately, her employee finally moseyed up—with only a broom and dustpan, but it was a start. And she could get away from this jerk.

But she couldn't resist having the last word.

"No worries, sugar pie," she said to the pirate, her voice taking on all the sickening sweetness his had lost.

Then, on an impulse, she sank her fingers into the cascade of ruffles on his chest and dragged his lips down to hers. She kissed him hard and thoroughly.

"Enjoy the rest of the party, sweet cheeks," she cooed, before turning to head back to the kitchen, not needing to make direct eye contact with her employee to know he was sporting a be- mused expression.

She didn't slow her departure even as she slipped slightly on a chunk of tuna still stuck to her shoe.

Of course by the time she reached the kitchen, she wasn't feel- ing so self-righteous. Why the hell had she done that? Really? After the mental lamenting about needing to be nothing but pro- fessional? Why would she potentially cause another round of raised eyebrows? And what if rubber-bound Barbie with her crop and black lipstick trotted over to the bride and groom and told them their caterer was busy playing kissy-face with the wedding pirate?

"And this, Josie Lynn, is why you are destined to be the Queen of Bad Decisions," she muttered to herself. She needed to use the damn brain God gave her.

And not for evil.

She pulled in a deep breath and tried to focus on the chaotic kitchen. She couldn't take back her behavior—or his, but she could finish this wedding with a bang. And that didn't mean banging a pirate.

Even though she could imagine it. His body had felt really nice against hers. And surprisingly, he sort of smelled like the sea, fresh and manly and a little salty.

She felt her body react, nipples hardening, moisture gathering between her thighs.

Enough! She shook her head. "So, the Queen."

"Huh?"

Josie Lynn turned to her other employee, a slender, pretty blonde who was sadly reinforcing all dumb blonde jokes. Apparently minimum wage got her minimum speed with Eric and minimum intelligence with Ashley. And as soon as she noticed what Ashley was doing, all thoughts of kissing pirates and poor decisions vanished.

"Ashley! What are you doing?"

The blonde made a startled squeak and dropped the food syringe she was holding.

"I—I'm filling the éclairs with cream."

"No," Josie Lynn said slowly, "you are filling the éclairs with a crawfish and crab cheese sauce."

She snatched up a pastry bag filled with vanilla bean and Grand Marnier crème and shoved it toward Ashley. "This is the right filling."

Ashley gave her a pained look, but Josie Lynn barely acknowledged it, instantly counting the number of desserts ruined beyond repair.

Only a dozen. Thank God.

"I'm so sorry, Josie."

"No worries," Josie Lynn said, realizing that response was becoming the mantra of the night. "Just do the rest with this filling." She pushed the metal bowl filled with more crème toward her employee. "Please."

"Of course," Ashley said. "I'm so—"

Josie Lynn raised a hand to stop her apology. "No worries, just finish the rest and I'll finish the minicrepes."

Which are filled with the crawfish-and-crab cheese sauce, she finished silently. And sarcastically.

"You can pull this off," she said quietly to herself, determined to make this her new mantra of the night. "You can pull this off."

Chapter Three

THE WEDDING CRASHERS

JOHNNY looked at the crappy punch on the table and said to Wyatt, "Seriously? This is a dry wedding? Who the hell has a dry wedding in New Orleans?"

"A dominatrix, apparently." Wyatt glanced around the court-yard before lifting up his pants leg. He had a flask strapped to his calf. "But I was prepared."

"You should have told me."

"You should have read your invitation. It said it right on there they weren't serving booze."

"I barely glanced at it." Johnny wasn't fond of paperwork. Or details. He wondered where Lizette was off cursing him at the moment. So he had beaten her to the apartment that morning. His apartment. Which contained *his* stuff, he might add. And so he had broken off the locks her goofy henchman had installed and liberated his drum kit. They were his drums and he had gotten them off of Keith Moon back in the sixties. They were sentimental, not to mention the most expensive thing he owned by far, including his car, and he was not about to let Dieter take a crap on them or whatever he was planning to do in there. In his apartment. Where he paid the rent. And did he mention it was *his* apartment? He was not going to feel guilty that he might just be making life slightly more difficult for her. She was the one making his life difficult.

Especially when she did things like walk over grates and have her skirt blow up where he could see her slim, milky legs.

"So Stella told me about the VA being up your ass," Wyatt said, retrieving his flask.

"Yeah. I ditched out on a meeting with her tonight. I figured if she's going to be taking her sweet time clearing this misunderstanding up, I can take my sweet time giving her answers." Johnny wasn't sure why he was having such a strong reaction to Lizette, but he suspected it had to do with the challenge she presented: so buttoned up, yet so feminine. That might explain the weird reason that he had dreamed about her all day while he had slept, and why he'd woken up with a giant erection and the vision of Lizette wearing librarian glasses while riding him like a mechanical bull dancing in front of his eyes.

It had made him edgy, and now he had every reason to believe this wedding reception was going to suck. At least the exchanging of the vows had been short and to the point, though he could have done without seeing Saxon crawl down the makeshift aisle.

"That may be slightly counterproductive, but I can understand your frustration." Wyatt unscrewed his flask and eyeballed the punch. "Do you think whiskey would taste good in that shit?"

Johnny eyed it. "Is that sherbet floating in there? That stuff is gross. It's like swallowing a lump of phlegm."

"Saxon loves the stuff."

"Saxon is a moron." Johnny normally loved that quality about him. It made life with him around highly entertaining. But at the moment, he would have preferred an open bar with top-shelf liquor. Or even cheap liquor. "Can I just have a sip of that straight? Please? I'll give you five bucks."

"You don't have five bucks. The VA froze your assets, remember?"

Like he could forget. "Thanks for reminding me."

But Wyatt took pity on him and handed him the flask. He took a nip off it, glancing around the reception. It was an odd assortment of vampires and mortals, the bride a vision in white leather, her crop whizzing through the air at random intervals and smacking the wall, causing Saxon to giggle. Saxon himself looked like a middle-school girl at her first dance, wearing skinny jeans, Converse, and a tuxedo T-shirt, his long blond hair crimped.

He looked happy.

Zelda looked happy.

Cort and Katie looked happy.

Wyatt and Stella were happy.

Johnny was happy they were all so goddamn happy.

Yet he couldn't help but feel less than happy for himself.

He was, for lack of a better word, lonely. Which wasn't an emotion he ever really felt. He was a social guy, and he surrounded himself with people. Friends, women, his sister. He was the guy who sat in the bar talking to the bartender, bouncers, and shot girls for hours, long after his shift playing drums for the night was over. So it was very unusual for him to feel like this. Maybe it was just all this coupling up and settling down that was going on around him. At least he still had Drake as his token single friend. They would have to start hanging out more while everyone else was at home getting laid.

Huh. That was not the least bit reassuring of a thought. Sex with a hot woman or trolling around with Drake. He would have run for the street and married the first woman in sight if those were really the only options, but unfortunately, marriage was a long time, and Johnny had generally found himself allergic to commitment. Which didn't really make sense, because it wasn't like he craved change. He hadn't moved in five years, had lived in New Orleans for thirty, still enjoyed his sister's company, and wore a pair of jeans he liked until they disintegrated. Even all his one-night stands over the years had turned into friends-with-benefits relationships. He'd never once had a true, never-see-her-again hookup.

So why had he always been so reluctant to commit? He had no idea. He had faked his own death to avoid a more serious turn in his relationship with Bambi. He'd never even lived with a girl-friend. The very idea seemed really . . . intimate.

"What's it like living with Stella?" he asked Wyatt. It had only been two weeks since his sister had moved in with the bass player, and he was curious if they were still in love, or if toothpaste disputes had already killed the burn of passion.

But Wyatt grinned, his smile so wide and goofy, he rivaled Saxon for a split second. "Dude, it's amazing. Everywhere I look, she's there, either literally, or just there in the sense that her stuff is, and her personal touch on my apartment."

Oh my God. That sounded like hell on earth. Johnny couldn't imagine looking in every direction and seeing the same woman over and over. It would be like watching *The Notebook* every day for a millennium. "Can I have that flask again?"

He took a long drink.

Then he forced himself to say the right thing, which was all true, but it didn't change the fact that his hand was shaking just a little. "Well, I'm happy for you guys, I really am. Stella is a lot looser with you. She's happy, bro, and I thank you for that."

Wyatt clapped him on the shoulder. "Thanks, man. And your turn will come, you know."

"I hope not." Johnny figured he was working on being more responsible and less impulsive, and that was hard enough as it was. Adding a serious relationship on top of all that just might make his head explode.

"Don't you ever want to wake up and just know that you're going to turn and the woman you love is lying next to you?"

Johnny stared at his friend, who looked like he'd not only been struck by Cupid's arrow, but had also eaten it. "I'm moving away from you because now you're starting to get on my nerves. Go find my sister and cuddle. I'm going to find Drake and then maybe a bridesmaid to flirt with."

But when he saw Drake, who had been forced to wear a puffy pirate's shirt at the bride's request in his role as best man, Johnny decided there would be no picking up women for Drake that night. He'd be better off flying solo.

There was no band, which seemed a little criminal to Johnny, but then again, as far as he was concerned, the best band on the street was theirs, and they weren't going to play Saxon's own wedding. Though Johnny could have tolerated the DJ a little more if he hadn't been alternating between Frank Sinatra and booty-grinding music, neither of which put him in a better mood than his current state. Wandering through the courtyard, ignoring the food that had been set out for the mortals, he narrowly missed getting hit by a leather whip as he passed the head table.

Darting out of the way, he saw that one of Zelda's bridesmaids was grinning at him, flicking her wrist teasingly, whip in hand.

She was wearing a top hat covered in black and red feathers, and she had drawn black tears trailing down her face in makeup and had smeared her lipstick across her cheeks like she was bleeding. There were further fake bloodstains on her substantial cleavage, and as she grinned, he noted that her tooth was blacked out. Or maybe it was really missing. Possibly a whip injury. In any case, Johnny immediately rethought his bridesmaid project. Flirting with a cute girl was usually a foolproof method of improving his mood, but this was one scary bridesmaid. She clearly wanted to hurt him.

Johnny gave her a half smile, then got the hell out of the range of her weapon. He may be a vampire with excellent healing properties, but that didn't mean it felt good to have his ass whipped.

Turning, he contemplated strangling himself with the leaves of a banana tree, and wondered when the last time was that he'd truly had fun. Probably at his own wake, if he had to be honest with himself. That had involved laughs, gambling, dancing, bull riding, and a spontaneous wedding that wasn't his. Unfortunately, he was the only one who remembered it. He had been hoping that tonight would be a great night, given the potential of a vampire marrying a dominatrix. Instead it was like cirque du freak meets Lawrence Welk. There were actually bubbles floating down from the misters, and if he wasn't mistaken, there was a transvestite dressed like Cher making her way across the dance floor with a very determined stride.

And Lizette Chastain was coming through the archway from the street into the courtyard, her posture angry as she marched straight toward him.

Shit.

Johnny contemplated hiding, but she had already spotted him.

Besides, he was trying to be more mature. Which meant that when he ditched out on a woman and completely disregarded her rules, he needed to stick around and take responsibility for it instead of hiding. Hey, growing up didn't happen over night. He was taking baby steps.

"Mr. Malone," Lizette said, her voice clipped as she stepped right up to him, dressed in a suit that, while a lighter gray, was essentially the same one as the day before, though she was wearing lower heels with a splash of red on them.

"Ms. Chastain, it's a pleasure to see you again. What brings you to a wedding you weren't invited to?" He turned so that he moved under the archway, away from the view of the majority of the courtyard. She shifted as well, and they stood under the red, uneven bricks of the arch, the twinkle lights and dull volume of the wedding to his right, the dim light from Chartres Street on his left. Her lips were pursed in agitation and again it struck him at a completely inappropriate time how attractive she was. Everything about her was delicate. Except her expression.

"You are not a gentleman," she accused him.

He wasn't sure that he had ever claimed to be one. Growing up potato-poor in Ireland, he had learned that his fists spoke volumes, and that stealing a loaf of bread filled his hungry belly faster than trying to find work that didn't exist. Then when he'd come to the States with Stella in the twenties, he had taken those lessons and applied them to running with the Chicago mob. In his immortal life, he had set aside crime and violence, and had established a pretty firm personal code of ethics, but that didn't mean he knew a whole lot about which fork to use and putting out his pinky and shit like that.

So he just agreed with her. "Probably not."

She gasped. "We had an agreement to meet at seven, and you did not attend our meeting. Not to mention that Dieter informed me you have stolen your drum set."

"I can't steal what I already own. Look, I didn't want to deal with this today. I'm sorry I no-showed on you, but I didn't want to sit there and answer questions for five hours when I had a wedding to go to. If I have a key to my apartment, and can tell you where everything is, and a couple dozen witnesses can back me up that I'm Johnny Malone, I don't see what the big deal is. Just take me off the list and we can forget this ever happened. You can even keep the twelve hundred bucks if it will get the VA off my back." The longer he spoke, the more irritated he felt. Seriously, where did they get off?

"That is not the way it works, as we discussed." It was clear she was struggling to contain her frustration.

"Well, why do I have to follow their dumb rules anyway? I didn't vote for any of those douchebags. This isn't a democracy."

Her face blanched. "We exist to ensure we *continue* to exist. Rules are in place to guarantee the safety of each and every one of our kind."

"I think we're doing just fine on our own. Here in New Orleans, people don't give a shit if you're a vampire. It's cool to be a vampire, hip even."

"You tell people the truth?" She sounded shocked to the core, and she actually swayed a little on her heels.

"No, not outright. But if we did, no one would believe us. They would just think we were pretending. Being a 'vampire' is part of a fetish lifestyle. People get fang implants and drink blood and dress Goth all over the city—and all over the country for that matter. This isn't the Middle Ages, it's a freaking great time to be a vampire. We're trendy." He had to say, he loved it. It made life a lot easier than trying to be something he wasn't. "I think it's awesome that Saxon could marry a mortal. If she makes him happy, he should enjoy it while he can." Before Zelda got old and wrinkly and couldn't lift her crop anymore.

"This is a *mixed* wedding?" Lizette looked like she might faint.

He frowned. "Sweetie, that sounds racist."

"We can't marry mortals. We can't. It's the antithesis of everything the VA stands for. I am shocked at the utter disregard for rules and self-preservation going on here. I can only tell you that my report back to my superiors will recommend a full investigation into the coven here and your misconduct."

Oh God. And he meant that most sincerely. He had just accidentally opened up Pandora's Parisian box in the form of Lizette Chastain, and everyone he knew was going to kill him if the Vampire Alliance suddenly showed up in New Orleans, taking attendance and inspecting their quarters. "I think *coven* is a strong word. We're just a cover band."

She kept swallowing and blinking, and Johnny was actually starting to worry about her. It looked like she was having some kind of aneurysm, which was of course, impossible. "Can I get you a drink? You look like you're overheated or something."

At first she started to shake her head, but then changed her mind. "Actually, yes, I would, thank you."

"Just stand here for a second. I'll get you a drink and a chair." She was actually scaring him a little. He didn't really know what the hell was wrong with her. Vampires didn't get sick, but she looked feverish.

It occurred to him maybe she needed to feed, but he could only imagine her reaction to his suggesting she have some blood to drink.

Which left him only the shitty sherbet punch to give her. Gag.

Even as he lifted the ladle and scooped it, he wanted to hurl a little. But he poured two glasses in case she really was dehydrated, went under the skirt of the table where Stella had left her messenger bag, and pulled a bag of blood out of it. His sister was always prepared. Pouring a little in each glass, he figured it was enough to cut off the urge to feed, but not enough to make Lizette even realize she was drinking it until she had already swallowed. He sniffed it. There was a slight hint of blood, but maybe she would be so thirsty she wouldn't question it.

When he got back, she was actually leaning on the wall, looking like she might slide down it at any given second. Johnny held out the glass in front of her, and slipped his arm around her. "When was the last time you fed?" he murmured.

"Before I left Paris."

"Are you crazy?" That had to have been at least three days. "Drink this."

"What is it?" She frowned at the glass.

"Punch. With ice cream in it."

She swallowed a huge gulp then promptly started coughing. "The texture is horrible."

"Just keep drinking, you'll feel better. Take it back in one whole shot, okay? We'll do it together." She looked unconvinced, but he raised the second glass to his lips. He may have been responsible for being a pain in her ass, but he didn't want her passing out from lack of blood in his presence. "Come on. One, two, three."

Johnny threw back the drink and let it slide down his throat in one massive, gelatinous glob of gross. He tried not to shudder and gave her a reassuring look. "Mmm. Good, huh?"

Lizette was shuddering and wiping her lips, but her glass was empty and there was already more color in her cheeks. "I am not sure if 'good' is the term I would use, but thank you. I do feel slightly better."

"I'll get you another glass."

She nodded, eyes glassy, posture still hunched.

Johnny repeated the process, trying to work around the ice cream, going mostly for the liquid and a healthy shot of blood. He himself was feeling a nice hint of warmth in his extremities from the drink. He hadn't thought he was particularly hungry, but now he had to wonder, given that he was definitely craving more. This time he had his glass halfway down before he even got to Lizette, and she drank it quickly as well, with no encouragement from him.

Within a minute, she was standing straighter and sighing. "Thank you, I feel much better."

He wanted to reprimand her for taxing her ability to go without feeding like that. But that really wasn't his style, nor was it any of his business why she had gone days without blood. Maybe she had her reasons. All he knew was that she looked better, and he was suddenly aware again of just how smoking-hot she was. He normally dated balls-to-the-wall kind of chicks, but that wasn't Lizette. She was elegant. She was beautiful in an ethereal, non-showy kind of way. He wanted to trace his hands over her delicate body and see if she would keep her eyes open or close them. He wanted to bite her, gently, suck her blood into his mouth, then smooth over the wound with his tongue while her dark hair tumbled over her petite shoulders.

Johnny blinked, his erection suddenly painfully obvious in his black jeans. Why his thoughts had taken a tumble into the French gutter, he wasn't sure. But if he didn't lighten the mood, he was going to end up in more than a disagreement with Lizette. She was going to call the cops on him. Or more likely, her brawny assistant. Johnny wondered where her muscle was tonight. Probably at his apartment, sitting on his couch, wearing his underwear, and downloading expensive movies on his TV. Fucker. Johnny laughed a little out loud, though he wasn't sure what was really so funny.

When he turned, it seemed like the twinkle lights shifted a little, undulating in and out. Weird. He was feeling a little strange. For a second he wasn't even sure what he had been doing.

Lizette. Right.

He gestured to the courtyard. "Do you want to dance?" he asked, because that seemed like a totally logical question to ask. Even though he never danced, and he didn't think Lizette was the bootygrind type. Who had almost just fainted. Yet, he asked.

Stranger yet, she nodded. "I'd love to."

The girl had moves like Jagger. She swayed back and forth, hips swirling, and Johnny had no sense of time or space or sound. Everything moved in sensual slow motion, a hazy, breezy, and dark erotic dance of their bodies next to each other, not touching, but speaking volumes, the banana trees fanning behind Lizette's head.

And that was just during the Cupid Shuffle. Johnny could only imagine how she would dance to Usher or Flo Rida.

The problem was, he could only imagine. Because after that, he didn't remember a single thing.

LIZETTE TRIED TO remember why she was at a wedding with Johnny Malone. She tried to remember why she was angry. It had something to do with Johnny not being Johnny and stealing something that was his, if he was he. But then she had felt faint from not feeding, which was odd, because she was old enough to be able to go days without blood. But for some reason, she had felt desperately hungry and that awful sherbet had caught in her throat and she'd been afraid she would vomit in front of Johnny.

Instead, she had immediately felt better. Much better. Like her inner thighs had been laid under a heat lamp and she was alone in a dark room, dancing for herself in the mirror kind of better. Like no one else existed but this charming man in front of her and a soft breeze. Which reminded her that she was actually outside. Wasn't she? Lizette turned and turned, taking in the fairy lights, and the thick green plant leaves, the rich red brick, and the parade of feathers on women's hats. Where was she?

Then Johnny Malone handed her another drink and she decided she didn't care, just as long as she could drink sherbet for the rest of her very long life.

It was the last coherent thought, if you could even call it that, she had that night.

Chapter Four

ONCE . . . TWICE . . . FIVE TIMES A CHER

DRAKE had to admit this wedding had suddenly become a lot more interesting. That little caterer was definitely sexy and had fit perfectly in his arms and against his body. And she could kiss—damn, she could kiss. But she was also a spitfire. He could see it, even though he knew she'd been trying to remain calm and businesslike. But her blue eyes had flashed with fire.

A woman who gave as good as she got—now that was hot.

He glanced at the maid of honor, who now chatted with a man in a dog collar who looked ready to drop to his knees at the first flick of her wrists. Definitely a better fit for her. Just like Cupcake was a better fit for him. He liked giving as good as he got, but only when it didn't involve whips, ball gags, or safe words.

Just call him old-fashioned. Plus you didn't live for two hundred years and not learn what you like. So now he had something to distract him from the horror of this wedding. He was going to convince the caterer to have a little fling with him. Maybe he should tell Saxon he was going to try a cupcake after all.

Yeah, no. But it was clear that he did need to get laid. That was probably why he was so irritated with all his "in love" friends. And why he was so cranky.

So he was going to go apologize appropriately to the caterer, then work on taking her home for the night.

He smiled broadly just thinking about it, but his grin faded as he watched the kid who worked for the caterer push the slimy tuna around on the slate tiles with a broom. He did feel bad about the ruined food and the mess he'd created.

All the more reason to go give her a very sincere apology. Maybe several. In his bed. In the shower. Maybe even in this courtyard once the freak-show wedding was done.

Another grin curved his lips. Oh yes, he was having a lot more fun.

Then he realized the maid of honor was watching him from the other side of the room, studying him over the rim of her punch glass as she took a sip of the vile Lake Ponchartrain punch. And Dog Collar Boy appeared to be nowhere in sight. He looked at the ground in front of her. Yeah, nowhere in sight.

Great.

She lowered her glass and continued to stare at him, but now she no longer looked flirty and determined. She looked angry and determined.

Shit, maybe a spurned dominatrix was scarier than a horny one.

Yeah, definitely time to go talk to the cute caterer in the kitchen.

The brunette was easy to find. She stood at a stainless steel counter that was littered with dirty dishes, utensils, and trays of food in various stages of preparation. She swiped at her bangs with the back of her wrist, the movement tired and a little agitated, then she started dolloping some kind of sauce onto minicrepes.

He walked up behind her.

"Hey," he said, keeping his voice low and gentle, not wanting to startle her. She seemed tense enough. But his strategy didn't work.

A small, surprised squeak escaped her, and she dropped the spoon she held. It clattered against the metal mixing bowl, then disappeared into the creamy concoction.

"Damn it," she muttered as she spun around to face him. Her startled expression quickly transformed to one of utter annoyance, but she quickly suppressed that look behind a mask of stoicism. Although her blue eyes still flashed with irritation.

Such blue eyes. The same bright, vivid blue as a clear summer sky. Or at least as he remembered it.

Shit, this woman was furious and he was thinking about her eyes. That was as crazy as everything else about the wedding. Or maybe it just further validated that he needed a little adult fun—with a woman like this. Adorable with big, blue eyes, pink lips, a pert little nose, and curves in all the right places.

"I'm sorry, sir," she said stiffly, "I'm going to have to ask you to leave."

"Sir? What happened to 'sugar pie,' cupcake?" he teased, but if the flash of irritation in her eyes was any indication, she didn't appreciate his joke.

"Fine, sugar pie, I need you to leave. Only employees are allowed in the kitchen."

"I understand, but I really wanted to apologize to you and explain my actions. I shouldn't have kissed you like that, but it was an impulse."

"Well, I'm glad you cleared that up for me," she said with feigned sincerity. "Otherwise I would have gone through my life thinking you had plotted that out for weeks. Now if you don't mind, I really do need to work."

Instead, Drake chuckled at her sassiness. "You're funny."

"No, I'm busy." She turned back to the counter and reached for a new serving spoon.

But Drake wasn't about to be dismissed so easily. This woman really did intrigue him. So instead he moved beside her, leaning a hip on the stainless steel counter.

She attempted to ignore him, probably hoping if she didn't acknowledge his presence, he'd get bored and wander away. And often he probably would have, but he wanted this woman and as flighty as he could be about some things, he could be very tenacious when he wanted something . . . or someone.

The brunette finally stopped scooping the filling onto the crepes and turned back to him. "I accepted your apology, why are you still here?"

He smiled at her brusque words. She was an interesting combination, physically all sweet and soft looking, but her personality was brisk and blunt—maybe with a hint of sarcasm.

"I wasn't actually done explaining why I behaved so badly," he said.

"You know, your explanation worked just fine for me. I'm good." She lifted the spoon again and returned her attention to her work.

"But I don't want you to think I'm some creep who just goes around kissing woman unsolicited."

"Too late."

Drake chuckled again. She was a delight.

"I did have a good reason. I was actually trying to dissuade unwanted attention from that woman who was standing beside me."

"You're right," she said, not pausing her work to look at him. "That totally makes me think you aren't a creep. Why not just tell the woman you aren't interested, when you can create an elaborate lie by grabbing a total stranger, kissing her *and* pretending to be involved with her, thereby dragging her unwillingly into your deceit? Nope, not creepy at all."

"Well," Drake said slowly, "when you say it like that, it does seem a little creepy."

She shot him a sidelong glance, then ladled more cheese sauce onto a crepe.

"Ashley," she said to the blonde who had been shooting curious looks at them as she struggled to inject pastries with some sort of filling.

"Please take this platter of crepes out to the buffet table."

Ashley hurried over to do as the brunette asked.

"Watch where you walk," the brunette added just as Ashley was about to disappear out the door.

Ashley gave her a muddled look.

"I dropped the skewered tuna on the floor," the brunette explained. "Eric is cleaning it up, but it could still be slippery."

Ashley nodded, but still looked confused as she left the kitchen.

JOSIE LYNN WASN'T sure she really wanted to be left alone in the kitchen with "sweet cheeks" here, but the food did need to get out to the guests and frankly, she didn't like Ashley being here to eavesdrop on this bizarre conversation.

"Let's face it, if anyone is going to fall on their ass, it's going to be that one," Drake said, shaking his head, still leaning on the counter, arms crossed over his chest, all relaxed as if he knew her well and it was completely normal for him to be there.

She scowled at him. Why didn't he just leave? Good lord.

"Oh, don't give me that look." He said, again in a tone that implied they were old friends. "I know you know I'm right. That's why you warned her."

He smiled, a lopsided smile that was endearing and charming and altogether too attractive.

She sighed. "Do you plan to hover here all night?"

"Hover, huh? Well, I could help. You look like you need it."

Oh, no he didn't.

Josie Lynn knew what the kitchen looked like. It looked like a disaster, but that comment was the final straw. She didn't need help. Especially from some pompous jerk dressed like he should be working a kiddies' pirate ride at an amusement park.

She spun toward him, waving the cheesy spoon in the man's face. "I absolutely do not need help. I happen to have everything under control."

"Josie Lynn," a tentative voice said from behind them. She turned to find Eric standing in the doorway, broom still in hand. God only knew where the dustpan was.

"What?" she snapped.

"Umm—some of the guests are asking for more rémoulade for the crawfish fritters."

"Okay," she said, some of her irritation fading. She was over-reacting. She knew it. "It's in the fridge over there."

Eric looked reluctant to enter the room, but came in anyway, heading to the large stainless steel refrigerator that she pointed to with her spoon. Yeah, she didn't look like she needed help. Totally in control here.

Eric located the bowl of rémoulade, without further guidance, and even moved rather quickly to exit the kitchen.

"You might want to leave the broom here," the pirate commented when Eric passed.

Eric looked slightly startled that the pirate had spoken to him, but then he leaned the broom against the wall and left.

"You might want to consider a little bit sharper staff down the road."

Josie Lynn glared at him. "Why the hell are you here? Honestly? Can't you see that I have a lot to do?"

She raised her hand to stop him as he opened his mouth to answer her.

"You know what, that was a rhetorical question," she said. "I don't give a rat's rear end why you are here. And I know I have a lot to do here. I know I could use more staff. Better staff. But I can do this, and frankly, I don't need or want your help—aside from you just leaving."

He didn't respond for a moment, and just when she wondered if he'd just chosen to completely ignore her, he finally nodded.

"Okay," he said, calmly. "I know you are busy."

Thank God, he was finally just going to go away. Yes.

"But—"

Josie Lynn fought back a groan. Really? Was this some kind of joke or something?

"I still don't feel like I've given you an appropriate apology. So let me take you out for a drink when the wedding is over. Then you can relax and we can just talk."

She gaped at him . . . clutching a cheese-caked spoon straight up in the air in front of her. Was he really that thick? Didn't he see she was annoyed with him? Beyond annoyed. She was a woman perilously close to the edge.

But instead of saying any of that, she simply said, "No."

He still remained rooted in the same spot, ass to edge of the counter. "Really? Because I think we'd have a great time."

"No."

"Not even just one dri—"

"No."

He stood there a moment longer, then shoved away from the counter. "Are you sure?"

"Absolutely."

He studied her for just a few seconds longer, then he bowed. The gesture should have looked silly, or patronizing, but Josie Lynn found his movement oddly elegant. Oddly appealing.

He straightened. "I do wish you would reconsider, but I also realize I overstepped proper etiquette and put you in an awkward and unfortunate position, and for that, I am truly sorry."

Josie Lynn stared at him. He looked sincere—and even stranger than that, his way of speaking seemed from another time, yet utterly natural to him. And maybe stress and anxiety had taken what was left of her mind, but had he suddenly acquired an English accent?

Then he smiled, that mischievous, roguish grin that she was already far too familiar with, and Josie Lynn immediately felt like a fool for being sucked in by his charm—even for a moment. It was an act. Like all men's charms.

The costume made total sense. He was dashing and dangerous and totally out for himself. And she wasn't about to let her emotions get ravished again. Even by a very pretty pirate.

"Great," she said with forced detachment. "Now please leave."

"Okay." In that one word all of his affected gallantry disappeared. In fact he sounded as if her rejection didn't matter in the least to him, and even though she didn't have any intention of going out with him, she was still hurt by the idea that he'd come on so strong, then was ultimately so apathetic about her rejection.

Don't worry about it, Josie Lynn. He did you a favor. He just re-

minded you why you are out of the dating scene for now—and possibly forever.

The pirate gave her another nod of his head and then sauntered out of the room.

She watched him leave, willing herself to not feel bad.

She refocused on her work. She needed to finish up two more platters of appetizers. She immediately went to the large fridge to pull out the spinach-and-feta turnovers that needed to be put in the oven now. And she needed to get the yogurt-dill dipping sauce into a serving bowl.

She checked the oven temperature and slid two baking sheets full of pastries inside. Then she returned to the refrigerator to get the sauce.

Where was her help? Eric was moving at the pace of a drowsy snail, no doubt. And God only knew what Ashley was doing. Probably flirting with one of the wedding guests.

An image of the pretty blonde smiling sweetly at the pirate popped into her head. She stirred the yogurt sauce with a little too much force, and some of the white mixture slopped over the side of the mixing bowl.

Okay, she needed to let this go. Who cared if the man was out there flirting with half the women in the room? Better them than her.

Yep. Better them than her.

She had just reached for a sponge to wipe up the glob of sauce on the counter, when she heard a sharp rap from across the room. She paused, surprised by the sound. Someone was at the back door.

She wasn't expecting anyone.

Another knock sounded. This one louder than the first.

She grabbed a paper towel, wiping her damp hands as she

headed tentatively toward the door. This was New Orleans, after all, and she wasn't sure if she should even answer it. Who knew what unsavory character could be on the other side? She paused, listening, not that she could hear anything over the din of voices, laughter, and the beat of "Gangnam Style."

Josie Lynn glanced back toward the kitchen door, wishing Ashley or Eric would come back so she wouldn't be alone. She was probably being too dramatic.

She jumped as the back door shook under another knock.

Or not.

She hesitated a moment longer, then reached for the doorknob. The truth was, she didn't have time for another distraction, and she needed to get rid of this one, too.

She jerked the door open, preparing herself for an unruly wedding guest, or maybe a vagrant coming to beg for food. She even considered someone shadier. So she wasn't at all prepared for . . . Cher.

Five Chers, to be exact. And to be more exact, they were five transvestites dressed as Cher in different stages of her career. At least, Josie Lynn thought they were transvestites. She had to admit they looked pretty good.

"Can—can I help you?"

The one closest to her was dressed as Cher from the sixties with long, straight hair, a fur vest and red, orange, yellow, and green striped pants.

She flipped her hair and said, "Hi. Sorry to interrupt you, but we have a favor to ask."

Wow, she/he even spoke like Cher.

"Okay," Josie Lynn said uncertainly.

"We are friends of the bride," Sixties Cher said.

"And we wanted to come in through the back to surprise her," said Half-Breed Cher.

Sixties Cher glared at the Half-Breed one, clearly not appreciating the help explaining. Half-Breed Cher shrugged, the feathers of the elaborate headdress she wore bobbing, and Believe Cher blew one of the errant feathers out of her face.

"We wanted to come in through the back to make a dramatic entrance," Bob Mackie Cher added, the thousands of sequins on her evening gown glittering in the light from the kitchen.

Josie Lynn looked at If I Could Turn Back Time Cher's huge, curly hair, studded leather jacket, stockings and garters, and a mesh and V-shaped bodysuit that just barely covered her breasts and vajayjay. Did she/he have a vajayjay? And how on earth was she/he hiding the additional . . . junk, if she/he still had it? Either way, all these Chers couldn't help but make an entrance no matter where or how they entered a room.

"We would be happy to pay you for your help," said Sixties Cher. Bob Mackie Cher ran a pointed tongue over her top lip in signature Cher style, then pulled something out of her cleavage. She held it up. A hundred-dollar bill.

Josie Lynn frowned. Why would they feel like they had to pay her to be allowed in? Especially if they were friends of the bride's?

Believe Cher seemed to see her concern, because she quickly said, "We know you're busy working and just wanted to pay you for your time."

"After all, we are all working girls here, right?" said Believe Cher, using an index finger to brush her black-and-red highlighted hair away from her face.

Josie Lynn hesitated, looking at the money. Then she thought about the sushi that had ended up on the floor. That money certainly would help with the loss of that. And given what she'd seen of the wedding guests, a gaggle of Chers certainly seemed like a natural fit as the bride's friends.

"Okay," Josie Lynn said as she took the money. She stood back opening the door wider. "Come on in."

DRAKE SIGHED AS he walked back into the reception. It looked as if there would be no distraction tonight. Cupcake was not only a spitfire, she was tough. He'd seen that there was no way he was going to charm her into going out with him. Much less fall into his bed for the night.

"Which just blows."

"What blows?"

Drake turned to see Obsidian beside him. He couldn't convince Cupcake to give him a chance, and apparently he couldn't convince the persistent maid of honor that he was not interested. But at least now she no longer carried her riding crop. Instead she held two champagne flutes of the wretched-looking punch.

She offered one to him and he accepted, seeing no way to deny her—at least if he didn't want her to head back and retrieve her crop.

She lifted her glass in salute. "Yo ho ho, blow the man down."

Drake lifted his glass in return, but didn't take a sip.

"I have to say, your girlfriend surprises me."

He frowned, just briefly confused by her statement. Then he understood whom she was talking about.

"Oh? Why is that?"

Obsidian pursed her dark red lips as if considering the right answer, which he highly doubted she needed to. He was certain she'd formulated her opinion about the caterer right away.

"She seems a little too—pedestrian for you."

Pedestrian? Really? Were they looking at the same woman? He considered asking this woman—who as far as he was concerned was trying far too hard not to be pedestrian and was only managing to be a bit of cliché—how she had come to that conclusion, but he realized she would answer him. And he didn't feel like hearing it.

So instead he simply smiled and said, "Don't let the ruffled shirt and breeches fool you, I'm a pretty average guy myself."

She raised a dark, thinly arched brow. "I don't see that."

He found it hard to believe she saw much of anything with the amount of black eyeliner she had caked around her eyes.

"Yes, well in some cases, looks can be deceiving," he stated, then without thinking, took a swallow of the disgusting-looking punch.

Holy shit, it tasted even worse than it looked. He forced the slimy, sort-of-clumpy concoction down, even though he really wanted to spit it out on the ground. Dear God, he needed a real drink more than ever.

"Will you excuse me?" he said to Obsidian, not managing to keep the disgust off his face, and frankly he didn't care if she thought it was directed at her or the drink.

He registered that she again raised an eyebrow at him, but she said nothing as he walked back toward the kitchen.

Drake knew Cupcake wouldn't be any more impressed to see him back than Obsidian had been to see him leave so abruptly, but he had to see if the little caterer had any sort of alcoholic beverage.

Tonight really had him out of sorts, and at this point even a few swigs of cooking sherry might take the edge off this weird feeling inside him. And truthfully, as he headed back to the kitchen, weaving through the crowd of guests, he felt even stranger.

But he ignored the almost dizzying feeling, blaming it on the circus sideshow feel of the wedding—the crazy clothing, the decorations, and the bizarre dance that many of the people were doing that looked like they were pretending to ride horses while spinning invisible lassos over their heads.

So weird. So almost surreal.

He just wanted to get to the kitchen. And hopefully get some booze. He'd grovel to Cupcake if he had to.

He giggled—yes, actually giggled. So not pirate-y. It was funny, because he suddenly felt kinda—good. Well, loose at least.

When he entered the kitchen, the light was glaringly bright, more so than he'd recalled from the last time he was in there. He paused, leaning against the doorway, having to blink several times to get his bearings.

Then he saw Cupcake, God she was so sexy. He was going to go tell her so, again, right now. But then he noticed she was holding the back door ajar and she was talking to . . . he blinked again, his vision seeming to swim in front of him. He gained a little control and squinted, trying to see clearer.

She was talking to several . . . Chers? He blinked again, and actually rested his head against the doorjamb. Was he seeing double? Or would that be multiple? There were a lot of Chers.

He giggled again. Funny, he didn't usually giggle.

Damn, he felt weird. What was happening? He took a few steps into the room, then had to catch himself from stumbling on the edge of the counter. From his vantage point, now he couldn't fully see the people she was talking to, and because of this odd underwater-type feeling, he wondered if he'd just imagined that.

But she was talking to someone and as he watched, still bracing himself on the counter, he saw Cupcake reach for something. He squinted again, the wooziness in his head growing. But he could still make out what she'd taken. Money.

Yes, money, he thought, proud that he'd had enough focus to make out that. But the lightheadedness intensified. The kitchen started to feel as surreal as the courtyard.

Maybe he should go find the others. Something was really wrong with him and he needed to find Cort or Wyatt. Even Johnny.

Johnny would probably tell him just to go with it. Saxon, too. Maybe he should; it wasn't unpleasant exactly.

He set down the glass he still held, not even realizing he had, until he slid it awkwardly onto the stainless steel. He looked back over to where Cupcake stood, debating if he should just call to her.

No, he'd already made a terrible impression on her. Acting like this would really convince her he was a loser. Not to mention, she'd probably just think it was some lame ploy to get her attention.

He had to find the others. He staggered back to the doorway, stopping again to catch his balance. He glanced back at Cupcake once more to see her opening the back door wider and allowing the Chers into the kitchen.

He stumbled back into the dim light of the courtyard, only making it a few feet, then he decided he couldn't face that crazy room of strange people. He turned to go back to the kitchen, and that was the last thing he remembered.

JOSIE LYNN WATCHED the Chers ready themselves for their grand entrance, adjusting their clothing and fluffing and flipping their hair. She looked down at the hundred-dollar bill still clutched in her hand, that same sinking feeling deep in the pit of her stomach.

Maybe she shouldn't have let them in.

But as If I Could Turn Back Time Cher gave her a wide smile and a salute, then turned her thong-exposed ass toward her as they all left the kitchen, Josie Lynn decided it was too late to worry about that now.

She had to worry about finishing this party with a bang.

Bang, bang, he shot me down.

Wasn't that a Cher song? Well, she sure as hell wasn't getting shot down. She headed back to the counter and her work. The turnovers should be almost done.

When she approached the workspace, she noticed a glass of punch that hadn't been there earlier. Had Ashley or Eric brought it for her? She looked at the frothy, oddly colored mixture, hating to admit, because she'd made it, that it looked awful.

She tucked the money into the pocket of her black work pants, then reached for the glass of punch. Maybe it tasted better than it looked.

She took a tentative sip, then grimaced.

Nope. No better. It was sweet and slimy. With a strange, bitter aftertaste.

Oh well, she couldn't take the blame for that one. She'd made it to the groom's specifications.

She set the glass aside, smacking her lips again in aversion, then reached for the mixing bowl of yogurt sauce. But she misjudged and stuck her hand right into the white dip.

"Oh my God," she muttered. What was wrong with her?

She extended her clean hand toward the paper towels, but when she was sure her fingers should connect with them, they grabbed air. Frowning, she really focused her eyes on the roll and tried again. Again she missed them.

What the hell? She moved her gaze from the towels to the rest of the room. The whole kitchen seemed to swim before her eyes. She felt instantly dizzy and had to steady herself against the counter.

Panic filled her chest, making it hard to breathe. What was wrong with her? She needed to get help. She started to head toward the courtyard, but paused to lean heavily against the counter again. She couldn't go out into the wedding weaving and confused. That would be the end of this job for her.

But she needed help. She forced her disobedient fingers into her pocket and tugged out her cell phone only for it to slip out of her hand and to the tile floor. She gripped the edge of the table to steady herself as she bent down to pick it up, but just as she would have fallen face-first on the floor, someone caught her.

She looked up at her savior. The pirate. Damn, he was so good-looking.

"You are so good-looking." Crap, did she just say that aloud? She thought she had. The words might have been thick and slurred in her mouth, but she did think she'd said them. And he understood, because a big, almost lazy smile turned up his lips.

"So good-looking," she repeated as if she couldn't control herself.

She couldn't control herself. She leaned heavily against him. His arms moved tighter around her.

"Thank you, gorgeousth," he said, his words sounding as slurred as her own. She felt his hands on her back, sliding downward. And his lips on her neck, warm and wonderful.

She closed her eyes and let her head fall back, loving the feeling of him against her, kissing her. She opened her eyes, focusing just briefly on the industrial fluorescent lights on the ceiling. Then everything swirled and blurred, except the pirate's pleasurable touch. Then she drifted, lost in a confusing haze.

Chapter Five

DUNGEONS AND DRAG QUEENS

DAMMIT, Drake thought, did these bitches have to wake him up the same way every goddamn morning? He was really tired of getting a boot to the ass as a wakeup call. And this kick was particularly forceful this morning. Not to mention whoever did the kicking had an unusually large foot and one sturdy boot.

He groaned, letting his head fall to the side as he struggled to stay asleep, willing his body to just move with the sway of the ship. The longer he slept the less he had to deal with his situation. He made another noise low in his throat. His shoulders and wrists ached from the manacles. But even worse than that was his head—it throbbed, an almost crippling pain ricocheting around his skull. Probably from dehydration and lack of sleep.

But none of this was new; he'd existed like this for . . . he'd lost count of the days. Being held in the dank hold, surrounded by stench and sickness, the days and nights running together. All he knew for sure was it felt endless.

He let his head loll to the side. More aching muscles. More

pounding in his head. But even through the pain, he did register that the hold didn't smell as awful as usual. Nor did he hear the customary coughs and retching of the other prisoners. Why?

It didn't matter, really. He still felt wretched and he was still restrained. A state that had gone on for an eternity with no end in sight.

Eternity. Eternity?

The word joined the pain in his head, bouncing around, causing no agony, just questions. Why did that word seem so significant? He wished he didn't feel so miserable and he could focus. Eternity.

Then slowly the explanation came back to him like a floodgate had been jimmied open, and memories rushed in.

The captain of this prison ship was female, and she was . . .

"A vampire," he said aloud before he could stop himself.

Another kick landed against his backside—this strike even harder than the first.

Shit, had one of the crew just heard him? Did they think he intended to reveal their secret? He knew that would mean certain death, and he had no intention of letting the truth about his captors be known. He didn't want to die. He wasn't sure he wanted to be a vampire either. But all he knew at this moment was that he did not want to die.

He needed to be sure whoever heard him knew that. He wasn't a thief, even though that was the accusation that had brought him to this hideous state. Nor was he a traitor. He'd vowed to the captain he would never expose the crew's secret if she spared him. Was that why it was quiet down here? Had the crew fed on the other prisoners? Shit, he had to scramble to make sure his confused slip of the tongue wouldn't be his undoing.

He opened his eyes, expecting his gaze to meet darkness. The fact that it didn't was almost as disorienting as the complete black-ness. He blinked, trying to get an idea of where he could be. In the Captain's quarters? On deck?

He blinked again. This was not the eighteenth-century prison ship he had been brought to Louisiana on. Unless his captors had miraculously turned the ship into a houseboat, because this was decidedly a house. He glanced around him to see an assortment of what appeared to be sex toys and restraint devices on the faux-marble walls. Okay, it was a strange house, and although he couldn't say exactly where he was, it was definitely not the ship. He looked down at himself. He wasn't manacled to the beams above, and the reason he thought he'd felt the rocking of the vessel was that he was dangling in the air. His ass was in a swing of sorts with his arms cuffed together above his head and to the swing itself.

What the hell?

But he was quickly distracted from his own predicament when a small person seemed to scramble out of nowhere, screaming. Really, really loudly. A very cruel joke when he couldn't get his hands free to cover his already-sensitive ears. The caterwauling certainly wasn't helping the pain in his head. But more than any-thing, he hated the fact that he was restrained, bad memories still clinging to him. He tugged at the cuffs binding his wrists, his movements erratic and panicked.

Only when he glared back at the woman, whose screams were not helping his situation, did everything completely fall into place.

"Cupcake?"

The woman stopped looking frantically around and stared at him, then her gaze dropped to what she was wearing. His puffy shirt. Her already-pale face turned ashen, and for a moment she looked as if she might pass out. Then her wide-eyed stare returned to him, roaming down over his body. Her eyes stopped and grew even rounder when she reached his crotch.

He looked down also, and saw that he wore nothing but chaps. And his Old Chap was lying against his thigh for the whole world to see. Or at least for Cupcake to see. Amazingly, her gray pallor turned pink almost instantaneously.

But with her reaction, a sheepish averting of her eyes and the realization that he wasn't back on Captain Morgan's Floating Ship of Bloodletting and Doom, he actually chuckled. Being in a sex swing with his Happy Jack swinging in the breeze was not the worst thing he'd ever experienced.

Especially when it was having such an interesting effect on Cupcake, who still averted her eyes—mostly. He noticed she took quick glances every now and then. Which was making old Happy Jack all the happier.

"I don't suppose you could help get me down?" he finally asked when it became clear that Cupcake had no intention of saying anything first.

She hesitated, shooting another quick glance at him, this one directed at his face. Mostly.

"Presumably you are the one who trussed me up here. So shouldn't you be the one to get me down?" he said pragmatically.

"I did not—truss—you up there."

He gave her an amused look.

"Well, I have to admit I don't remember. Unfortunately. But since I'm wearing no pants . . ." He glanced down at himself. "Well, virtually no pants. And you are wearing my shirt, I'm thinking something happened between us."

She cast a look down at herself, too, then crossed her arms over her ample chest as if that would somehow nullify the fact that that was his shirt . . . ruffles, lace, and all.

"Some help," he prompted again.

She hesitated a moment longer, then dropped her arms and let out a sigh. Apparently she saw no other way around helping him, for which he was thankful. His shoulders and arm were killing him. Still, she only took a few steps closer to him, clearly trying to decide what would be the best strategy to get him down.

"You're not going to be able to avoid getting up close and personal," he said with a grin, then spread his legs so she could move between them and reach the cuffs.

Her cheeks grew redder, but rather than move between his legs, she placed a hand on his leather-clad knee and shoved it toward the other one, closing his legs. She still had to press up against his outer thigh and side of his chest to reach the lock.

"Or you can do it that way," he said wryly. It was on the tip of his tongue to point out that one of her very full, very perky breasts was still right there in his face, but decided against it.

He didn't know Cupcake well, but he knew her well enough to know she'd just leave him hanging if she got pissed off.

"How long have I been up here?" he asked, trying not to think about how amazingly tempting that breast was—so close to his face. His mouth.

"I have no idea," she said absently, focused on undoing the lock. "Don't even know where we are or who those other people are, for that matter."

"Other people?" He tried to look around, but his position made it impossible. The deeper meaning of her words hit him and his gaze shifted to her face. "Wait, you mean you don't remember either?"

Her fingers faltered and her face grew redder, if that were possible. "No."

He was silent for a moment. "Shit. Not again."

This time her hands dropped completely from the cuff and she gaped at him, her eyes huge and startlingly blue.

"What do you mean, 'not again?'"

He gave her a pained look. "Well, this memory loss thing . . . it happened another time, too."

WAS HE FREAKING kidding? He'd had this happen before? Because Josie Lynn could absolutely assure him this had *never* happened to her before. Waking up in some sort of sex room? Wearing only a men's shirt? With other scantily clad people passed out around her? Yeah. This had never happened. Ever. Frankly, she couldn't recommend it.

And of course it would be the sexy pirate she would wake up with . . . well, sort of with. She was wearing his shirt, so clearly she'd been with him for a least part of the time that she couldn't remember. Very possibly *really* been with him.

She shot a quick glance past him to the couple only a few feet away. Had she also been with that guy? At least she recognized the pirate, but this other guy . . . oh dear God. And the woman. Then she realized another woman lay on the floor, still unconscious. Or at least she hoped the woman was unconscious.

She had to be. Josie Lynn didn't want to contemplate other alternatives. Nor did she want to think about what they had all done in this room together. What if they'd had an orgy . . . ?

Oh, this could be really bad.

"Okay, you kind of look like you might pass out again," the

pirate said, drawing his attention away from the others. "So could you get me down before you do that?"

Josie Lynn gave him a dirty look. "I love the concern."

"I assure you, I'm very concerned," he told her. "But I'm also a little concerned that I have no feeling in my hands, too."

Begrudgingly, Josie Lynn supposed that was an understandable reason to be worried and set back to getting him unlocked. This time, maybe because she just wanted some answers, then out of here and away from all of these people, she managed to unfasten the locks without too much struggle.

"Thanks," he said, wincing as he lowered his arms and flexed his fingers.

"So you said this has happened before?" she said, ignoring his gratitude. "How many forgotten orgies have you had, exactly?"

The pirate stopped rotating his shoulder and looked at her. "Whoa now, who said anything about orgies? Why would you think we had an orgy?"

She lifted her hands and looked around the room, ending her tour on him and his lack of attire.

He shrugged. "Okay, I can see where you would conclude something sexual happened last night, but if we all did have a forgotten orgy, it would be my first."

"So what happened again?"

"I think someone must have drugged us."

"Drugged us?"

How could he stand there, his penis hanging out for all the world to see, and calmly tell her that he thought they'd been drugged?

"And do you and your friends get drugged often?"

"No," he said with the same nonchalance. "But it did happen once before."

Josie Lynn stared at him, trying to stay calm. "And do you know who did it?"

"The first time?"

She nodded slowly, starting to wonder if he could possibly be serious, or if maybe he was just nuts.

"Yeah, we know who did it the first time," he said, again amazing her with his matter-of-factness. "But I highly doubt he'd do it again. It was an accident."

Okay, yeah, nuts seemed like the most likely explanation here, but before she got the chance to tell him that, the other man, who thankfully had clothes on, called to him.

So this other guy knew the pirate. And, she realized as she looked closer at both the man and woman, they were handcuffed together.

Of course they were handcuffed together. Yeah, this was effin' nuts.

LIZETTE WAS HAVING a rather pleasant dream of riding in a hot air balloon over the French countryside after the Parisian World's Fair back in 1889, when she had the sensation of being tugged, accompanied by an irritating rattling. She wanted to suggest to whoever was creating the ruckus to please cease, but she was alone in the balloon.

Then a scream cut through the air, ripping her balloon and sending her basket plunging to the ground and her certain death.

If she wasn't a vampire, that is, and if she wasn't dreaming.

Lizette jerked awake and shot her gaze around the dim room,

not recognizing her hotel room. This was not the Royal Sonesta. This was not her room. Where on earth was she?

She realized what had woken her up was a woman she did not recognize screaming at the top of her lungs as she stood in the middle of the room, looking down at her rather unusual outfit, which consisted of a puffy blouse and nothing else. Lizette frantically looked down at her own attire, and while she was still wearing her skirt, her jacket was gone, and her blouse was unbuttoned almost to her navel. Her bra was showing.

Letting out a little squawk herself, Lizette moved to rebutton it.

But when she pulled her right hand toward her breasts, a man's hand came with it.

Lizette swallowed hard and stared in bewilderment at the faint dark hair on the back of the callused hand, not entirely sure what she was looking at.

Hand. Metal. Oh my.

Her sluggish brain processed the fact that she was handcuffed to a man. The silver ovals encased both of their wrists, and his hand was now flopping on her lace bra. This was not a good sign. Her gaze shot to her right as she shook her hand, trying to force the man's hand off of her, which as much as she would like it to be, was not in fact dismembered.

It did belong to a living vampire, possibly the last vampire she would like to be chained to in a dark room that she didn't recognize.

Oh dear. It was Johnny Malone who was handcuffed to her.

"Oh, good, you're awake," he said with a half smile.

"What is the meaning of this?"

"I have no idea." Johnny swept his free hand through his short hair. "I was actually hoping you had some idea of what happened last night, because I don't. Never once have I blacked out, and yet . . . nothing."

She didn't remember anything either, and frankly, that was terrifying. "I don't remember a thing! This is awful. Where are we?"

"Zelda's dominatrix dungeon."

"*What?*"

"And no, that's not a fetish game show. We're at the bride's house, in her special soundproof room."

Bride. That's right. Lizette had gone to the wedding of Johnny's friend to confront Johnny for missing their appointment and removing his drums from the apartment before the investigation had been concluded. Or had even really started, frankly. She remembered arguing with him, feeling a bit faint, drinking a horrible-tasting punch. Then mostly nothing.

"Did I dance with you?" she asked him in horror.

Johnny gave her a rueful look. "I think we danced together and then some."

Oh dear. Did he mean . . .

Lizette's head was throbbing. Her eyes were gritty. Her shoulders and legs were stiff.

But those were not the only parts of her that were sore. As she sat on the carpeted floor of Zelda's dominatrix dungeon, she stared at the handcuffs attaching her wrist to Johnny Malone's, and had the horrible suspicion that he was the party responsible for the unmistakable well-loved sensation between her legs.

She wouldn't have slept with him. She couldn't have. Except there was no denying a few particular facts.

She was handcuffed to him.

A quick shift confirmed she was no longer wearing panties.

And despite the way her head ached, whenever she glanced over at him, there was a sizzling awareness between them, like their bodies remembered what had happened even if neither of their brains did.

"I don't know what to say. I am mortified," she told him honestly. "I have never blacked out from drinking. Ever. I would have declined the toxic punch if I had known it would result in . . . *this*. Whatever this is." Overcome with the sudden desperate need to get out of the room and distance herself from Johnny and the knowledge that she had behaved like a complete wanton, she tried to stand up.

Only to wind up falling down on her backside when the weight of Johnny's attached limb pulled her straight back down. "Stand up!" she snapped.

"Fine. Jesus. How was I supposed to know you were going to stand up? I'm not psychic," he mumbled. "On the count of three, we'll stand, okay?"

She nodded, realizing he was right.

"*Un. Deux. Trois.*"

He spoke French. Amazed, Lizette pushed off the floor with him as they stood together. He didn't look like the type of man who would know a second language, whatever that might look like. She realized that this could work to her advantage, because she remembered a key piece of information. "Saxon's new wife is mortal, yes?" she asked quietly.

He nodded.

"Is that her?" she asked, gesturing with her head to the screaming blouse-wearer.

"No. I have no idea who that is." He edged forward in the dark a little. "I think that's Zelda on the floor, passed out, but holy crap, why is she almost naked? And where is Saxon?"

Lizette found that she could not care where Saxon was, as she had suddenly become aware by their forward shuffling that there was a man wearing leather pants that had no back to them so that his entire posterior was exposed. He turned around to face them. Nor was there a front.

Oh my.

She swallowed and averted her gaze, suddenly wishing she had resisted the urge to tell Johnny Malone exactly what she thought of his defiance and had waited until after the wedding to speak with him. She had heard tales of wild partying in New Orleans, and clearly here was her evidence. There were far too many people in this room in various states of undress, and a glance over to the right revealed an entire wall of sex toys and props. She couldn't look at them.

But she couldn't look at the naked man either.

Or the woman sprawled out on her back in nothing but a bra and sheer panties.

Which left her nowhere to look but at her feet, which were bare. Those were expensive pumps she'd been wearing, and she glanced back to where they had been sitting, suddenly frantic at the realization that her purse wasn't on her shoulder. She went nowhere without her handbag. It was a third arm, and she would be profoundly unnerved if it was missing, given its contents. Her passport was in there. She gave a sigh of relief when she saw it was lying on the floor. That was a start. And at least Johnny was fully dressed. She had checked. It was slightly reassuring, but honestly she'd feel much better with her panties on and her hair back up in a bun. Why would she have taken her hair down?

That was probably a stupid question. During dancing or whatever had come after that.

"Drake! Dude, how many times do I have to tell you to put some clothes on? Damn." Johnny looked pained himself as he shielded his eyes from the view. "And where the hell is Saxon?"

"I have no idea, man. You know about as much as I do, which is nothing. Your foot on my ass woke me up, then Cupcake got me down out of the sex swing. Saxon is gone. Zelda is passed out. You're handcuffed to a chick I've never seen before in my life, and none of us remember what happened last night." He looked at Lizette hopefully. "Unless you do?"

"No, sorry." She wasn't sure if that was a curse or a blessing. She suspected it might be better to be lacking in details of the events of the night. "I'm Lizette Chastain, by the way. It's a pleasure to meet you." She stuck out her free hand, realizing it was a bit ridiculous under the circumstances, but feeling that manners should never be abandoned, especially in times of crisis.

He gave her a grin and shook her hand enthusiastically. "Drake Hanover, at your service."

He gave her a leg, eighteenth-century style, which would have been significantly more charming if he weren't fully naked from hip to hip. His wrist wasn't the only thing that gave a flourish.

"I take it you're French? I spent time on the Continent in my youth," he told her. "My father was British, my mother Spanish, but I spent time in Paris."

"Oh, indeed?" Under normal circumstances, she would have loved to discuss his youth, which she suspected was of a similar time to her own, but the girl in the blouse was clearly mortal. Lizette could hear her heartbeat and smell the blood pumping through her veins. She turned to her. "I'm Lizette, it's a pleasure. And you are?"

The girl didn't look particularly scared. She looked angry. Very, very angry. "I'm Josie Lynn."

"*Enchanté*," Lizette added, because there just wasn't an English equivalent that sounded as pleasing to her French ear.

"I'm Cajun but I don't speak French," Josie Lynn said. "And I want to know who the hell drugged me last night!"

That startled Lizette. "We were drugged?" she asked Johnny.

"It certainly seems like a reasonable explanation," he said. "Which means we should probably be a little concerned about Zelda. She is out cold, and I would cover her up with my shirt but I can't get my shirt off with this handcuff on. Is there a blanket or something around here? Maybe we should call for backup from Stella and Katie."

Lizette knew Stella was of course Johnny's sister and that Katie was married to Berto Cortez. She realized that Johnny was concerned about Zelda, and it did touch her just a tiny bit. Not wanting to reveal anything vampiric to Josie Lynn, she spoke French to Johnny. "So you think Zelda may be in danger, given that she is a mortal? If a drug could affect us as vampires that dramatically, what could it do to her, yes?"

"Exactly," he said, nodding.

The truth was, Johnny had no clue what the hell Lizette was saying. He didn't speak French. He barely spoke English with any sort of rhyme or reason, and certainly without any regard for proper grammar. But for some reason, Lizette thought he was worldly enough to speak her language, and he wasn't about to disabuse her of that notion right now. It must have been his counting to three in French, but that was all he knew how to speak in about six languages. Along with the obvious *yes* and *no*. But he just didn't want to admit that. Maybe it was because they might have had sex with each other, but Johnny felt compelled to impress Lizette. He knew she thought he was a jackass, and normally, that wouldn't bother him. He also thought she was perhaps the most irritating woman he'd ever met, with her clipboard and her lists and her rules. But she had danced like a French hooker the night before, and with her hair down now . . . looking luscious and carefree, well, he didn't find her quite as annoying.

He hoped the sex had been good. Even if she never remembered it, he'd like to think that he'd kept it up for a good long haul, and that she had screamed his name in violent orgasm at least three times. That was the way he was going to remember it. If they'd actually had sex. He wasn't exactly sure. Did women have a secret way of knowing that? They always seemed to have a longer post-sex satisfaction. Ten minutes after he pulled out, it was like he'd never had sex in the first place, but women were wired different. So if they had, chances were Lizette would know in some mysterious female way.

Maybe he would ask her later.

"Okay, I'm calling Stella," he said. "I think Zelda should be checked out by a doctor, just in case." He turned to Josie Lynn. "How are you feeling? Do you feel okay?"

"I have a splitting headache and I'm wearing the stupidest shirt I've ever seen in my life, but other than that, I'll live."

"Good." Johnny shot a glance at Drake, wondering what exactly had gone down between him and this girl. He didn't even remember seeing her at the wedding, though admittedly, his memories didn't extend much past the first bridal dance. "So what did we all drink in common, the punch?"

"I had one sip," Josie Lynn said. "One lousy sip."

"Lizette and I had like three glasses each."

"I had about six," Drake said. "Dude, I was thirsty."

Johnny pulled his phone out of his pocket and called his sister while Drake went in search of better pants. Any pants would be better than those. Tighty whities would be better than those.

It took ten rings for Stella to answer. "Hey, Stella, have you seen Saxon? And did you drink that punch last night? Because I'm here with Drake and we're hungover and can't remember a damn thing. It's like my wake all over again, only I'm not dead and this time I'm one of the victims, so actually, it's much less fun." Especially considering what he'd most like to remember was who had done the unbuttoning on Lizette's blouse. Him or her?

"Same thing here," Stella said, her voice gravely. "Wyatt and I don't even remember going home. That is so damn scary, I hate it. Anything could have happened! You think it was the punch?"

"Pretty sure. And Zelda is here but she's out stone cold. I was wondering if you could come over and get her dressed and take her to the ER. I think maybe she should be checked out, maybe given some fluids."

"Oh, geez, sure, of course. Give us ten minutes. Wyatt's in the shower. Have you talked to Cort or Katie?"

"No. Can you call them and have them meet us?"

"Where are you, by the way?"

"Zelda's apartment, in the domme room. You know, her special little dungeon."

Stella gave a startled laugh. "What the hell are you doing there?"

"I would tell you, but I have no idea." Johnny tried to move away from Lizette, feeling the conversation was more than a little private, when he realized he couldn't get more than two feet from her without dragging her like a poodle on a leash. "Bring metal cutters, by the way."

"Metal cutters? Do I even want to know?"

"No. Just hurry please."

He hung up the phone and tried to call Saxon, but it went to voice mail. Then he asked Lizette, "Any word on who Josie Lynn is?"

"The caterer. Apparently she and Drake met last night in the kitchen and she was unimpressed."

"I guess at some point she got impressed."

"Like me?" Lizette shot him a look.

"Um, yeah, about that." Johnny leaned his head down so they weren't overheard. "Maybe we should talk about that. Alone. Would you mind going upstairs with me? We have to let Stella in anyway."

"Shouldn't we be looking for the key to these handcuffs?"

"Sure, in a minute, but I doubt we're going to be able to find them. This room is full of *objects* if you noticed."

Lizette sighed. Johnny felt kind of bad. It was one thing for her to catalog every crappy ashtray in his apartment, it was another thing for her to have to deal with Zelda and Saxon's getting-their-freak-on equipment. Which reminded him. "By the way, the VA can keep my ashtray collection. I quit smoking five weeks ago. It was starting to stain my fangs." He was pretty proud of that fact. It wasn't easy to give up the nicotine or the oral fixation.

"Congratulations. We will dispose of them regardless of the findings."

So they were back to that. He'd probably showed the woman a helluva time last night and she still couldn't cut him any slack.

Johnny yanked open the soundproof door to the room and stepped out. Lizette's shriek stopped him cold. "What? What the hell is the matter?"

She pointed behind him. "Alligator."

"What?" Her accent was particularly thick, and he couldn't figure out what she was saying.

She pointed again. "Alligator!"

Johnny turned. "Holy shit! There's an alligator in the hallway!"

"That's what I said! Get back before he . . ." Lizette made a snapping motion with her left hand. "Chomp, chomp!"

Johnny almost laughed. Almost.

Instead he jumped back into the room and slammed the door. Then he laughed. "Oh my God, there's an alligator in the hallway."

"That's insane!" Lizette said.

"Very." Johnny looked back to Drake for assistance, but he and Josie Lynn seemed to be arguing. "I guess we can bum-rush him. Otherwise we're trapped here."

"Are you sure that's wise?"

"Well, we are vampires. We'll live."

"Shh!" Lizette covered his mouth with her free hand. "You cannot speak of such things!"

Johnny pursed his lips and again fought the urge to laugh. She was so damn earnest. Slowly, he stuck the tip of his tongue out and licked her fingers.

She let out a yelp and yanked her hand back, eyes wide. "What are you doing?"

Now he did laugh. "Just trying to lighten the mood."

Her eyes narrowed in anger. "We need to remove these handcuffs immediately. It will make it easier for us to rush past the alligator."

"I could probably try to yank them. I do have supernatural strength. It might tear our flesh, but it will heal."

His suggestion got the exact response he'd expected from Lizette. "We can't do that in front of Josie Lynn. It won't look normal."

"Then let's get out of here and do it in the other room. Then we can go our separate ways." He would continue to look for Saxon, and she could go write a list detailing the ways they should look normal.

"Fine. Let me get my purse." The haughty Frenchwoman was back in place, her delicate nose in the air as she marched over to the spot where they'd been sleeping, or more accurately, where they'd been passed out cold. It took them a second to get their walking coordinated, because she strode and he ambled, but they only needed to make it a few feet across the room.

When she bent over, Johnny had to admit he eyeballed her ass. It was a good ass, what could he say? He adjusted his pants a little. What a shame to make the ice princess thaw and not even be able to remember it. It was an actual tragedy.

"Hey, Drake," he said. "There's an alligator in the hallway, so be careful. We're going to head out and look for Saxon and the key to these handcuffs." He gave the cuffs a more thorough inspection. "They look like titanium to me, which will make this more of a challenge. Stella and Katie are on their way to get Zelda dressed and off to the ER."

Drake just nodded, like none of that was particularly strange.

"An alligator?" Josie Lynn asked. "Are you freaking kidding me? What kind of a weirdo fun house is this?"

"If this is a fun house, it's a terrible one," Lizette said, sounding put out. "I think it's time to leave. Has anyone seen my shoes?"

Johnny gave a cursory glance around the room. There were a few whips and ball gags strewn about, and the sex swing dominated the center of the room, but he didn't see any clothes or shoes. He had a hard time picturing Saxon spending hours of pleasure in here with Zelda, who was actually much smarter than

Saxon. The woman ran her own business and had raised two kids, so she clearly had more than cotton between her ears. Saxon, on the other hand? He wasn't so sure.

Johnny had to admit he was ready for some fresh air. This was all just a little too much togetherness and more of a glimpse into his friends' private lives than he needed. "I don't see your shoes. We can see if Zelda has flip-flops. You shouldn't be walking around the quarter barefoot."

"Oh, heavens, no." Lizette gave a delicate shudder. Her fingers fluttered over her chest.

It was then that he realized she was in fact far too classy for him. Here she had woken up in a strange place surrounded by sex paraphernalia and people she didn't know in various states of undress, and she was completely holding it together. In fact, she was buttoning her blouse one-handed, and despite their being attached at the wrist, she was assessing him coolly, like nothing was out of the ordinary whatsoever. Johnny did not have that kind of self-control. He'd never had that. Most likely he never would, given that he was damn near a century old and it hadn't happened yet. Which meant Lizette was out of his league.

Which suddenly pissed him off.

Chapter Six

THE LEGEND OF ZELDA

LIZETTE didn't want to admit it to Johnny, but she was terrified of the alligator. So while she knew intellectually that it couldn't kill her, she still couldn't help but imagine that teeth crushing her flesh and bones would not feel particularly wonderful. So she was hiding her fear under an aristocratic veneer. It was something her mother had taught her back when she was a child in France. Her mother had frequently been afraid in the tumultuous days of the Terror but she wouldn't let her tormentors have the satisfaction of seeing they had made her so. Lizette wasn't going to let Johnny see that she was quite possibly on the verge of having a complete meltdown.

It was becoming more and more clear that she was attached to Johnny for at least the next hour or so, when all she really wanted to do was run away to her hotel room to take a long shower, before putting on her most demure panties and business suit, so that she could pretend none of this had ever happened. It was a little hard to pretend nothing untoward had happened, when the evidence was a living male attached to her wrist.

She supposed that she only had one option: She needed to get past the alligator so they could proceed with their lives outside of this windowless room.

Johnny pulled a riding crop down off the wall.

"What are you doing with that?" She was simultaneously horrified and just a teensy bit aroused, which then horrified her all over again. What on earth was she thinking? One night in a sex dungeon and she was willing to be spanked? Her cheeks heated as she wondered what exactly had transpired between her and Johnny. And had there been witnesses? It didn't bear considering.

"I'm going to give the alligator a whack if I need to."

"Oh." Right. Of course. He was thinking about their safety, not about the sexual escapades they might have engaged in. Lizette cleared her throat and put her purse firmly over her shoulder. "*Bonsoir*," she called to Josie Lynn and Drake. "It was a pleasure meeting you, and please extend my felicitations to Zelda when she awakens."

Johnny just stared at her.

"What?"

"Nothing."

Drake waved and gave her a smile. Lizette kept her eyes firmly above his waist as she waved in return, then she nodded to Johnny. "I'm ready. What is our plan?"

"The plan is to run past the alligator. If he snaps, I whack. That's it. Nothing fancy."

"In other words, you do not really know what to do."

"Exactly."

Well, she supposed she could appreciate his honesty. "Understood. Shall we? On the count of three?"

"Let's just go." Johnny pulled open the door and they both ran.

Which was something of a challenge, given that they were attached at the wrist and they both tried to squeeze to the left, out of the path of the alligator's jaw. They were stumbling and bouncing, Johnny's free arm swinging with the crop even though the alligator wasn't doing a damn thing. He just sat there looking like they were a couple of complete idiots. He was probably right.

Johnny was dragging her down the hallway and he opened the first doorway on the right. It was the bathroom. "Shit!" he said. He kept dragging her, and the next door was a bedroom. They ran in and Lizette slammed the door shut. Then locked it. She'd seen *Jurassic Park*. Who knew if an alligator could figure out how to push open a door?

They stood there, both moving away from the door before Johnny burst out laughing. Lizette couldn't help but smile with him. It was more than a bit absurd.

As was Zelda's bedroom. Lizette felt like she'd fallen into Barbie's dream house. There was hot pink everywhere and lots of shiny surfaces and crystal, from the chandelier to the candlesticks on the dresser, to the gigantic crystal-rimmed mirror. Where there wasn't bling, there was pink, and as Lizette turned, she could see six of herself in the many mirrors and reflective surfaces.

Johnny laughed even harder. "Wow, when you're on the bed, you can see yourself getting plugged from every angle. That Zelda. What a fun gal."

"Plugged . . ." Lizette suddenly realized what Johnny meant. "Why I've never even considered . . ." Then she cut herself off. Johnny Malone didn't need to know the details of her sex life, or lack thereof. Even if she had slept with him the night before.

"Maybe you should," he said mildly.

That annoyed her. "Can we just get some shoes please and get out of here?"

"Of course. Though looking at your feet, Zelda isn't going to have much you can wear. What size are you?"

"I don't know American sizing." Lizette went with him to the closet, because of course, she had to go wherever he went.

"You are size teeny weeny. Zelda is American-basketball-player size. But maybe these will work." He held up a pair of heels with pink poufs on the ends.

"I'm not wearing those!" Those were stripper shoes. She did not wear her sexuality so blatantly on her feet. She just didn't.

"How about these?"

They were flats, a big improvement, but they were bedazzled. "I am going to look ridiculous if I wear those. Everyone will be staring at me."

"So?"

"So the point is to blend in, not to stand out. We're vampires already, with odd habits. If we draw attention to ourselves, we're at risk."

Johnny scoffed at her and pulled out a pair of boots that had a mouth painted on the front. "That's ridiculous."

"I don't want to argue with you about this again. That is how I feel." And she was right.

"What do you think is going to happen?"

"I could be killed! I don't want to die!" What was difficult for him to comprehend about what she was saying? Lizette grabbed the boots out of his hands and tossed them back in the closet.

"Well, I want to live," he told her emphatically. "What's the point of being here if we have to be afraid of our own shadow? I'd rather die than live forever as a pale, boring, zero-fun version of myself slinking around in the dark."

"That's not what I'm doing," she insisted, though she had to admit, there was something about his statement that stung. She lashed out at him, unwilling to admit he could be right. "And I was never fun!"

Wait a minute. That wasn't what she'd meant to say.

What she meant was that she had seen horrible things done to first her parents, then Jean-Baptiste, and it had changed her forever. She wasn't carefree, and that wasn't a crime. There was nothing wrong with exercising caution.

So why did she suddenly feel so terrible?

Lizette lifted her right hand and eyed the handcuffs. "We should try to get these off now."

"You want me to yank? There's going to be blood. And then we'll still both have a handcuff ring around our wrists. Is that really what you want?" He eyed her. "Cause I'll do it. If that's what you want."

Why did he sound so belligerent? She was the one being put in an impossibly awkward position of jeopardizing her job at the VA. Speaking of which, she needed to call Dieter and see if he had any idea what had happened the evening before. She was torn between wanting answers and not wanting Dieter to know anything out of the ordinary had happened.

"Yes, that's what I want." Blood would wash off, and unattached to Johnny she could at least go back to her hotel and shower off the remnants of the tawdry whore that seemed to be clinging to her. Every time she shifted, she smelled a man's cologne wafting off her blouse and other areas.

Johnny lifted his hand and then dropped it again. "Shit. I can't do it."

"Why not?" Once again, Lizette found herself among the many women who were mystified by men.

"I can't hurt you. I just can't."

"I'm asking you to." Yes, it would hurt, but she was an aging vampire, and would heal fairly rapidly. She wasn't looking forward to the pain, but of course, she would live. "It will be easier to move around."

"Sorry." Johnny bit his fingernail, a habit she found both disgusting and endearing. "I don't want to see you bleed. It's not right. We'll find another way."

Suddenly aware of how close they were standing, Lizette averted her gaze. It was far too easy to stare at him, far too easy to imagine the power he would have in his thighs as he rose over a woman. Over her. These weren't things she thought about particularly often, but now that she was almost positive she had slept with him, she couldn't keep her mind from straying in that direction. It was embarrassing, yes, to think that she had done whatever it was she had done, when she didn't know him at all, and was supposed to be in New Orleans in an official capacity, but at the same time, it was even more upsetting to think that if she had done such things, she couldn't even remember them. Shouldn't she at least be afforded the right to have her curiosity appeased? It had been nearly fifty years since she had taken a lover, and that had been something of a letdown.

Her body seemed pleased to have been reawakened the night before, and she found herself wanting to touch his arm, his chest, wanting to slide her tongue across his bottom lip. It was disconcerting.

"That's very gentlemanly of you," she told him, because it was. There was something pleasing about his discomfit with causing her pain.

"I don't think I've ever been accused of that before, but I suppose you might actually be right. Maybe I'm improving." He grinned. "Now let's find a shoe that fits, shall we? Or at least something that isn't going to fall off of you."

What they settled on were little stretchy slippers that women were supposed to put on when their feet hurt from wearing high heels. Because of their stretchy nature, they weren't as huge as other options would have been, and they were black, which was a relief to Lizette. It was not a relief that Johnny had to help her put them on, lifting her leg up with his hand, his flesh cool and smooth on her calf as he helped guide the slipper. Lizette held on to his shoulders and tried not to think about her body or his body or any bodies, just on getting her foot into the fabric. Except that she was acutely aware of the fact that she wasn't wearing panties, and that vampires had excellent powers of scent. If she could smell his cologne on her, what else could he smell? Besides, it was not her imagination that his hand was lingering.

He glanced up at her, his black eyes intense. "Do you think something happened between us last night?" he asked her.

So to the point. Lizette would have blushed if she had been able to, and reminded herself that Johnny had lived in America for a long time. He wasn't going to dance around a topic for ages with flowery expressions like European men. Clearing the air was definitely advisable. "Well," she told him, lowering her newly slippered foot to the floor. "I would say that there are indications that something of a sexual nature occurred."

"Really? Are you sure?" He stood, slowly, and his male presence overwhelmed her as he rose, occupying her space and dominating her thoughts, unnerving her.

"Yes. I'm fairly sure."

"How do you know?"

She was regretting that he wasn't beating around the bush with charm and obscure entendres. "I just know."

"How?"

He was going to make her say it. Irritated with his persistence, she told him, "I seem to have lost my panties. And I seem to be experiencing a certain soreness that is not from sleeping on the floor."

Understanding finally seemed to dawn on him. "Ooohh. I see. Sucks we don't remember, doesn't it?"

"I'm not sure if it does or not," she told him truthfully.

Johnny laughed. But his thumb traced across her palm teasingly. "I think it's a damn shame, actually."

"THAT'S ZELDA."

Drake glanced back, surprised to see that Cupcake—or rather, Josie Lynn—was following him. Until this moment, she'd seemed like she wanted nothing more than to be far away from him, both last night and tonight. Yet, here she was. Maybe the allure of his bare ass had finally swayed her. Of course.

"You're right, that is."

She stopped and wrapped her arms around herself. She worried her full, pretty lower lip. "This is awful."

He frowned. Yeah, it was definitely awful. Not remembering what happened to you for hours was not a good feeling. But he wasn't sure why she was particularly worried about Zelda. Personally, he was far more upset that he'd very likely gotten a little taste of Cupcake and had not a single memory about it. He glanced over at the Amazon still sprawled on the floor.

If there had been any Zelda action, he was glad he'd blacked that out.

Josie Lynn stared at the unconscious dominatrix, looking almost—forlorn. Which struck Drake as an odd reaction.

"Listen," he said, returning to her side, "I know all of this is overwhelming, but it's really not that bad."

Josie Lynn spun toward him, that strangely hopeless look in her blue eyes replaced by a flash of anger.

"Not that bad! This is so far beyond bad, I—I," she threw up her hands. "I don't even know what to say. You are acting like this is just another wild weekend in the Big Easy. Well, this may be normal for you, but it sure as hell isn't normal for me."

Drake looked down at himself. "And you think this is normal for me? I woke up in a sex swing in a dominatrix's dungeon. I might have had sex with a woman that I just met last night. And now I'm arguing with that very same woman with my schlong hanging out. Believe me, this is not normal."

She glanced downward, and to Drake's dismay his dick reacted instantly, bobbing outward. *Damn.*

"Well I think we both know the part about sleeping with a woman you just met is probably a pretty normal occurrence for you."

Something about the disgust on her face bothered him, even though he couldn't really deny that fact. Hell, he was a single vampire in a band on Bourbon Street. Women just happened. But somehow her expression made him feel—bad. Sleazy, even. But why the hell should it?

Okay, the current outfit really didn't help.

"You don't know that," he finally said, realizing he sounded more petulant than persuasive.

She snorted, a sound that, as much as Drake hated to admit it, sounded cute. "Well I do know that you came into the kitchen while I was working to try to get me to go out with you after the wedding. And I'm pretty sure you didn't mean just for drinks."

"That's exactly what I meant. To apologize."

"You mean for the unsolicited kiss?"

"Exactly."

She gave him a dubious look. "You wanted it to be more than drinks. Admit it."

"No," he said. "Because that isn't true."

She made another face, one that hinted at dimples at either side of her mouth and made her lips look utterly kissable. His dick hardened more and poked out in front of him like Pinocchio's nose when telling a lie.

He was telling a lie, too, and they both knew it.

But instead of continuing this conversation, which just appeared to be getting him in more and more trouble, he said, "I need to find some pants."

To his relief, Josie Lynn let him walk away with as much dignity as his assless chaps would afford him.

But after walking a few feet, he realized he didn't know where he was going exactly. Where the hell would he find pants—or any clothing—in this room? Now, if he wanted a ginormous purple dildo or a . . .

He tilted his head to study one of the items hanging on the wall. Was that a mace?

Yeah, he could find any item of sexual torture, but he was pretty sure a pair of size 34 Levi's was not happening.

He glanced back to Josie Lynn, who stood in the same place, her arms curled around herself again as if she was cold.

Or protecting herself.

He moved back toward her, debating what he could say to her to help. She had that worried, almost defeated expression again, and despite her obvious dislike of him, he felt the need to comfort her. Of course that was all he'd been trying to do before their conversation went badly just moments earlier.

He paused, trying to think of the right thing to say, when he heard her say to herself, "This was not how this job was supposed to go. How the hell am I going to get the money now?"

Drake frowned. This job? The money? What was she talking about? Then a memory, although somewhat hazy, came back to him. One of the last he remembered from last night. Josie Lynn taking money. Taking money for what?

Could Josie Lynn be involved in whatever had happened to cause their memory loss? And now that he thought about it, where was all their stuff? His wallet was gone. His cell phone. Hell, even his pants. Maybe they hadn't been just misplaced during a night of debauchery. And he imagined everyone else's stuff was gone, too. Had this been a robbery of some sort? And was Josie Lynn somehow involved?

If she was, the plan had clearly backfired, at least for her. But she was involved in something. He knew he'd seen her take money and let some people in the back door. He thought about the people he'd seen, trying to remember what they looked like.

They'd looked like . . . Cher. Multiple Chers.

He frowned. Maybe the drug had already started to take effect at that point. Chers. That couldn't be right.

He looked at Josie Lynn, who was again chewing at her lower lip and looking very, very anxious. Whether his memory of Cher en masse was accurate or not, one thing was for certain; he wasn't letting Cupcake out of his sight until he got the truth.

JOSIE LYNN STARED at the motionless body of the bride, Zelda.

Well, there was no denying this bride would remember her wedding night. Or if she was like the rest of them, remember that she didn't remember her wedding night. Josie Lynn was also pretty sure she wasn't going to be pleased to find her wedding dress, her gifts, and her groom for God's sake, all missing. This was a nightmare.

Josie Lynn wondered if all of her catering supplies were gone, too. Her cookie tins and serving platters. Her mixing bowls and serving spoons. Everything could very well be gone, and she had no means to replace it. She didn't see how she could recover from another major financial hit. If those items were all gone—stolen or whatever happened to them—she didn't think she could salvage her catering career. If she could anyway. It was safe to say the bride and groom probably weren't going to have anything positive to say about their wedding reception, period.

So much for rave reviews.

She immediately felt selfish. Everyone had lost things last night. And a person was missing. That was far more serious than her nonstick pots and pans.

She curled her arms tighter around herself. And there was another niggling thought that wouldn't leave her mind. What if she was somehow inadvertently involved? Everything had gone crazy after she let those transvestites into the reception. But how could they be involved in the drugging? After all, they'd just entered the party moments before Josie Lynn had started to feel so funny.

It didn't make sense.

But Josie Lynn didn't have time to ponder other explanations, because her thoughts were interrupted by the other guy, Johnny, she thought she heard his name was, shouting to the pirate.

"Hey Drake, there's an alligator in the hallway, so be careful."

An alligator? In the hallway? This had to be a joke, right?

She looked over at the pirate—Drake, who was regarding her rather than reacting to what his friend had said. Looking at her? Rather than reacting to a deadly reptile on the loose? She didn't think that could be a good sign.

He walked back over to her, and he obviously hadn't found anything to use as pants or a diaper or even a loincloth. But she must have been growing accustomed to his state of undress, because she was definitely more concerned about the expression on his face than his wiener hanging out.

"Did they say alligator?" she said once he got closer.

He nodded.

She looked toward the other couple just as they called out they were leaving.

Josie Lynn gave Drake a startled look. "They are going into the hallway with the alligator? Do you think that's a wise idea?"

"They'll be fine," he said, almost as if he were distracted. But still, there was an alligator out there. She'd grown up on the bayou and knew gators were no joke. And frankly, that French woman didn't look like she could hold her own with a kitten, much less a vicious beast with a gazillion teeth and a jaw like a steel trap.

"I'm not sure they should go out there," she said, and again he repeated that they would be fine.

She watched the door close behind the couple, feeling certain she would soon be hearing shrieks of terror and pain.

"Who were those people you let in the back door at the reception?"

Josie Lynn's stomach dropped and all thoughts of impending gator death vanished. Slowly she looked back to Drake. He'd seen her take the money. Great, he thought she was involved. Hell, she thought she might be involved, too, but purely by accident.

"They were a group of transvestites who said they were friends of the bride."

"All dressed like Cher, right?"

Josie Lynn nodded, and he looked almost relieved, but that

expression quickly faded as his dark eyes narrowed with suspicion.

"You didn't think it was weird a group of trannies wanted to come in through the back door?"

"Yes I did, but they said they wanted to surprise the bride, and given what the rest of the wedding guests looked like"—she gestured to the shirt she now wore, his shirt—"I didn't think it was terribly weird that transvestites all dressed like Cher would be her friends."

He didn't argue that, but he did bring up the very thing that had troubled her for the moment it happened.

"So why did they give you money?"

She had wondered that, too. Would they have done that if they were just friends? There was something rather desperate about that action. And she'd been rather desperate to take the money.

"They just offered it to me as—a way of thanks, I guess."

"Or as a payoff."

"No," she said shaking her head, even though she wasn't sure that wasn't what it was.

"And we've already figured out the one thing we have in common is the punch. And who made the punch?" He gave her a pointed look.

Josie Lynn gaped at him. Now that she knew she'd had no part in. "I did not tamper with the punch."

"Well, you're going to say that, aren't you?"

"But I didn't. That punch was right out in the open on the buffet table. Anyone could have laced it. Besides I drank some, too. Why would I drug myself?"

"It's a pretty good alibi," he said, eyeing her even more distrustfully. "If you are drugged-out and with us, then your band of

Chers can do the dirty work and split the money with you at a later date."

"That isn't what's going on. My stuff is missing, too. Including the money they gave me for letting them in." She frantically gestured to the fact that all she wore was his shirt. She had nothing, just like everyone else. Except—

"That Frenchwoman with your friend. Who is she? And why is she the only one who has a purse? Or a cell phone? Maybe she's somehow involved."

He seemed to consider her suggestion, then shrugged as if he didn't really care and he'd already made up his mind that Josie Lynn was the culprit.

"The way I see it, there is only one solid lead, and that's to find the Chers and find out what they did with all the stuff you guys stole."

"I didn't steal anything," she insisted more frantically. He had to believe her. His accusation was a whole lot worse than just losing her catering company. If he told his friends about her taking the money and his theory that she was involved, who were they going to believe? Even she could admit that she looked like a likely suspect.

"I want to help you find them," she said, knowing she had to locate these guys—gals—to clear her own name.

"Oh, I have no intention of letting you out of my sight," he informed her. "A woman who is willing to drug herself, even sleep with one of her victims—"

"One of *my* victims!" she exclaimed. He could not be serious. "You are not one of my victims. If anything, I was your victim. You forced yourself on me at the reception. You grabbed me and kissed me."

"I seem to recall you grabbing me and kissing me, too," he pointed out.

"One of my many stupid mistakes last night," she muttered.

"Like getting involved with underworld Chers, who got you to do their dirty work, then left you out to dry?"

She clenched her teeth and groaned. There was no point defending herself to his man. He'd clearly already made up his mind about her, and the only way to defend herself was to find the Chers and find out the truth.

Which meant staying with this jerk. Great. And she likely did have sex with him last night. This was just great.

Behind them she heard the door open. She turned, expecting to see the handcuffed couple darting back into the room, but instead two women sauntered in looking so calm that Josie Lynn wondered if the alligator had somehow gotten out of the hallway and was now lying in wait somewhere else.

One of the women was tall and svelte with red hair and pale skin, while the other was petite and almost waifish with blond hair and a wide smile. They were both stunning and utterly unfazed by the scene before them.

"Drake, how unusual to see you with your pants down," the blonde said with a laugh.

Drake gave her a look, although Josie Lynn could see fondness in the grimace. "Isn't that part of the fun of living with me, Katie?"

This Katie lived with him? Josie Lynn suddenly felt all the more self-conscious to be standing there in nothing but his shirt. Although the blonde didn't look upset. Maybe they were truly roommates. Maybe they had an open relationship. But no maybe about it, Josie Lynn did not like the sharp pang of jealousy that had shot through her when he'd said they lived together.

Why the hell would she be jealous—or feel anything for that

matter—for this jerk? He was accusing her of being a thief, for God's sake.

The redhead stepped closer to him and tilted her head, inspecting his look, then said, "It's not really 'with your pants down.' They don't seem to be intact. What *are* you wearing?"

"They are chaps, Stella," Drake said with the odd air of haughty dignity that he seemed to acquire every so often. "I would think being married to a cowboy, you'd be quite familiar with them."

Stella laughed. "Well he never wears them like that, that's for sure."

"See what you're missing," Drake stated. Clearly done with the women's teasing, he gestured to the prone bride. "Zelda is over there. She's breathing, but I do think she should be brought to the hospital."

Josie Lynn wondered how he knew she was breathing. As far as she'd seen, he hadn't gotten anywhere near her.

"Hi," the blonde said, suddenly appearing at Josie Lynn's side with her hand extended. "I'm Katie Cortez. I live with Drake. I'm married to one of his best friends."

Josie Lynn ignored the wave of relief that washed over her as unexpectedly as the jealousy had.

You just don't want to have had a potential one-night stand with a man who was involved with another woman, she assured herself, not quite believing the reasoning even as she thought it.

She accepted the blonde's hand. Her fingers were small and cool.

"And they are also in the band together. Maybe you've met my husband. Cort?"

Josie Lynn shook her head. It was on the tip of her tongue to say she didn't even know Drake was in a band, but she didn't want to reveal to this clearly nice woman that she was in a sex dungeon with a man she didn't really know. And again, wearing nothing but his shirt.

"Okay," Stella said, drawing everyone's attention to her. For which Josie Lynn was very grateful. "I know where Zelda and Saxon's room is—"

"I'm not even going to ask why you know that," Drake said wryly.

"Because I've come over to feed Waldo, you perv," Stella said.

"Waldo?" he asked.

"The alligator."

"You knew about the alligator?" he asked, surprised.

"Yeah, it was Saxon's one-year anniversary gift to Zelda. Although he's normally not hanging out in the hallway," Stella said. "Anyway, their room is two doors down on the right. Drake, go get Zelda some clothes. And something for yourself while you're at it."

"Like Saxon's clothes will fit me," he said.

"But Zelda's probably will," Katie pointed out.

Josie Lynn actually smiled slightly at the horrified expression on Drake's face. God, this was all so weird.

"Okay," Drake said, once recovered from the idea of wearing Zelda's clothes. "Josie Lynn and I will go do that. While you figure out the best way to get Zelda to the hospital."

"Don't you think maybe Josie Lynn should stay here?" Stella said, giving Drake a look Josie Lynn didn't quite understand, but she wondered if the redhead somehow knew he thought she was a part of last night's debacle. Although Josie Lynn didn't know how she would know. Drake couldn't have told her. Maybe nerves were just getting to her.

"You know she'll be fine with me," Drake said again with that haughty air.

Stella looked like she wanted to argue, but then just shrugged. Clearly she knew that it would be a waste of breath to argue with him. Josie Lynn had already figured that out about him, too.

"Just be careful. Waldo is a little cranky."

Not just Waldo, all gators, Josie Lynn thought reluctantly following Drake to the door, but not before grabbing a bungee cord that dangled down from the bottom of the sex swing. She didn't know what it was for on the swing, but she knew it just might come in handy when facing Waldo.

Chapter Seven

LOVE BITES, LOVE BLEEDS

DRAKE hesitated just slightly before he opened the door. He wasn't scared about the alligator for himself. Shit, he was a vampire. He could take his knocks, even from a wannabe dinosaur. But Josie Lynn was another story. Being human, one bite could be fatal. And that scared him. A lot.

More than he really understood, actually. Sure, he wouldn't want to see anyone maimed and killed by an alligator, but the idea of Cupcake getting hurt. That really bothered him.

Because you want to see her brought to justice in a way Captain Morgan never had been, he told himself. This was about a lying woman getting what she deserved. This was about comeuppance.

Or so he would tell himself.

Slowly he opened the door, and there Waldo lay, his back to them, looking more like a stuffed gator than the real McCoy. Unfortunately he was dead center in the hallway, making it hard to stay to one side of him. They were going to have to get pretty damn close to him to make it past.

So that meant one thing; he was going to have to go first. That way if Waldo decided to go all prehistoric, he'd hopefully attack Drake first, while Josie Lynn fled to safety.

"Follow me," he said, whispering, though he wasn't sure why. Did alligators even have ears?

"Maybe I should go first," Josie Lynn suggested, and Drake shot her an astonished look. Was she crazy? That would be like sending old Waldo an appetizer.

"No way." He stepped out the door, staying to the left of the hallway, since that seemed to be the side with the most space between the wall and the animal. He walked carefully, being as quiet as he could. Which was very quiet. That whole vampire thing.

Behind him Josie Lynn was being quiet, too, although he could hear the soft pats of her feet on the bare wood. He just hoped his vampire hearing was more acute than the alligator's.

Once he reached the beast, he debated where the best place to step was. It was like a bizarre game of Twister, except in this game if you didn't pick the right spot, you didn't collapse into a tangled pile of limbs and laughter. In this game, you just lost a limb.

He carefully took a step over the curve of the gator's tail. Then another over his back leg. So far, so good. Waldo hadn't even twitched. He took another small step, bringing him up to Waldo's front leg. At this point the best bet seemed to be to quickly step over that front leg, then run as fast as possible past his head and the long snout.

He looked over his shoulder to tell Josie Lynn his strategy, and that was the exact moment he heard the swish of Waldo's scaly skin on the floor and a noise that was somewhere between a snarl and a hiss.

Then Drake was on the floor right beside the beast. Shit, the damn thing had swung its head and knocked him down. Now he was right near that huge mouth, stuck between the animal's side and the wall.

He lay still for a second, debating at this angle if he could shove himself backward fast enough to avoid those teeth. His vampire abilities made him very fast, but this was a weird position.

But before he could do anything, Josie Lynn was on top of the gator, her bare legs straddling its back. She lay down on the beast, pressing both her forearms down as hard as she could on the alligator's snout.

"What the hell are you doing?" he cried.

"Shut up," she yelled back. "Take this cord and wrap it around his snout."

Drake didn't argue, taking the bungee cord from her and circling it quickly around the alligator's long nose and mouth.

"Higher up," she said, still using all her strength to keep his huge jaws shut. "That's it."

When it was secured, Josie Lynn sat up, still straddling the beast, her legs bare and her coffee-colored hair tangled around her face. Her chest rose and fell as she struggled to catch her breath.

Holy shit, she was sexy.

His dick shot straight up against his stomach, painfully hard and swollen, but fortunately she didn't seem to notice.

"How—how the hell did you learn to do that?" he asked, struggling to catch his own breath.

She smiled then, the first time he'd seen her genuinely smile.

"I'm Cajun. This is what we do."

Damn, he was in love.

. . .

JOHNNY WAS PUSHING his luck, and he knew it. But Lizette looked so disheveled and sexy that he couldn't resist. Besides, the fact that she had said she wasn't wearing panties had him hard in two seconds. All he could think was that his dick was currently so close to her pantyless deliciousness, and all it would take was a little tug of her skirt and he'd give her something she wouldn't forget this time. He could take her wrist that was attached to his, raise it above her head on the hot pink wall behind her, and make her sore all over again in the best way possible.

Before he could do something that would get him slapped though, there was a knock on the door, causing Lizette to jerk away. "Yeah?" he called out.

Drake opened the door. "I thought I'd see if I could borrow some pants from Zelda."

"Please do." There was just far too much of Drake hanging around lately. "Where is the alligator? Is it watching TV or something?"

"Josie Lynn tied off his snout. She's Cajun," he said, like that explained everything. "She made it look easy, and basically made you look like a pussy."

Great. "I was trying not to show off." He turned back to Lizette. "Are you ready?"

"Yes."

"Is Zelda awake yet?"

"No, but she's definitely breathing. And just so you know, I don't think Katie and Stella came bearing metal cutters."

Johnny hadn't really thought they would. They were undead musicians; they had stuff like guitar picks and guitar strings, drumsticks and plasma bags lying around, not tools designed to slice through metal. Although it might not be a bad idea to get some, given how this evening was going.

"Still no word from Saxon?" Drake asked

"Nope. Keep in touch, man. Somebody let me know how Zelda is doing and I'll let you know if I find Saxon." Normally Johnny would have clapped Drake on the back or something as he passed, but he'd just as soon keep his hands to himself at the moment.

Heading into the hallway, he glanced back toward the dungeon and was amazed to see that the alligator was on a leash hooked to the bathroom doorknob, his snout tied shut with the bungee cord from the sex swing. Josie Lynn was tossing her hair back and tugging Drake's pirate shirt down toward her knees.

Wow. Impressive. He waved and continued in the opposite direction. He had to say, he was done with the freak factor for the night. He just wanted to find Saxon, make sure the little idiot was okay, and go home to his apartment that he wasn't allowed to go home to. Damn it. This was going to be a long night, and he was really starting to be confused about his feelings toward Lizette. He alternated between extreme irritation and total horniness. Maybe the night before would work in his favor though. She had seemed really embarrassed by what happened, so maybe she wouldn't argue if he said he wanted to go home. After they separated their cuffs, that is.

When they stepped out the front door of Zelda's and paused on her front stoop, he realized Lizette was very quiet again, her lips pursed, bag clutched tightly against her chest.

"What's wrong?"

"I just looked in my purse."

"Yeah?" Johnny couldn't even imagine what would put that

look on her face. Actually, he could think of a lot of things, each more bizarre than the last, starting with dildos and ending with sherbet vomit.

She opened it up for him to see and he to admit, he was a little surprised. There was a thick stack of dollar bills. "I take it you didn't have those before last night?"

"No! There must be several hundred dollars in small bills in here. Where did I get those from?"

He couldn't even begin to guess. "I have no idea." It was then he realized that the back of her shirt was darker than the front. "Hey, turn a little bit for me." He studied the spot and realized that was why he was feeling so thirsty. Lizette had dried blood on her shirt.

"What, what is it?"

Crap. She wasn't going to like this. "You have blood on the back of your shirt. A lot of it."

"That's why I keep smelling blood. I thought it was just Josie Lynn."

"Huh." Because really, what else could he say? "It's only a couple of blocks to Saxon's. Hopefully he just got cold feet last night or forgot where Zelda lived or something."

"How could he forget where his fiancée lives?"

"Trust me, Saxon could."

She bit her lip. "I'm going to call Dieter. Maybe he knows what happened last night."

"Who is Dieter?" Johnny asked, even though he knew exactly who her beefcake assistant was. He just wanted to hear her say yet again that her relationship with him was strictly platonic.

"My assistant."

"He has a thing for you," Johnny told her, just to hear her protest, and because he was suddenly feeling particularly ornery.

"He does not!" Lizette actually starting walking faster than him, like she could walk ahead of his questions, even though she had no idea which direction they were going in.

A sudden thought occurred to Johnny, one he had to say he didn't like at all. "How do you know it's me you had sex with? I mean, we don't know how long we've been handcuffed together." Maybe he hadn't had sex at all. Maybe that's why he felt such an urgent need to hump Lizette. Maybe he'd been blue-balled. No. He couldn't believe it. He'd made her come three times. That was the only story he was willing to believe.

Apparently Lizette agreed with him on that because she stopped walking, turned around, and slapped him.

Holy crap. His head snapped back and he stared at her, stunned, cheekbone aching. She had some force behind those little hands. "What the hell was that for?" He could honestly say he'd never been slapped before in his whole life. Not even by Bambi, and she had been hot tempered. He had assumed slapping was reserved for eighties soap operas and *Tom and Jerry* episodes.

It was kind of hot, he had to admit.

"For calling me a slut!" she said hotly, eyes flashing, mouth trembling with rage.

Whoa now. "I did not call you . . . that. I was just saying that maybe we were making an assumption, that we don't know for sure what happened."

"Why, are you horrified at the mere thought of having slept with me?"

Ninety-some years alive and he still couldn't figure out women. Why would she get a stupid idea like that? "Of course not! I'm *fascinated* at the idea that we might have had sex. It just seems like the last way things would have turned out last night. You know, since we get along so well. But the very idea of seeing you naked and kissing your cherry lips has me totally hard." And just to prove his point, he brought her hand with his and ground it onto his cock, which was starting to feel like a rattling pressure cooker.

"Oh! *Mon dieu!*"

"He's got nothing to do with it," Johnny assured her.

Lizette made a sound of exasperation, yanked her hand away, then whirled back around and started walking, muttering in French and dragging Johnny along with her.

He had no idea what she was saying, but he could guess it was filled with name-calling and her affronted dignity. "You're going the wrong way," he pointed out. "We need to turn left here."

She practically hissed at him, then followed it up with more rapid-fire French. But she did turn left.

"It's not my fault I don't remember," he told her, because he was feeling a little bitter about that. "I wish I did, trust me. And just for the record, I would be jealous if you slept with someone else." It was true, and he figured it would win him points. Women liked jealous guys, didn't they? They did in movies, anyways.

Johnny walked down Dumaine and pondered how it was that he'd never really understood women. His relationships such as they were had been like origami, full of little folds, then when he tugged one piece the whole thing collapsed. Here it was happening already with Lizette and he wasn't even sure he actually liked her. He was pretty damn sure she didn't like him.

He really hadn't been passing judgment, but he knew he was right; they had no way of knowing if they'd really had sex. If she had banged someone else, well, she had been out of her mind. Hell, if she had banged him she had clearly been out of her mind. Not drugged, he was 100 percent positive she would not have come near him. He wouldn't have hit on her sober either. Because he would have gotten slapped.

Johnny worked his jaw and fought the urge to grin. Yeah, she was hot, there was no doubt about it. The uptight paper-pusher had a fiery side, and he couldn't help but want to explore that side of her.

Lizette had dug her phone out and was speaking into it in French, which made Johnny wonder if it was Dieter, because he could have sworn her assistant was German, but then again, what did he know? Besides, Germans probably spoke French. He was starting to feel like a real potato farmer next to her, which was stupid. He was a musician and chicks everywhere dug that. He wasn't a loser. Even if he was walking behind her, attached to her like a disobedient dog.

The submissive lifestyle wasn't for him, he had to say. He was happy for Saxon if that was his thing, but Johnny didn't like to take orders. He liked to coax and tease and charm his way to get what he wanted. What he wanted right now was Lizette, naked, below him, quivering, her plump lips parted.

"Hey, brother, what's up?" A man on the corner of St. Philip and Bourbon Street outside of Lafitte's gave him a wave and a friendly smile. "Where's your bucket tonight? My wife loved the picture of her with you guys."

Okay. What picture might that be? And why the hell would he have a bucket? Johnny figured this was a good opportunity to gather some information. He touched Lizette's arm so she would stop marching down the street. "That's awesome. I'd love to see it if you have it on your phone."

"Sure, sure, no problem." The guy was wearing a golf shirt with large sweat stains in both pits, and he wiped his forehead with a hankie. "I'll tell you, it's hot out here. Okay, let me pull it up on my phone. The wife is inside having a hurricane. Little hair of the dog, if you know what I mean."

Johnny smiled back at him. "That sounds about right for a Saturday night in New Orleans. Hope you're having a good trip."

"Oh, the best, absolutely the best." He glanced at Lizette, who had turned her head and was still on her cell phone. "I'll tell ya, you're a lucky son of a gun. Your girlfriend is beautiful."

"Thank you." Johnny felt a ridiculous sense of pride, even though Lizette didn't belong to him in any way.

"Here it is." The man turned his camera and showed Johnny the image on the screen. "It was so real. My wife loved it!"

Holy fuck. Lizette was going to birth a cow. Johnny tried not to react, but it was hard not to at least go a little buggy-eyed as he stared at the picture of him biting Lizette's neck, her eyes rolled back in ecstasy, blood trailing down the back of her shirt. The tourist's wife was standing next to them grinning and pointing. Lizette was perched on a bucket, and in front of them was a pile of money on the street. Oh God, they had been charging tourists cash to watch him suck her blood.

"That is a great shot," he told the man with as much enthusiasm as he could muster.

"How do you get the blood so realistic? I could swear it even smelled like blood."

Johnny gave him a shaky smile and a wink. "Trade secret, buddy. Can't give that away or we'll be out of business."

The tourist laughed. "Sure, sure, I understand. You want me to send you a copy of this picture? I can shoot it to you in an email."

"Great, thanks." Johnny gave him The Impalers email address and debated if he could get away with never telling Lizette about this. Ever. But he wasn't about to turn down a copy of that picture. It was intensely erotic and he wanted to blow it up and study Lizette's expression alone in a dark room.

"I'm Mike, by the way."

Johnny exchanged a few more pleasantries with Mike, then said good-bye as the guy headed back into the bar to find his wife, probably excited to tell her that he had seen the fake vampires again. Little did he know.

Lizette put her phone away. "Who was that?"

Johnny wrestled for a few seconds, a little afraid of the fallout if he told her the truth. Yet he knew if she found out later she would decapitate him for not telling her. He kind of liked his head right where it was, so he cleared his throat as they started walking again and gave her a smile. He'd just ease into it. "Was that Dieter? Does he know anything?"

"No, that was his Parisian assistant."

"Your assistant has an assistant?"

"*Oui.* So what is going on? Who was that man?"

There was no way out of it so he bit the bullet and tried to sound charming. "Well, the good news is I know where you got all that cash from and it wasn't from stripping, if that's what you were worried about."

"Of course not!" she said, but she sounded relieved. "How did I get it?"

"It seems we set ourselves up on Bourbon Street with a bucket. You know, like the living statues who paint themselves silver or like a ghost and stand there and don't move while people take their picture. They have a donation bucket out. Apparently we put out a donation bucket."

Lizette gave him a look of bemused bewilderment. "Why would people pay to see us standing there? I doubt either one of us is that interesting standing on a bucket."

"Speak for yourself," he teased. "But um, well, the thing is . . . we seemed to be reenacting a vampire bite." Reenacting. Actually doing it. Almost the same thing.

"What? What do you mean? Like how?"

"You know, like my fangs on your neck. Breaking your skin. Sucking whatever blood didn't run down your shirt. You know. Like that." Johnny braced himself for a second slap.

Fortunately, she appeared too stunned to even consider it. "Why would you do that? Are you insane?"

"I don't know! Maybe we needed cab fare. You did freeze my assets." He wasn't going to take the full blame for this either. He dug out his phone to see if Mike had emailed him the picture yet. "Besides, you looked like you were enjoying yourself." She did. So there.

"I highly doubt that!" she said with extreme indignation.

Thank God for technology and Mike's eagerness. "Ha! Look at this!" Johnny shoved the image in her face. "Tell me you're not enjoying that."

She so clearly was, it made him horny all over again, if he had ever actually stopped. The way her head was thrown back in complete abandon, her eyes half-closed, tongue out on her bottom lip. It was the hottest thing he'd ever seen.

Lizette grabbed his phone and stared closer. Then the phone tumbled out of her hand down onto the sidewalk. "That isn't me. That can't be me. I would never . . . I couldn't . . . it's not possible . . ." Her voice trailed off, her eyes glazed, her free hand fluttered aimlessly over her chest.

After rescuing his phone and making sure it still worked despite the screen kissing the concrete, he eyeballed her, a little worried at her tone. "Do you need to stick your head between your legs or something?"

"Excuse me? How dare you!"

Maybe that didn't sound right. "I don't want you fainting!"

But Lizette was tugging at their attached wrists. "I want this thing off of me right now! I want away from you. I want to leave this street, this city, and go back to Paris."

People were stopping to stare at them. Johnny gave the observers a casual smile. "She's drunk," he told them.

"I am not drunk!" She whacked his arm with her giant purse.

"Look, we're home," he told her, pointing to the door that led up to Saxon's second-floor apartment. "Maybe we can talk about this inside. You know, away from total strangers."

"As if it matters! After last night, apparently there is nothing left to hide!"

Yeah, she was flipping her wig. Johnny debated calling Stella or Dieter for backup, but Stella was busy with Zelda and he hated Dieter, purely on principle. He was on his own. "Lizette, obviously nothing bad happened last night, because we're still here. No one is in jail or in a science lab, so let's just go inside and keep it that way, okay?"

"Oh, now you are so reasonable?"

She was fairly quivering with indignation, and she was so tiny and cute that Johnny couldn't help himself. He bent over and kissed the tip of her petite nose. "Yes. I'm being reasonable, so we should probably make note of this. It doesn't happen all that often."

His kiss rendered her speechless. She blinked up at him, eyes wide, mouth open, anger deflated. She murmured something in French.

"I know," he told her soothingly. At some point he probably needed to confess that he didn't speak French, but so far, it didn't seem to matter. The extent of their conversations was about how he was screwing up and her fears of exposure. All he really needed to do was agree.

The nosy partiers had lost interest and had kept walking, so he took her hand, the one attached to his, and held it like they were teen lovers. It felt oddly comforting, and made the handcuffs irrelevant. He held open the door for her and led her into the courtyard. Up some groaning wooden steps and they were at Saxon's front door. His apartment was essentially just a long narrow room, originally slaves' quarters to the town house facing Dumaine. It was perfect for a vampire who didn't want a lot of natural light, but it was too small for Johnny. He felt claustrophobic inside it, and the feeling immediately came over him as he pushed open the door.

"It isn't locked?"

"Nah. Saxon doesn't have much to steal and he could defend himself. He may look like a twelve-year-old girl, but he is an immortal."

"That's true." Lizette looked around. "Well, obviously he is not here."

"Yeah." Johnny frowned at the empty room. "I am starting to get a little worried. I mean, I could see him coming back here to sleep or get some stuff, but where else would he be on his own wedding night? Everyone wants booty on their wedding night."

"I think everyone got booty but him."

Johnny laughed. "It was definitely a wedding to remember. Except no one remembers it." He went over to Saxon's tiny fridge. "Want a drink?" There was blood in there, and suddenly Johnny just wanted a drink and a cigarette. But he had quit smoking, so he would have to settle for a glass of red.

"I think perhaps that would be wise." Then Lizette surprised him by opening her purse and pulling out the wad of cash. "I suppose we should split this, yes? I believe you earned it."

Johnny grinned, but as he poured them both a drink into jelly jars from Saxon's cupboard, he wondered if her thoughts were taking the same turn his were—straight back to the image of him biting her neck and drawing her blood into his mouth.

He wanted to bite her again. Now.

"Don't even think about it," she told him, proving that not only was she adorable, she could read minds as well.

"I have no idea what you're talking about," he lied.

Chapter Eight

THE RAGIN' CAJUN

"**YOU** know, you'd think she'd have something basic I could wear. Sweatpants. Plain old jeans. Hell, a plain pair of black leather pants."

Josie Lynn stood by the door, watching Drake rifle through Zelda's closet like a teenage girl trying to choose a dress for the prom.

He pulled out another pair of pants. They were pink leather with silver studding around the pockets and down the leg.

"This is like the fourth pair of pink pants. She's a dominatrix for God's sake." He shoved the pants back into the closet.

Josie Lynn could no longer suppress her amusement. She giggled.

He shot her a look. "What's so funny?"

"You must be a nightmare to shop with," she said, shaking her head and laughing again.

He looked grumpy for a moment, then he begrudgingly smiled.

"Well, I don't usually buy clothing in the tacky section." He pulled out a pair of silver, almost plastic-looking leggings to demonstrate his issue.

"But you are wandering around with your junk hanging out," she said. "I think this is a prime example of beggars can't be choosers."

He shrugged, still not conceding she might have a point.

She levered herself away from the doorjamb and moved so she could see into the closet a little better, but still left plenty of space between herself and Drake. There were too many things that had happened between them for her to feel comfortable getting too close.

"Why don't you just hand me something to bring the others?" she suggested. "They need to get Zelda to the hospital."

Drake glanced at her, and she could tell he was undecided about letting her out of his sight. Clearly his admiration of how she'd wrangled the gator had worn off, and he was back to distrusting her.

"I'm not going to take off," she assured him. "I have just as much reason to want to find those transvestites as you do." Probably even more. Her name, her livelihood, everything rested on figuring out what had happened last night.

He nodded, and handed the silver leggings to her, then he grabbed a T-shirt that actually said, DOMMES HAVE IT ALL TIED UP.

She made a face as she took the garments. "Okay, she does have questionable taste."

"Well, if you knew Saxon—the groom, you'd know that is really true."

She looked down at the clothes, then asked, "Are you worried about your friend?"

Drake pulled out another pair of pants, these ones white with more metal studding. "Saxon? I'm sure he'll turn up. This wouldn't be the first time he's gone missing. Last year, he disappeared for about a week. Turns out he got lost in Metairie."

"Metairie—as in the suburb only a few miles from here?"

"That's the one."

"How did he manage that? Drugs? Drinking?"

He shook his head. "Nope, he was just going to Walmart. He gets confused sometimes. Well, a lot of the time. So aside from her abominable taste, I guess Zelda is good for him. At least she knows where she is most of the time."

"Unfortunately, she doesn't right now," Josie Lynn said, then held up the clothes. "I better get these to your friends."

"I'll be right there," he told her, his tone harder than it had been, and she realized he still didn't trust her. And in truth, she supposed she didn't blame him. If the tables were turned, she would think he looked pretty guilty, too.

So she was going to have to stay with him and figure this mess out. She paused on the way out of the room to snag a thick black belt, with studs of course, that was lying on the dresser.

The hallway was quiet. Waldo lay by the bathroom door, looking rather pathetic tied to the bathroom doorknob with his large snout wrapped in cord.

"Sorry, big guy," she said on the way by him. "But you do live with a dominatrix. I suspect bondage is kind of par for the course around here."

Waldo didn't respond, not even with a blink of his reptilian eyes or a swish of his scaly tail, but Josie Lynn did hear something behind her. Expecting to see Drake already following her, she was surprised to see the hallway and bedroom door empty.

She must have heard Drake moving inside the room. She returned her attention to getting the clothes to Drake's friends. Ev-

eryone seemed pretty confident that Zelda was okay, but they
should probably hurry and get her checked out. Who knew what
kind of drugs had been slipped in the punch, if that was even
what they had been slipped into, and who knew how much Zelda
had gotten.

She opened the dungeon door and hurried inside.

DRAKE DUCKED BACK into Zelda's bedroom before Josie Lynn
could see him and paused, listening, hoping she'd continue talking to herself. Or Waldo, as the case may be. Talking sweetly to an
alligator like she was talking to the family dog.

He had to admit, she didn't seem like a hardened criminal. Or
a criminal at all. Okay, she could wrestle an alligator, which was
thoroughly impressive. And she definitely had no qualms about
stating her mind. He was pretty sure neither of those things were
on any lists of top traits for criminal offenders. But those two
things made her interesting as hell. And very appealing—in this
oddly paradoxical way. She was clearly tough, yet she had this
sweet, angel face and soft, curvy body.

He just didn't know. Maybe she wasn't involved in the events
of last night.

And maybe he was just getting suckered in by a lovely face
and sexy body. God knows he had an MO for that sort of thing.
How many of his worst choices in life were made because he'd
fallen for a pretty face?

He looked down at his dick—blessedly flaccid at the moment,
and it wasn't many times in a man's life that he thought that. But
his buddy down there had made far too many of the most important life decisions for him.

"And you are not a good judge of character, my friend," he informed his penis.

Still, he was having doubts about Josie Lynn's guilt. He did see her take the money, but she hadn't denied that fact. And while she did make and have access to the punch, she'd also made a valid point about that, too; dozens of people had had access to it.

He guessed that the only way he was going to figure out the truth was to find the gang of transvestites, and just to be safe, he was going to keep Cupcake with him. He was sure she wouldn't like it. She'd made it abundantly clear last night and tonight that he was not one of her favorite people. But he couldn't risk her possibly being a part of this mess and getting away with robbery. So they would go search the French Quarter for clues.

How hard could it be to find five drag queens dressed like Cher?

"SO HOW LONG have you known Drake?" Katie asked as she hefted Zelda's leg in the air.

Josie Lynn instantly felt her cheeks burn.

"Umm, I just met him last night." She started to fidget with his pirate shirt, but caught herself.

"Well, welcome to the weird world of The Impalers."

Josie Lynn frowned at Stella, who struggled to get the silver legging over one of Zelda's large feet. "The Impalers?"

"Hold her leg still," Stella told Katie, then answered Josie Lynn, "The Impalers is the name of the band that all of our boys are in. Wyatt, my boyfriend, plays rhythm guitar and tries to sing." The redhead stopped her exertion to shoot Josie Lynn a conspiratorial smile. "Don't tell him I said that. He thinks he's got a great voice."

Josie Lynn readily nodded, although she wondered when exactly she would ever meet her boyfriend. She didn't expect to see these people again after tonight.

"And my husband," Katie said, trying to get a better grip on Zelda's long leg, "actually can sing. He's the lead singer."

Josie Lynn nodded, a little surprised and overwhelmed by the two women's friendliness, but she supposed they didn't know that Drake thought she was the villain of last night. They probably wouldn't be so nice if they knew that. There was still every chance Drake might tell them, too. Not that any of that mattered as long as she found out the truth.

But even as her thoughts went to all those places, she found herself asking, "What does Drake play?"

"Oh, he's the lead guitarist," Katie said smiling at her. She had such a lovely smile. One of those smiles that made the person she was smiling at want to smile, too.

"Probably the best guitarist on Bourbon," said Stella, still focused on dressing Zelda, a satisfied smile curving her lips as she finally managed to get the legging over Zelda's foot. "Maybe even all of New Orleans. He's amazingly talented."

"Although he'd deny that," Katie added. "He can be very humble about his talent."

Humble? Josie Lynn hadn't gotten that vibe from him. But these were his friends; they would see him differently than she would.

"But only about his talent," Stella said, waiting for Katie to step over Zelda and raise her other leg. "About everything else, he can be pretty arrogant."

"Well, I think that's because of how he was raised, don't you?" Katie said.

"Probably," Stella agreed, then bit her lips as she concentrated on lining up the leg hole of the legging with other Zelda's foot.

Again, almost against her will, Josie Lynn found herself asking, "How was he raised?"

Stella's stopped her lining up, and Katie almost dropped Zelda's leg. Josie Lynn didn't miss the look the two women exchanged. They thought they had said too much.

"He was raised . . ." Katie looked at Stella for help.

"He was raised very privileged."

Josie Lynn got the feeling that wasn't exactly the word either of the women wanted to use, but she didn't get the chance to ask more, because the door opened and the privileged Drake strode into the room. She was pretty sure none of them were thinking about his past now. All eyes and thoughts were locked on his outfit. Wow, and what a look it was.

He'd managed to find pants that fit him and that weren't pink or white or sparkly. However, they were turquoise. Skintight, shiny, vinyl turquoise pants. And with that he wore a plain black T-shirt, except it was also skintight and had a low V-neck, exposing his lightly hairy chest. On his feet, he wore black flip-flops that were a little too small, so that his heels hung off the back, and there were silver metal studs along the straps.

Josie Lynn smiled despite herself. So he hadn't totally avoided the studding.

"Drake," Stella said, "you look so . . ."

"Fashion forward?" Katie suggested.

"That wasn't exactly the description I would have gone for, but it will do," Stella said, then laughed.

Katie smiled. Josie Lynn had already figured out the pretty blonde was too sweet to outright laugh at him. Josie Lynn didn't have such qualms, but she did try to hide her amusement behind a hand.

"Laugh it up, ladies," Drake said. "I can go back to wandering around with Mr. Big hanging out."

He started to reach for the top button of the pants and all of them shouted, "No!"

He dropped his hands to hips. "Then don't be mocking the look."

Then to Josie Lynn's utter surprise, he cat-walked over to join them, singing "I'm Sexy and I Know It." She laughed again, as did the others. Clearly he didn't really mind that they found his clothing amusing. He did, too. He may be arrogant, but he also didn't take himself too seriously. She also learned that he couldn't sing either.

He stopped his out-of-tune singing and asked how Zelda was. Then he crouched down to check Zelda, his fingers deftly finding her pulse. Again there was a confidence about him that Josie Lynn found very appealing.

"I think she's fine," he said to Katie, then smiled to reassure his friend. That smile was very, very appealing, too.

Stop it! She didn't want to find more things to like about this man, because she was far too attracted to him already. Yet here she was, finding him funny and sweet and totally sexy, while he thought she was a liar and a thief. Okay, a liar and a thief he'd do the dirty with, but not one he respected. Or believed.

Again, leave it to her to get all moony about a man who didn't respect her in the least. Hmm, that was another pattern in her life, though, wasn't it?

"I really think she'd just passed out," he said after a minute. The vinyl of the turquoise pants creaked as he stood.

Katie straddled Zelda, her back to the prone woman's face.

She bent forward and grabbed both of Zelda's ankles and yanked them upward. At the same time, Stella tugged the leggings up the unconscious woman's legs toward her hips.

"Well, we'll take her to the hospital anyway," Stella said, then grunted slightly as she tried to get the pants the rest of the way under Zelda's butt. "Better safe than sorry."

Then she paused her pulling and added, "So why don't you let us handle this, and maybe you two can start trying to figure out what happened to all of us."

Stella raised an eyebrow at Drake when he didn't react right away.

"Right," Drake said, seeming to get the unspoken hint. He looked at Josie Lynn. "We do have some leads we need to follow."

Josie Lynn waited for Drake to elaborate, to finally tell these women that he'd already figured out that she was involved in last night's disaster. But instead he walked over to Josie Lynn.

"Are you ready to go see what we can find out?"

She nodded, wondering why he hadn't shared what he'd seen last night.

He looked her up and down, his expression unreadable, and her stomach sank. Now he was going to announce her suspected involvement.

"You definitely pull off that shirt a lot better than I did."

Josie Lynn stared at him, almost sagging with relief. "Th—thanks."

"It looks cute," Katie said. "That belt really works."

"Yes, you can definitely pull off 'pirate chic,'" Drake said with a slight smile. "But then you are already a pro at pillaging and plundering."

Josie Lynn's relieved expression disappeared. She shot an awkward glance toward the two women, who both looked curious about his comment. Josie Lynn waited with them for his explanation. The explanation that would definitely make her look guilty.

"Because she's already stolen my heart," he said pressing his hand to his chest in an overly dramatic way.

Josie Lynn felt her cheeks burning. He hadn't told them about the fact that she'd taken money to let strangers in to the wedding reception. But he had made the comment to let her know he still thought she was guilty. And then the second comment was obviously to mock her.

And she'd just been thinking how likeable this guy seemed to be. Again, that was just another sign of her colossally bad judgment.

"Aww," Katie said, clearly missing any of Drake's sarcastic undertone. Stella didn't seem to notice either, although from the roll of her eyes, she clearly thought his vow was corny.

But Josie Lynn knew it wasn't meant to be corny, it was designed to make sure she knew she had to clear herself tonight. Or she would be in trouble with him and all of the wedding guests.

And she was going to clear herself.

"Let's get going," she said, her tone cool. She needed to keep her emotions in check, and the best way to do that was to stay as removed from Drake's charms as possible. He didn't believe her. He wasn't going on this search with her to see if she was telling the truth. He was going with her to make sure she didn't get away and that she paid. That was it.

She had to prove herself, and protect herself. Period.

DRAKE FOLLOWED JOSIE Lynn, who didn't wait to see if he was going to join her. He was a little baffled by her sudden shift in mood. Probably he shouldn't have flirted with her so blatantly in front of Stella and Katie. That had made her uncomfortable, which wasn't his intention, but he should have known that would be her reaction. He had seen a lighter, more open side of her and thought he could get away with a little flirting. Obviously not.

He found her attractive when she was guarded and serious. But damn, he'd found her outright stunning when she let her guard down and laughed and smiled. She was gorgeous. He really did want to get to know her. She fascinated him. But that openness was gone. He didn't like that she was all shut down again.

They stepped back into the hallway where Waldo sat looking decidedly uncomfortable in his makeshift muzzle.

"I bet you'd like to wrap a bungee cord around my mouth, too," he said as they skirted the big animal and headed to the door at the end of the hall.

"Or neck," she muttered, and Drake actually found himself amused.

"So vicious," he said.

She spun toward him just as they would have reached to door. "And let me guess, you are now going to add potentially violent to liar and thief."

Drake frowned. "No, I don't get any real violence vibe from you, Cupcake. But I am going to keep you in my sight until we sort out exactly what happened last night. I'm quite sure you'd do that same thing in my shoes."

She stared at him, and he could see some of the defensiveness fade from her bright blue eyes.

"Yes," she finally admitted. "Yes, I would."

"So why don't we call a truce for now."

She considered him, then nodded. "Truce."

He nodded, too, and pushed open the door to the main rooms

of Zelda's house. Even though Drake had never been here before, since he liked to avoid the whole domme thing, it wasn't hard to find the front door.

When they stepped out onto the street, Josie Lynn paused, looking around as if she was trying to get her bearings.

"Don't worry, I know where we are."

She shook her head, still looking around. "It's not that. It's just—I didn't expect it to be nighttime."

"Of course, it's nighttime," he said automatically, then realized that wouldn't make sense to her. She had the luxury of being awake either night or day, unlike him.

She turned her quizzical gaze toward him. "Why 'of course'?"

"Well, I just figured we had to have been out for a long time, you know, since we were drugged."

She seemed to accept his explanation. She started down the sidewalk, and he fell into step beside her.

"So where should we go first?" he asked. "Is your place nearby? Do you want to change?"

"I don't live walking distance from here," she said, then looked down at herself. "I think this looks all right."

Drake nodded. His shirt as a dress was more than all right. She'd rolled back the sleeves so the ruffles at the wrist were less noticeable. She'd also undone a couple of buttons to give glimpses of her pale neck and chest, while only hinting at her full breasts under the cascade of linen and lace that was cinched at the waist with a wide belt. The hem fell a few inches above her knees, far longer than Zelda's wedding dress, and on her feet, she somehow still had the black utility-style boots that had been a part of her work uniform.

Josie Lynn looked cute and sexy and kind of hip. Even the boots worked with the outfit.

But he'd already learned where saying anything flirty would

get him: standing outside the walls she put around herself. So he simply nodded. "It looks fine."

She inspected it once more, tugging down the hem a little, then said, "I'd like to go back to Gautreaux's. I want to see if my stuff is still there, and maybe if it is, we could test the punch bowl or glasses for traces of whatever drug was used."

"Good idea."

They headed down St. Louis toward Chartres, where the reception venue was.

"If it is the band of marauding Chers who did this, do you think robbery was their main goal?"

Drake shrugged. "Who can know what marauding Chers want, but since we don't have any of our valuables, it seems likely."

"But why were we missing our clothing, too?"

"Well, I don't know if you recall how you felt before you blacked out, but I do, and I definitely wanted to be doing things that required me losing my clothes."

Josie Lynn didn't say anything, but her deep pink blush was answer enough.

They both fell silent.

"Do—do you think we did have sex?" she asked, her voice quieter than normal. Her cheeks pinker still.

"I don't know," he answered honestly. "But I think it's very possible. What do you think?"

When she fell quiet again, he glanced at her profile. Her lips were pressed firmly together, and she blinked several times as if she was fighting tears. That was answer enough, too.

It was on the tip of his tongue to ask if she felt different, if she thought she could even tell, physically, if something might have happened. But her forlorn expression stopped him. He reached out to touch her arm. "Are you okay?"

She nodded. "I—I just hope all my catering stuff is still at Gautreaux's."

Drake didn't doubt she was concerned about that, but he knew that wasn't what had her ready to cry. He tried not to be offended that the idea of possibly having had sex with him brought her to tears. After all, she had made it clear, pre-drugging, that she wasn't interested in him, and if they had done the dirty, the act hadn't been her choice, but because of the effects of the drug.

He had to admit that he didn't like the idea either.

"You know what, we probably didn't," he said with feigned decisiveness.

"You don't think so?"

He shook his head. "Nope, and since we don't remember what happened anyway, I think we might as well assume nothing did."

She didn't say anything more, and he got the distinct feeling that plan didn't soothe her as much as she'd like.

Chapter Nine

VOULEZ-VOUS COUCHER AVEC MOI?

"So how do you think we wound up wearing handcuffs?" Lizette asked Johnny as they sat outside of Saxon's apartment on two rickety iron chairs on the narrow balcony. The drink he had handed her was resting in her grip, and she had her legs crossed, giving her appearance a sense of propriety she didn't feel. But it was actually pleasant to finally stop tromping around and just sit in the warm air and try to calm down. The courtyard was completely empty, only two apartments having access to it, and it felt safe to Lizette.

"Your guess is as good as mine."

Not normally prone to hysterics, she had been quite close to having a complete breakdown when she had seen the picture of Johnny biting her neck. It had looked so . . . sexy. So . . . public. "Were we wearing handcuffs in the photo?"

"No. So I guess we can still assume that it happened at Zelda's later in the night."

"Perhaps you meant it as a flirtation."

"Hey!" He smiled at her. "How do you know it was my idea?

Maybe it was your way of keeping me close at hand until you could get all your questions about 'The List' answered."

It was clear what he thought of her job. It should have bothered her more than it actually did. But he sounded more teasing than anything else, and she had to admit that was something she appreciated about Johnny. He didn't seem prone to hysterics either, and he definitely took the approach that life was meant for laughing. Lizette found that a refreshing change from the ancient and dusty vampires in the VA who clung to brooding traditions. To them, shopping for a new coffin was a hot night on the town. Johnny didn't even have a coffin. She knew because it wasn't on the list.

"I highly doubt that I would resort to handcuffs. Then again, I can't say I behaved the way I normally would have last night." She stared down into her glass. "I have compromised this case, you know. I will have to return to Paris and have it reassigned. It wouldn't be ethical for me to be the one investigating your identity when I have . . . when we . . ." Lizette forced herself to say it. "When we have been sexually intimate."

"At least you can verify my penis size. I'm sure the VA knows that, too."

She wanted to be offended, but it was probably true. Lizette laughed. "I would if I could remember."

"Want to check now?" Johnny put his hand on the button of his jeans, clearly joking.

"No!" She said the first thing that came to mind, a joke she normally would have kept to herself. But she let it out. "I don't have a ruler on me, so what good would that do? Though I suppose I could gauge it with my mouth."

Johnny choked on his blood, actually spraying some across the banisters of the balcony. "Holy crap. I cannot believe you just said that."

She had her moments. "I can have a sense of humor as well, Johnny. If your name is really Johnny."

He gave her an eye roll. "Well, how else can we verify that I'm Johnny Malone? There has to be a way. I don't want you to get in trouble because my friends throw weddings with seriously spiked punch. I can answer any question you have, because I am me, you know."

She did believe him actually. He was too well-known by the other vampires, too aware of everything in the apartment, too casually comfortable. Unless he was an astonishing con artist, he was in fact, Johnny Malone. "What is your birthday?"

"That's easy. Born April 17, 1899 in Cork to Mary and John Malone. My sister Stella was born two years later, followed by three girls, one born each year. Molly, Maggie, and Maeve. My mom had an *M* thing going there for some reason. She and my three little sisters all died in the influenza outbreak of 1918, and my father buried his grief in the bottle. A few years later Stella and I came to America, and fell in with the mob in Chicago after I proved a dab hand with me fists." He turned up his slight accent until it was thickly Irish, his fists in front of him. He gave her a mock jab with a grin. "It kept us from starving. Until it also got us caught in the line of a machine gun. Woke up a vampire, thank God. I wasn't ready to go out yet, you know what I mean?"

She nodded. "I do." She had seen an extraordinary amount of death. It had made her even more fearful of dying.

"When were you born?"

It wasn't relevant to his case, of course, and she never shared her personal details with anyone outside of the inner council, but he had been so open, and she was feeling oddly melancholy, so she told him the truth. "I was born in 1770 in Lyons, France, though my family spent most of the year outside of Paris at the court of Versailles with the royal family. My parents were murdered during the Terror and I was a witness to it. I myself was scheduled for decapitation at the guillotine, but the blade was dull and did not complete the execution. However, I was tossed in the pile of bodies and well on my way to death, though I have no memory of it. But I awoke as I am today, a vampire by the name of Jean-Baptiste having saved me."

"Jesus. That's horrible."

"Yes." Lizette drained her glass. "But no more horrible than your history. You lost your family as well."

"I did." Johnny leaned forward, his palm on his knee, the hand connected to hers dangling by her side. "Stella and I never knew who turned us. We just woke up frightened and undead. Was Jean-Baptiste a good mentor?"

"Yes." Her throat felt a little tight, as it always did when she thought of him. "We spent a century together."

"As friends or as something more?"

"More. Much more." He had not been the most affectionate of men, but he had been loyal, steady. He had taken care of her. Which seemed ironic now that she had become so independent in the hundred years since his death. She no longer needed that from a man. But she did miss the companionship.

"I can tell by the look on your face you either broke up or he died. I'm sorry." His fingers enclosed around hers on their mutually dangling hands.

"Thank you. Yes, he died." Though she wasn't going to talk about it. Lizette looked over at Johnny, studying the straight line of his jaw. There was something that bothered her if he was telling the truth and he was Johnny. "Why did you fake your death?"

The look he gave her was sheepish and uncomfortable, but she just waited and he finally spoke. "Well, this girl I was dating, she got pregnant."

"And you were clearly not the father."

"Exactly. And the thing was, it was like I've known for a long time I couldn't have children, but in that moment it hit me like a ton of bricks. I will never be a father. I'll never pass any of myself on down to a miniature human. I'll never get to hold a baby or teach a son how to play ball or grow old while my kids and grand-kids sit around a huge dinner table. It all hit me, hard, in a way it hasn't in decades, that this is it, you know. Just me, and everyone except my few vampire friends will all die, and I won't. I guess I wanted to see what it would feel like to die." He finished his drink. "That sounds really damn stupid now."

But Lizette understood. It had taken her years to accept the fact that she would never be a mother. She squeezed his hand. "Mortality is a strange paradox for vampires. Sometimes we crave death, yet we fear it even more than mortals because it is not inevitable. Vampire death shocks us in a way human death does not any longer."

"Exactly." He smiled at her. "How did you get to be so smart?"

When he smiled like that, it was easy to see how she could have been persuaded to have sex with him, especially under the influence of a drug. "I am not smart enough to pass on drugged punch."

"That's the thing with drugged punch though. It looks innocent but it has a real kick. Like you, I would imagine." His thumb was stroking her palm again, not a touch of comfort, but one of intimacy and sexual suggestion.

"You think I have a kick? That I bite?" Lizette set her glass down on the wooden floorboards. "I don't believe that's true. I think I have become quite dull." Actually, she knew she had. Normally it didn't bother her, but tonight it felt wearisome. There was something to what Johnny had said: If life was eternal, shouldn't it be enjoyable?

"Then obviously last night was good for you. You needed to come out of your shell a little."

"Perhaps. Though it would be better if I remembered it." Then the image of her head thrown back popped into her head. Yes, she would definitely like to remember that. She wasn't sure she wanted any memory of how she'd wound up in a sex dungeon with four other people though. That went a bit beyond loosening up.

"Not remembering last night is one of my true regrets in life," he told her, in a way that was so sincere she actually believed him. "But I'm happy to repeat certain parts of it if you'd like."

It was on her lips to say no automatically. To protest and demure, because that was the appropriate thing to do. But then she thought about it. If she already had compromised the case and would need to reassign another agent to the investigation, what difference did it make if she slept with Johnny again? The cat was already out of the bag, so to speak. So she told him, "I just might like that before the evening has concluded."

His eyes widened. "Really?"

"We'll see." It would take a huge dose of courage on her part, but the idea seriously intrigued her. "That is, if you're truly interested, and not just jesting."

"I don't even know how to jest about sex. I most definitely, absolutely, one hundred percent want you with every fiber of my immortal being." His eyes had darkened to black and he shifted in his chair. "It was that picture that clinched it, you know. You look so damn sexy with my fangs in your flesh."

Lizette fought the urge to squirm. She wanted to see the picture again because it had been sexy. They had looked so intimate. So into each other. It was a passionate side of herself she had never seen captured. Yet, it was something that shouldn't exist, and she knew it.

"You should delete that picture."

"Fuck that. The dude on the street still has it, so even if I deleted it, it still exists. So why shouldn't I enjoy it? I may even frame it, put it on the mantel."

Lizette rolled her eyes, which made him laugh.

"Hey, I'm going to try Saxon again. If I can't get a hold of him, I think we should go to my place. It's closer to Zelda's. Maybe he was wandering around drunk and went to my place by accident."

It didn't seem plausible, but she wasn't going to argue. She didn't have a better solution and she didn't know Saxon or what he might do. "Sure. I'm going to call, now as well."

Not that she knew what to say to him without sounding completely unprofessional. While Johnny dialed on his phone, she dialed on hers, reflecting that it was strange that it no longer seemed to be bothering her as dramatically that she and Johnny had to sit next to each other at all times. She was getting used to their hands hanging in tandem.

"Hello?" Dieter said, voice slightly muffled.

"It is Lizette. Do you have a minute?" she asked, suddenly feeling nervous. What did Dieter know of her behavior?

"Sure."

"Yes, well, I believe that tomorrow I am going to return to Paris and send a replacement. You will need to stay here to keep an eye on things."

"Does this have something to do with the drunk text you sent me last night?"

Her face heated. "I sent you a drunk text?"

"Well, I can only assume you were drunk as you don't usually ask me why I've never wanted to fuck you."

Lizette almost dropped her phone. "What? I did not."

"You did. And I wasn't even aware that my fuck factor mattered to you." He sounded amused, damn him. She was not amused.

"Oh, dear." She wasn't sure she could be any more embarrassed. "I can't imagine why I would say such a thing."

"Maybe because you were worried that no one would ever fuck you again. That's the way you put it—that no man ever wants you."

She had been wrong. She could be more embarrassed. She was going to throw herself off the balcony and run away and start a new life in Mongolia.

"Just kill me now," she told him. "I am surely not so pathetic as that." Her celibacy had been a choice, so she couldn't even imagine why she'd been so weirdly desperate for male approval.

"Lizette, I don't think that your attractiveness has ever been in question. But you have the Great Wall of China in front of your emotions, and most men don't have the tools to climb it. So maybe throw a rope down to Johnny and you can get yourself a little bit of cuddle time."

"Why would you suggest him?" she asked, not about to admit that she already had indulged in cuddle time. Big time. Panty-free time. Probably. She wasn't entirely sure. As to Dieter's wall theory, she could not argue with it. It was true, no question about it.

"Anyone could see the sexual tension between you two."

Ignoring that, she asked, "So did I happen to say anything else? Perhaps detailing my whereabouts or my plans? My memory is a bit hazy." As in gone. Completely. A glance over at Johnny showed that he had heard her. He shot her a wink.

"Something about sitting at a bar while you shopped on the Internet."

"I was shopping on the Internet?" What things were showing up at her apartment in Paris as they spoke? She lived in 700 square feet, so whatever it was, hopefully it was small. "*Zut alors.*" She really wanted to say fuckity fuck fuck, but she had already ruined her reputation with Dieter. No reason to cause his doubt in her when she was sober as well.

"Are you sure you need to turn this case over? I won't say anything about last night and I don't think any harm was done."

Lizette closed her eyes. "Trust me. Harm was done."

When she hung up the phone, she scrolled through her email and found that she had been quite the busy shopper. "Oh dear." She had purchased twelve-hundred-dollar Christian Louboutin shoes, probably in a drunken attempt to replace the shoes that had been lost somewhere along the way.

She had purchased several new blouses, a Chanel lipstick in Rich Red, and an excessively large amount of sexy underwear. A *lot* of underwear, all in lace and sheer materials, in soft shades of pink and ivory. Then there was a red number that was one piece, and when she clicked on the image to expand it, she read the description. It was a crotchless teddy. Apparently she had been much more than drunk the night before. She had been horny. Which was confirmed by the next email, which showed she had purchased a substantial vibrator with remote-control operation.

Clearing her throat, she closed the email quickly and glanced over at Johnny, worried that he was watching her. He was. He raised his eyebrows. "Everything okay?"

"I may have overspent with some online shopping last night." She picked her phone back up. "Around four a.m. We must have been apart at that time as I can't imagine you were interested in helping me online shoe shop." Though he might have been all or partially responsible for the other purchases. A sudden thought occurred to her. Those had been American sales sites written in English. Clicking on the lingerie email, she groaned out loud.

"Damn it! Not only did I spend nearly two thousand dollars in sexy high heels and lingerie, I entered the shipping address as your apartment!"

"What? Let me see."

While she was still recovering from the knowledge that she was a slutty shopaholic who clearly didn't even remember her own address when intoxicated, Johnny looked at her emails. Belatedly she realized that meant he would see what she . . .

"You ordered a *vibrator*?" Johnny yelled much louder than she appreciated. "I don't know whether to be turned on or offended."

"It was probably your idea!" she said, suddenly wanting to laugh. This was all so ridiculous. "Same for the lingerie."

His eyes had widened and he pinched the screen on her phone to expand the picture of the red scrap of lace. "Yeah, this might have been my idea. I could totally picture you wearing this and honestly, it's making my pants hurt."

"I can't picture me wearing that." She couldn't. That wasn't her style. She was more of a turn-off-the-lights-and-never-look kind of woman.

"Hey, Lizette?"

"Yes?"

Johnny handed her the phone back. "I know you were saying a little while ago that you were planning to return to Paris soon, but um, it looks like you canceled your return flight." He pointed to an email from the airline.

"What?" She scanned the email. She had canceled her return flight and had shipped a bunch of panties to Johnny's apartment. In her drunken mind, had she been planning to stay longer? That was either one compelling drug she had taken or he was impressive in bed. "I suppose it doesn't matter at this point, since the damage is done, but what on earth was I thinking?"

"I don't think we were. Though I have to say, your choice of vibrator intrigues me. That is no baby carrot."

Her cheeks burned. "You are incorrigible."

He laughed. "I'm just speaking the truth."

Unfortunately, he had a point. "I imagine if I act quickly, I can cancel some of these purchase orders."

"Now where would the fun be in that? I say we get the party started." Johnny winked at her.

Lizette rolled her eyes. "Are you ready to leave? By the way, I am assuming you were unable to reach Saxon?"

"No, he didn't pick up. I called Stella and Zelda is fine. She was dehydrated, so they gave her fluids."

"I'm glad she is well, though I find being drugged more than a little unnerving."

"You're an investigator, right? How would you approach finding out what happened?"

"I would start with the guest list and question the caterer as to who she saw in the kitchen before the punch was brought out. But honestly, it could have been anyone. It was just sitting on that table for hours, yes?"

"I would think so." Johnny picked up their empty glasses. "You ready?"

"Yes." They stood in tandem.

"We need to cover your shirt," Johnny said. "The blood is a little too realistic looking. Let's see if Saxon has a jacket or something."

He had a point. Lizette imagined she looked like a secretary who had been stabbed. It was not conducive to blending in.

"This will work." Johnny pulled an olive-colored button-up sweater off the couch. Trying not to wrinkle her nose, she let him drape it over her shoulders, effectively covering her back and shielding her handcuffed hand from view.

It smelled like patchouli and didn't match her outfit, but she supposed she had no right to be picky. Johnny smiled at her. "You look adorable. Like Mister Rogers."

She had no idea who that was, but she suspected it wasn't a comparison she was going to like. Nor did she have it in her to suggest they stop at the drugstore so she could purchase a pack of panties, which was what she really wanted to do.

THERE WAS NO way Lizette looked like Mister Rogers, but it was amusing to Johnny to see the old-man sweater draped over her. She looked exactly like what she was—an elegant, classy woman who had taken her hair out of her bun and had some fun. Johnny just wished he could remember it.

As they left Saxon's, he said, "Does all this architecture here in the Quarter remind you of home? I've never been to Paris."

"Actually, the majority of this is Spanish architecture. Most of the French buildings burned down in the late eighteenth century. It does feel very European though."

Of course she knew the history of New Orleans better than he did, because she was that kind of woman. Intelligent and well-read, and in desperate need of someone to shove her slightly off balance so she didn't end up shitting diamonds. He was just the man to do it.

"Is that so?" he asked her mildly. "It looks as French as a poodle to me."

"Poodles originated in Germany."

Johnny laughed. "Thanks, Miss Encyclopedia Britannica. This is why I like hanging out with older women."

"Older women? *Pardon!*"

She looked severely put out by the idea, which was ludicrous, given they were immortal and she would never physically age, so Johnny knew he had hit on a fun way to rib her. "Turn left here. And yes, you are older than me. Substantially older. I've always wanted to make it with a wise woman. I'll be the student, you can be the teacher." He gave her a wink.

"Is that a sexual reference?"

"Absolutely."

Glancing at him from under her dark, luscious eyelashes, Lizette said with an honesty that he had come to realize characterized her, "Then I don't imagine I can be much of an instructor to you. My sexual experience is rather limited."

Now why was that suddenly so arousing to him? Johnny stopped walking and nudged Lizette until she was back up against a wooden door.

"What are you doing?" she asked, sounding suddenly breathless. "This is inappropriate."

"I'm going to kiss you. Something I've been wanting to do for an hour."

"I don't think that is wise. We're on the street."

"Haven't you noticed that sex and alcohol cling to all the dark corners of New Orleans? Everywhere you turn someone is making out or flirting or drinking. Normally I don't act like a tourist, but I do like the freedom it gives me. No one is going to look at us if I kiss you." Johnny studied Lizette, marveling at how delicate and sensual she was, and she seemed to have no idea. Her rich brown hair was thick and came down over the hills of her breasts in chocolate waves. He touched it, stroking his fingers back into it to get a sense of its weight, its soft silken texture.

Her eyes had widened, her shoulders stiffening, but she didn't push him away and she didn't tell him to stop. "I suppose I have no objections then," she said, her French accent one of the sexiest damn things he'd ever heard, even when she was saying something as priggish as that.

"Good." Johnny leaned forward, shifting his body in closer to hers. She smelled like a soft floral perfume, blood, and the tangy musk of desire. He briefly closed his eyes and drank in the scent. Normally, he wasn't the least bit grateful for his heightened sense of smell, and he had long suspected it was why he'd taken up smoking. The cloying sweet cloud of cigarettes muffled the assault on his nose of everyday smells like garbage, fried foods, and the body odor of tourists sweating in the Louisiana sun.

But now he was glad for his sense of smell, because Lizette smelled beautiful, like everything feminine and delicious, a perfect aphrodisiac.

"Are you sniffing me?" she asked.

"No. I'm breathing you in." Johnny leaned down over her neck, her breasts, hand still buried in her hair, torturing himself, dragging out the anticipation.

"This is where the student becomes the teacher then," she said, "because while you may be substantially younger than me, you are most effectively seducing me."

Male pride swelled, along with his cock. "That's good to know." He kissed the soft flesh of her neck, and moved down to rub his lips over the cleavage peeking demurely out of her blouse. "And here European men get all the credit for being romantic."

"Aren't you European?" she asked, her voice breathless, her lithe fingers gripping his bare arms. "You are Irish."

"It's not the same as being from the Continent. No one has accused Irishmen of being romantic like Italians or the French." He lightly kissed just her bottom lip, enjoying the way she shifted restlessly, his slow brushes of flesh on flesh clearly stirring her arousal. "You know the Irish curse, don't you?"

She shook her head.

"They say Irishmen in general are underendowed." It was the rumor. Johnny couldn't say with any sort of certainty whether it was true or not. Certainly in his youth, the lads had all bragged about their prowess.

"Oh dear," she said, her head falling back as he nuzzled along her jaw to her ear. "You are not giving a glowing report for your countrymen. How do you compare then?"

"Well, you've said my charm is adequate. And I can assure you that you will be equally satisfied with the rest of me." He was no porn star, but he hadn't heard any complaints.

"So is my impending knowledge of your anatomy such a foregone conclusion then?"

"That's entirely up to you." Johnny finally kissed Lizette fully on the lips, tilting his head and taking her mouth with confidence, ready to taste her.

She didn't disappoint. He'd known from staring at her all night that her lips would be soft and full beneath his, and as he kissed her, Johnny decided that he had found the perfect fit for his mouth. The connection felt amazing, like the closest a vampire was ever going to get to heaven, their bodies in sync and intimate, yet not exactly touching. It was satisfying, yet it wasn't enough. It was a teasing taste of how far he wanted to go if she would let him.

Lizette gave a soft sigh between kisses, an acquiescence that made him feel oddly happy. If anyone had told him two nights before that he would be pleased that Lizette Chastain was giving in to his advances, he would have laughed himself sick. He still wasn't sure even now why he wanted to so desperately, other than that he was of course attracted to her. But it was more than that. It was her sincerity, her unwavering honesty, her clear loyalty that appealed to him. Plus she was damn cute when she was quivering in indignation. It wasn't indignation that was making her shift restlessly against the wall in front of him now though.

"So what do you think?" he asked her, spreading his hand across her waist to the small of her back, enjoying how petite she was, how big and powerful he felt standing in front of her. He kept his tone casual, but he had a deep desire to give her the most intense pleasure she'd ever known. "Want to see what I've got? *Voulez-vous coucher avec moi?*"

It was about the only French he knew besides counting to ten, and he sure as hell couldn't spell it, but it seemed if there was ever going to be a time he could bust the phrase out, it was now.

"I suppose there is no harm in it," she responded in her usual formal speech. Yet her tone was different. It had dropped lower and carried a slight tremor in it.

She was in. It was there in her voice.

He stepped away from her. "Then let's start walking again before I compromise you right here and now. And while having your back up against the wall never feels good, considering this is brick it really won't."

Their cuffs rattled as she smoothed her hair back and moistened her lips, purse firmly on her shoulder. Johnny had almost forgotten they were attached at the wrist. He was getting used to it, which made him pause for a second. Could he get used to a woman in his life, like Wyatt had with Stella? He hadn't thought so.

He still didn't. Did he?

Maybe he did.

That thought scared the living shit out of him.

Chapter Ten

DUDE LOOKS LIKE A LADY

"**E**VERYTHING is gone." Josie Lynn said as soon as she saw the barren courtyard. Nothing remained of the gothic wedding but the tables and chairs that belonged to Gautreaux's.

"Probably the venue employees cleaned up everything," Drake said, his voice low and calm.

He probably saw she was about to have a panic attack. What if all her catering supplies were gone? Her career was over before it even started.

"Let's check the kitchen," Drake said, placing his hand on the small of her back. She didn't pull away from the touch, actually appreciating his support. He'd been nothing but polite and conversational since their talk about whether they'd had sex last night. Which she found nice, but also a little unnerving. It made her have those feelings again that Drake could honestly be a good guy. Even though with those smoldering dark eyes, naughty smile, and killer body, he looked the epitome of bad boy.

Just as they reached the swinging kitchen door, it whipped

open. Drake looped his arm around Josie Lynn's waist, pulling her back against him to avoid them both being hit.

"Oh. I didn't know anyone was here."

"Eric?" He was the last person Josie Lynn would have expected to be here, and he carried a bucket of sudsy water and a rag. He appeared to be working. The king of the slackers—working? When there was actually no reason he should be?

"What are you doing here?"

"I came back to see what happened last night," he said, shifting awkwardly from one sneakered foot to the other. "I—I kind of blacked out or something."

"Yeah, that seemed to be going around last night," Drake said.

"Yeah," Eric nodded.

"So what did you find when you got here?" Josie Lynn asked.

"The place was pretty much a mess. Nothing had been cleaned up, so I decided I should probably do some picking up," Eric explained.

Josie Lynn looked back at the nearly spotless courtyard. "That was a lot of work. Did you call Ashley? Did you try to call me?"

"Umm—" He shook his head, brushing his disheveled hair back in an almost agitated way. "Nah. I didn't think to call anyone. I just decided to get to work myself."

Josie Lynn nodded, but she found his story strange. Since he'd started working for her, Eric had needed his hand held. Unlike Ashley, who would take initiative and do tasks on her own, usually wrong, but at least she tried, Eric waited to be told what to do. And then he moved at the pace of a snail with mono.

So why was he cleaning now?

"Where are all the dishes that were on the buffet?" she asked.

"I washed them and loaded them into your van."

Oh yeah, this was suspicious. Definitely.

She wasn't going to let her employee know that was what she was thinking, but she did want to talk to Drake about her suspicions.

"Well, thank you, Eric. I'm going to go—see how the kitchen is looking," she said. She didn't give Drake a look to indicate she wanted him to follow, afraid Eric might notice it.

But she didn't need to give Drake a sign. He followed her anyway.

Once in the kitchen, which was almost as tidy as the courtyard, she turned to him.

"Something is not right about this," she whispered.

"I was thinking the same thing. I watched him just cleaning up the spilled tuna last night. He was being totally half-assed about it. Yet he's cleaning this whole place, without any go-ahead from you." Drake shook his head. "Something is fishy about that."

"I agree. So do you think *he* drugged the punch?"

"Possibly." Drake walked over to look in the fridge and near the sink. "There is no punch left. Even the punchbowl is washed and gone."

Josie Lynn went to the back door. Her van was still in the back alley and she could see Eric had indeed put all her supplies into the beaten-up old Chevy. For a second she wondered if he had her keys. That might be a sign he was involved, too, but then she remembered that the back of the van had been open last night when everything had gone down. So he probably just loaded the already-opened van without the need of her keys.

"Why would he drug us though?"

"Robbery," Drake suggested. "Maybe the Chers aren't really involved. Maybe it was just this guy alone."

Josie Lynn considered that possibility, but that didn't totally add up to her. "Okay, if he drugged all of us to steal our money, cell phones, etc. . . . then why come back to clean up? He could have just taken off and been long gone by now. He wouldn't even need to clean up any evidence, because there still would have been no way to pin anything on him. Yeah, he was near the punch, but so was everyone. So if he did it, why come back?"

"You're right," Drake said. "It doesn't add up. Hey Eric!" he called behind him. "Come out here a second."

"Yeah?" Eric poked his head out the door.

"Is there anything you want to tell me?" Josie Lynn asked gently.

Drake snorted. "It's a miracle you haven't been robbed blind." He turned to Eric. "Dude, why the hell are you here cleaning up without a word to your boss?"

Eric gave a reluctant shrug. "I don't want to get fired." With that, he went back to banging around in the kitchen.

Josie Lynn looked thoughtfully after him. "Wow. I'm kind of impressed."

"But he could still be involved. I think we have to find those Chers."

Josie Lynn nodded. "But where do we even start?"

Drake gave her a knowing look. "You start at the top. Come on."

He caught her hand, and they left out the back door.

JOSIE LYNN GRIMACED as a raucous college student in a football jersey and baseball cap staggered into her. He gave her a cursory, and slightly slurred, apology, then kept moving with his group of equally wild and inebriated friends. Josie Lynn had been to Bourbon Street many times, but it had never been her thing—for reasons like that.

Growing up in a family of wild Cajuns, she'd seen her share of partying and fights and craziness. She didn't need to come to Bourbon to experience that. But as they kept walking, she realized Drake was leading her to a section she didn't know that well.

The first thing she noticed was that that clubs and bars looked better kept up than the places below the 800 block of Bourbon. The balconies were decorated with plants and lights. And while the party was still happening full tilt here, it did look less seedy.

Then she glanced over toward a beautifully decorated bar front, only to do a double take. Lined up in the opened windows were bare-assed men, shaking their naked cheeks to the pulsating music from inside the bar.

Okay, so not less seedy after all. Not to mention, she'd seen plenty of bare ass tonight already.

"Where are we going, exactly?" she asked once she managed to look away from the booty-grinding.

"Here," Drake said, pointing toward a doorway Josie Lynn would never have noticed amid all the other lights and decorations. And butts.

"Where is here?" she asked as she followed him into the smoky darkness.

"The home of Madame Renee Chevalier."

Josie Lynn looked around. Home? This was a bar. And honestly not a very nice one. In fact, the one with all the man butts looked considerably nicer than this place.

They walked down the length of a narrow bar toward the back and through another set of doors that opened into a larger room. This room was no less rundown and dingy. Wooden tables that had long since lost their polish were scattered around and surrounded by wing-back chairs covered in worn, red velvet. A few people, predominately men, sat at the tables, sipping drinks and smoking.

It reminded Josie Lynn of a gentlemen's club that had seen better days. And as if to validate that image, curtains at the far end of the room parted to reveal a woman lounging provocatively across a chaise.

Drake took Josie Lynn's hand, as he had when they had left Gautreaux's, and led her toward the stage. He chose a table right in front of the woman languishing on stage. Pulling out a chair, he waited for Josie Lynn to sit.

She was about to ask him why they were here, when music began to play. She sat down and Drake hurried to take the chair next to her. They both turned their attention to the stage.

The woman, despite the heavy makeup and fall of bright auburn waves, looked like she was in her fifties, maybe sixties. She reminded Josie Lynn of what Ginger from *Gilligan's Island* might have looked like when she aged. Well, except for the woman's bosom, which was enormous under her gauzy white peignoir and robe. Actually, she looked more like Ginger and Dolly Parton melded together.

Then she started to sing in a voice so deep and husky that it startled Josie Lynn. She watched, amazed as the woman sang "Perhaps, Perhaps, Perhaps," lolling on her golden brocade chaise, occasionally waving a hand for emphasis or to flip back her hair. Josie Lynn was certain the woman thought her performance was provocative. Which it was, Josie Lynn supposed. Just not in the way the performer probably intended.

Just as Josie Lynn started to lean toward Drake to ask again why they were here, the music suddenly changed and with another flip of her hair, the woman started to croon "Three Times a Lady."

Really? This woman was doing a Doris Day/Commodores mashup?

"Why are we here?" she finally asked once the shock subsided.

Drake leaned closer, but his gaze shifted between Josie Lynn and the woman on stage as if he couldn't quite manage to tear his attention away. Josie Lynn had to admit the woman was oddly fascinating in a train-wreck sort of way.

"If anyone in the French Quarter is going to know of a band of Chers, it is this woman." Drake then added, "Well, you know, this man who impersonates a woman. She's been working here for over three decades. She knows everyone."

Ah, now it made sense. It also did a lot to explain her low, husky voice, too.

"Well hello, loves," a very tall woman, who Josie Lynn assumed was also a female impersonator, sashayed over to the table, working her short skirt and high heels a heck of a lot better than Josie Lynn ever could. There was no way she could wait tables in a pair of four-inch heels.

"What can I get you to drink?"

"I'll take a whiskey, straight up," Drake said, then looked to Josie Lynn.

"I'll just have a Diet Coke."

The waitress gave her a regretful look. "We have a two-drink minimum."

After last night Josie Lynn wasn't sure she could handle alcohol. The idea made her stomach churn, but she also realized places like this that supplied entertainment needed to make their money somehow. In fact, places all over Bourbon Street counted on booze to make their money.

"I'll take a white wine."

"Chardonnay, lovey?" She said, batting her very long, very dark, very fake lashes at Josie Lynn.

Josie Lynn found herself smiling. The waitress really was quite charming.

"That's great."

Drake settled back in his chair. "Renee should be done with her set in just another few songs, then I'll see what she knows about those guys."

The waitress returned with their drinks.

"That was quick," Josie Lynn said, accepting her glass.

The waitress gestured around them. "Well, we're not exactly packed tonight."

That was true. It probably wasn't too hard for the wait staff to keep up with the handful of people in here.

Josie Lynn took a sip of her wine, grimacing slightly at the acrid taste. But as it slipped down her throat, she could also feel its warming effect, even as it hit her stomach, and she was surprised and pleased the sensation wasn't quite as unpleasant as she'd imagined it would be.

"So do you know Renee?" she asked after she'd taken a second sip.

"Yeah." He took a swallow of his drink, polishing off half of it.

"How? You don't seem like you'd hang out here much." She didn't know why she thought that. It wasn't as if she knew much about this man.

"No, I don't. But both Renee and I have been around New Orleans for a long time."

"How long?"

Drake shook his head. "Damn, longer than I care to remember. Renee has been bringing down the house for forty years. You should have seen him back when he was young." He finished the rest of his drink.

Josie Lynn smiled. "Well, it's not like you saw him when he was young either. You can't be much older than me."

There was a pause, then he just shrugged. "I've seen pictures. It's a small world when you're working in this business."

"So you aren't from here?"

"Originally? No."

"Where then?"

Josie Lynn knew she should just stop questioning him, but she was curious about this man. Why? Well, that was a question she wasn't sure she could answer. Or better yet, she'd be reluctant to answer, because she'd have to admit that she was intrigued by him. Despite her better judgment—which as always was debatable anyway.

He looked around for the waitress, waving to her before he answered Josie Lynn. "I grew up in England."

Stella and Katie had said he'd come from a privileged background, and she got the sudden image of a sprawling estate, and private boys' schools with uniforms. He probably even played cricket, although she wasn't sure exactly what the sport was.

But that did also explain something else. "I thought I noticed you had an accent occasionally."

Drake frowned at her. "My accent is long gone."

"Did you want the same, sweetie?" the waitress asked, giving Josie Lynn a moment to study Drake without his noticing. He definitely didn't seem to want to discuss his past, which she could understand. Her upbringing was far from her favorite topic. But why even deny the remnants of an accent? Most people loved a British accent, herself included.

"Please," he told the waitress, handing her his empty glass.

"Are you good, precious?" the waitress asked her.

Josie Lynn nodded and the waitress left.

Drake watched Renee, who now sang "The Lady Is a Tramp," and strutted around the stage, her gown billowing out behind her.

Again, Josie Lynn got oddly entranced by the performance, but only until the waitress returned with Drake's fresh drink.

He took another long drink, and again Josie Lynn got the feeling he was very uncomfortable with her line of questioning.

"So what about you?" he asked as he set down his highball glass. "How long have you lived in New Orleans?"

It was her turn to take a sip of her drink. "I actually live in Westwego."

"That's a bit of a trek, but not bad. Is that where you grew up?"

Yeah, it was definitely her turn to be reluctant to answer. "I grew up near Atchafalaya Swamp. My dad and brothers are fisherman and—well, you know they have some experience with gators. And some of them take tourists out to fish."

She waited for more questions. Stereotypical questions about how it was to grow up Cajun, running wild in the bayous.

But he didn't say anything more, he simply nodded. Somehow that felt just as awkward as more questions.

She took another sip of her wine, then added almost self-consciously, "I'm sure your life was very different from how I grew up."

Drake made a face that Josie Lynn couldn't quite decipher. "My whole existence in general has been very different. Although I'm certainly familiar with the bayous and rivers of this area."

"Really? Why's that?"

"Well, because I was a pirate," he stated, and then smiled that lopsided smile of his.

She rolled her eyes at him, but smiled, too. "Right. How could I forget?"

"Arrgh," he said, squinting up his handsome face in a way that he clearly thought was pirate-y. "Would you like to walk my plank, matey?"

She laughed despite herself. Maybe it was the wine. "I'd watch yourself, pirate, you saw what I did to the gator."

He chuckled, then he looked back to the stage. Josie Lynn did, too, realizing the music had stopped. Wow, had Drake held her attention so thoroughly she hadn't noticed that until now?

"My lovely crowd," Renee said, in a husky, sultry voice.

Josie Lynn looked around again. *Crowd* seemed a rather lavish term for the six people scattered around the room.

"I will be taking a short break. But please don't leave us, because the stunning Clarisse Dubois will be joining you to delight with her magnificent vocal stylings. So please, sit back and enjoy."

As Renee sauntered toward the stage exit, Drake rose and waved to her. Renee gave him a vague wave back, then recognition lit her heavily shadowed eyes. She smiled, her ruby lips revealing startlingly white teeth. She gestured toward the backstage, then raised a manicured finger to indicate that she just needed a minute.

Drake nodded and returned to his chair.

"I guarantee she will know where to find the Chers," he said to Josie Lynn.

"Excuse me." A male voice drew their attention away from the stage.

Both Josie Lynn and Drake turned to see a man standing behind them. From the looks of the satiny shirt, the buttons straining over his rotund belly, and the light blue polyester pants, he looked as if he hadn't gone shopping since the seventies. He pushed at his comb-over and offered them an oddly knowing smile.

Right away the man made Josie Lynn feel uncomfortable. Something about that gleam in his dark eyes. They roamed over her, lustfully. Drake seemed to notice, too, because he moved his chair so his knee was against hers. The movement was not overt, but still a subtle sign of possessiveness and protection. Josie Lynn didn't shift her leg away.

"Can we help you?" Drake said, his tone cool.

"You don't remember me?"

Drake gave the man a once-over that silently stated he wasn't likely to forget this guy, then shook his head. "Sorry."

"Well, you two were pretty—busy last night." The man shot Josie Lynn another lascivious look, actually licking his lips.

Josie Lynn knew she didn't contain her repulsion.

Drake placed a hand on hers, another protective move that she wasn't going to discourage. But the man didn't seem to see it as protective warning. In fact, as his gaze dropped to where they touched, he licked his lips again.

Disgust darkened Drake's eyes, and his jaw flexed as if he was clenching his teeth. But he managed to sound relatively unperturbed as he asked, "And where exactly did you see us?"

"In the back room at The Dungeon."

The Dungeon? Had this guy somehow been in Zelda's sex room? That idea made Josie Lynn shudder. This guy and sex toys and all drugged out of their heads. Oh. Dear. God.

"The Dungeon," Drake said, his tone curious and apparently not as disturbed by the idea as Josie Lynn was. "What time?"

"Oh, I'm not sure. Late." Again the man eyed Josie Lynn, and she found herself squeezing Drake's hand. God, this creeper made her skin crawl.

"Can you tell us who was with us?"

"A tall, very attractive woman in nothing but a bra and panties and thigh-high boots."

Oh, dear God, he was describing Zelda. He had been in the sex room with them.

"Another woman in some sort of black leather catsuit and high heels."

Zelda and that woman Drake had been using Josie Lynn to get rid of. At least that seemed like to the two most likely women.

"And," the man added with any unnervingly excited grin, "your lady here was not happy with the catsuit gal. They got into quite a shouting match."

Josie Lynn gaped at Drake. She'd got into a fight? With that woman? Why?

Drake's expression wasn't one of shock, but rather intrigue.

"Really? What did they fight about?" he asked the man.

"Well, your lady here didn't like that Catsuit was hitting on you," the man said, then looked at Josie Lynn. "In fact, you can be quite a spitfire when angry. The bouncer made the woman in the catsuit leave."

Bouncer? Oh, wait, the man was talking about a Goth bar called The Dungeon just off Bourbon on Toulouse. But Josie Lynn's relief that this man hadn't been in Zelda's sex dungeon was short-lived, as her gaze inadvertently fell on his weirdo polyester-covered crotch, which was unfortunately at eye level with where she sat.

She made a small, appalled noise and shifted her gaze to Drake, although his expression wasn't any more comforting. He looked highly amused.

She squeezed his hand again, this time very tightly.

Drake chuckled. "Oh, she is definitely a little spitfire. You should see her wrassle a gator."

"Really?" The man looked even more titillated, although she didn't check his trousers to see how much more so. Damn Drake.

"Oh yeah," Drake said with feeling. "So my cupcake here didn't like the other woman's attention, huh?"

Josie Lynn shot Drake a dirt look. He was enjoying this far too much.

"Not at all," the man said. "In fact, she popped the woman. Probably blackened her eye in good shape."

This time, Josie Lynn's mouth dropped open. She'd punched that woman? No. No.

Beside her, Drake laughed out loud. "Wow. Popped her, huh?"

The man nodded, grinning, too. "Socked her good."

Drake chuckled again.

But Josie Lynn managed to gather herself. "What happened after—I hit her?"

"The tall woman in her bra and panties left with the catsuit woman. You wanted to follow them, but your man here found some other ways to distract you." The creeper licked his lips again.

Josie Lynn tried not to vomit in her mouth, and definitely not about what she might have done with Drake, but because this freaky dude had watched them. Probably not unlike he was watching her now.

"Did anything else happen?" Drake said, his tone sharp and thick with warning. He clearly didn't care for this man's look either.

"Then the bra-and-panties woman returned. She was upset about something. I'm not sure what. But you all left together."

"Donald." Another voice snapped from the other side of the table, startling Josie Lynn. "Stop pestering the guests."

Josie Lynn turned, relieved to see the person they'd come to see had finally joined them.

Renee posed before them, in all her primped and painted glory. She'd changed from her peignoir and robe into a glittery gold evening gown. Josie Lynn's first thought was that she was much taller and more intimidating up close.

Clearly Donald agreed, because he immediately backed away from their table.

"I wasn't pestering, Renee," he said, his tone somewhere between wheedling and worshiping. "I was just talking."

"Well go talk somewhere else," Renee said, clearly unimpressed with his sycophantic behavior.

The man didn't say anything more as he scurried away.

"Sorry about that," Renee said, collapsing dramatically into one of the worn, red velvet chairs. "Donald is a regular here. Such a strange little man. He's relatively harmless, but his attention can become a bit too much. Even for me." Then she smiled.

Then her heavily made-up eyes shifted to Drake, clearly done with the topic of Donald. She leaned forward to give Drake an air kiss on either cheek. Drake accepted the greeting comfortably, which Josie Lynn found kind of cool. Many men would not be comfortable with another man dressed as a woman being affectionate—even in such an affected way.

"So why are you here, rock star?" Renee said, lounging back against her chair.

"Do you know of a group of female impersonators who dress as Cher through the decades?"

Renee rolled her eyes, disdain very clear in her face. "Cher. So cliché. All female impersonators imitate her at some point in their career." Then she acknowledged Josie Lynn for the first time. "Not me, mind you. I was always too old to imitate her. But then you know I never went for the easy applause anyway."

Josie Lynn found herself nodding, although she didn't really understand why it was any easier to dress up as Cher than any other female. In fact, Cher seemed like she'd be pretty hard to imitate. God knows, she couldn't pull off that "If I Could Turn Back Time" getup. That took some serious balls and a really great tushy. Not to mention, in reality, Cher couldn't be much younger than Renee.

"So you don't know of any impersonators working together," Drake said, trying to keep Madame Renee on track. "There would be five of them."

Renee sighed. "Not working together, per se, but I do know several here and there. But if I had to guess what place might be doing a Cher Extravaganza, it would probably be the new club down on Royal. Queen Mary's."

Queen Mary's on Royal, there was something apropos about that.

Although it was clear Renee did not think highly of this new place. Probably because it was competition. Josie Lynn glanced around, not that any place would have to be much to be competition for this place.

The waitress who'd been helping them came over and placed a three-olive martini in front of Renee, who didn't even acknowledge the gesture. Apparently when you were Madame Renee, it was assumed your needs would be met without having to ask.

She took a ladylike sip, her ring-clad pinky extended, then she patted her ruby-red lips with a hankie she discreetly—or what she thought was discreetly—pulled out of her cleavage.

"The thing about these new, flashy nightclubs, my darling Drake," she said, settling back in her chair as if she planned to give a long diatribe on the matter, "is that there is no appreciation for the subtlety of our art."

Subtlety wouldn't exactly have been the word Josie Lynn would have used.

"These nightclubs are all about flash and glitz, not about appreciating the intricacy of being a true lady. And performing like a true lady."

Drake nodded, appearing to be listening with rapt attention, then Josie Lynn noticed he was inconspicuously patting his pockets, looking for his wallet, only to realize he didn't have it. And Josie Lynn was willing to bet there was no money squeezed into those shiny, turquoise pants.

Damn, now they were really stuck listening to Madame Renee lament the days of true burlesque.

But to Josie Lynn's surprise, Drake seemed to feel something and managed to squeeze his fingers in the tight pocket. Miraculously, he pulled out a twenty. He subtly waved it under the edge of the table for Josie Lynn to see.

"You know how it was in the day," Renee was saying. "The talent, the delivery, the elegance, those were the things people came to see. Not just some rote imitation of someone else's expressions and moves. Any tranny with a mirror and a record player could practice those things until they were passable. True talent is original. Unique."

"I know," Drake agreed emphatically. "It really is a shame."

"A shame? My dear boy, it's a crime."

Drake took that segue to place the twenty on the table. "You are so very right, Renee, which is why we have to try to find these Chers. We have every reason to believe they were involved in some illegal activity."

Renee perked up, leaning forward in her chair again. "Nefarious deeds?"

"Yes. So you will have to forgive us for not staying for your second performance."

Renee nodded instantly. "Most certainly. I understand if you must go."

Drake leaned down and kissed the woman's rouged cheek. "Thank you for your help, Madame."

"Ah, Drake, I'm happy to help any way I can. You know our kind must stick together."

The older woman caught his hand and squeezed it briefly, more in a gesture of some unspoken camaraderie than affection.

Our kind? What did that mean?

Okay, Drake had been dressed as a pirate when she met him. And now he wore skintight vinyl pants that belonged to a dominatrix. And there were, of course, the assless chaps, but she still didn't get any vibe from Drake that he was normally a cross-dresser.

Drake finished his good-bye and Josie Lynn mumbled her own, then followed him back through the narrow bar.

Once they were back on Bourbon, she asked him over the cacophony of people and music, "What did she mean when she said *our kind*?"

Chapter Eleven

ROCK YOU LIKE A HURRICANE

JOHNNY remembered when he reached the front door of his apartment that Lizette had changed the locks after he had gone in and taken his drum kit. Or more likely Dieter had. But either way, his key wasn't going to work. See what happened when you let a woman into your life? She locked you out of your apartment. Okay, so maybe Lizette had locked him out because he'd faked his own death, but the point was, he didn't like his world being disrupted. Even if he was the one who had started it.

Damn it. Feeling aroused and annoyed all at once because he was having emotions he didn't entirely understand, he was fully prepared to break a window to get in, but Lizette held up a key.

"My apologies for the inconvenience," she said politely, because Lizette was always polite. When she wasn't yelling at him. Or letting him kiss her.

He wondered what she had been like in bed. If she had screamed or if she had been silent in her pleasure. Here was to finding out. "Thanks. I was just going to break the door down."

She gave a cluck of disapproval that made him laugh. He pushed open the door, having a momentary fear that the place looked like crap, then realizing it didn't make any difference. Lizette knew everything he owned, right down to his last pair of underwear. There was no impressing her at this point. Still, he was a little self-conscious about the fact that despite quitting smoking a month ago, there was still a stale lingering aftereffect of the cigarettes in his apartment. The drapes were drawn tightly closed, but he led her across the floor and pulled them open, wanting to see the moonlight spilling into the living room.

"Make yourself at home," he told her. "Clearly Saxon isn't here, and there is no sign he was." The room was still and everything was undisturbed. Apparently Dieter put things back the way he found them as he check-listed other people's shit. What a douchebag job.

"I suppose we should have realized that Saxon wouldn't be able to enter the apartment," she said, pulling the sweater off her shoulders one-handed.

"He would have just broken in if he wanted to crash here," he reassured her, then realized that probably wasn't reassuring to a woman like Lizette.

"There is a lot of breaking and entering going on," she said, shooting him a long look.

"Being a vampire does have it advantages." Lizette looked like she wanted to sit, but he desperately wanted a drink. He suspected he was still dehydrated from the night before. "Can I get you a drink? Have you had a hurricane yet? They're the local classic."

"No, I have not. What is in one?"

A crapload of alcohol. "Rum. It's a sweet drink." He was a rum kind of guy, though he usually didn't add fruit juice to it. Drake always gave him a hard time about it, given that it was the guitar player who had been the pirate, not Johnny. But rum had a smoother flow to it than whiskey, and gin tasted like lighter fluid. Every man had his drink, but Lizette looked like she needed some pineapple juice added to her booze to take the edge off.

"Sure. I am thirsty."

"How many rules are you breaking by being in here with me?" Johnny asked, moving into the kitchen and pulling ingredients out of the cupboard.

"More than I care to consider."

"I'm sorry that you got wrapped up in all this, Lizette, I honestly am." He was. He didn't dig that they'd been drugged. He could only imagine how she must feel.

"Thank you. Though you aren't ultimately responsible for what happened at the wedding reception."

"It was my fault you were there. You were tracking me down."

"Good point. So you need to make it up to me." She leaned on the counter, the front of her blouse gaping a little, her tongue slipping across her lush lower lip.

Holy hell, she was flirting with him. He liked it.

"I can forward your vibrator to you when it arrives." Johnny grinned, pouring rum into two glasses while Lizette blushed. "But that's for next week. Tonight, I can think of even better ways I can make it up to you."

"Is that so?" She propped her chin up with her hand and gazed out at him from under her thick lashes. "You will need to prove it to me."

She had no idea who she was challenging. Johnny may not have been well educated or rich, but there were three things he prided himself on—his boxing, his drumming, and his sexual skill. Since he had no intention of punching Lizette and he was off work for the next three nights, he would have to make sure the final one counted. "I can do that." He lifted the drink to her mouth. "Take a taste."

Most women would insist on taking the glass from him, but she didn't. She let him tilt the glass and she opened her mouth willingly, tilting her head to let the drink easily slide back down her throat. Johnny waited for her to hold her hand up or move her head away, but she didn't, so when the glass was half empty he pulled it back, impressed. She licked the moisture off her lips.

"Mmm," she said. "That's tasty."

"Let me see." Johnny reached out and flicked his tongue across her bottom lip, the sweetness of the juice and the tang of the rum light notes to the heavy syrup of the blood he had added. It was delicious. Just like her.

He took a swallow straight from the glass, then offered her the rest. She willingly drank it.

"It's making me warm," she told him.

Her cheeks had gained color instantly, going from the smooth marble of her vampire complexion to a more human peachy cream. She was still alabaster and unflawed, but with a hint of color to her cheeks and her neck. The tops of her breasts, which were revealed when her blouse shifted with her movements, looked warm and healthy, a vein visible and pumping her sweet blood with hypnotic vigor.

"Where are you warm?" he asked her, taking his finger and tracing it across that blue trail beneath her flesh.

"It seems to be settling in my hands and between my thighs."

Again, he had to say he loved her honesty. Johnny's cock tightened in his jeans. "Not a bad place to feel warm."

"Not at all."

Johnny kissed her, still letting her rest on her hand while he took her mouth, his eyes drifting closed. She sighed against his lips. When he pulled back, she stood up and dropped her hands from her chin.

"Is this going to be a challenge with these handcuffs on?"

"No." In fact, he found it arousing.

"I suppose I cannot remove my blouse."

Oh, no. He was not about to settle for Lizette half-dressed. He wanted to see every inch of her bared out for him. "I can fix that." Reaching back, he pulled a knife out of a drawer. He didn't use it for cooking, but the apartment had come furnished and sometimes it came in handy. Like right now.

Her eyes widened. "You cannot be serious. It will ruin my blouse."

"Your blouse is already ruined. There is no way you'll be able to dry-clean the blood out of it."

"But what will I wear after?" But then Lizette shook her head. "Never mind. I did not say that. I'm going to be spontaneous. I am going to enjoy the moment and not worry about the consequences. It will be good for my soul, yes?"

She looked so earnest, so nervous, that Johnny leaned down and kissed her gently, his own emotional response a little puzzling to him. How was it that he could want to protect Lizette and pound the hell out of her with his cock all at the same time? It seemed weird to want to have rough sex with someone and yet cuddle with her before and after. But that was how he felt, and she was clearly experiencing her own sense of mixed feelings and anxiety.

"Yes," he told her. "It will be good for your soul and your body." He brushed her hair back off her forehead. "It's going to be good for mine, too, you know. You make me want to be less of an idiot. More respectable. That's no small feat."

She gave a soft laugh. "You make me want to relax."

"Win-win, baby. Now hold still so I don't cut you." It was just a matter of slicing down the one sleeve, then letting her slip out of the other, and Lizette was free of the bloodied fabric, her black lace bra displaying her small breasts damn well. She had a slender body, and the skirt she was wearing accentuated her narrow waist. Johnny had never thought he had a particular type with women—if he did, it was for big-breasted, ballsy blondes. But Lizette was nothing like that, and yet, there was something so intensely feminine about her that he decided she was definitely the most beautiful woman he had ever met. The delicacy of the bra, the hourglass waist, the smooth pale arms, and the red nails that matched her red lips, it was all turning him on a whole hell of a lot.

Time seemed to be standing still, and there were no distractions, no noises from outside, no light to take away his focus from her. There was just a moonlit room and a beautiful woman who was crazy enough to get it on with him. One who was not wearing panties, if he remembered correctly.

As they kissed again, he let his hands wander, up her soft back, over her shoulder, to where he peeled her bra strap off, then back down to her waist. The hands that were still cuffed together were clasped, fingers interwoven for ease, and her free hand splayed across his chest. She seemed as intrigued about exploring his body as he was about hers, though neither of them was in a particular rush. Johnny didn't want to wham-bam her. He wanted to take his time, ensure she was enjoying herself, stretch it out as long as possible so that he would really have something to remember her by.

Once Lizette went back to Paris, he most likely would never see her again, and he wanted to savor the moment. He stripped his T-shirt off as much as their cuffs would allow and let it dangle, wanting his skin on hers, wanting to be as close to her as possible.

It felt like they were dancing, Lizette thought. Like they were engaged in a sensual tango in a dank basement a hundred years ago. Though she would have never done something like that. Since the death of Jean-Baptiste, she may have had sex rarely, but she had never been intimate. She had never taken the physical and the emotional exploration of a man and blended them together the way she had Johnny were doing here. His eyes were glassy in the moonlight, and he looked at her like he thought she was beautiful. She felt beautiful. She felt not reckless, but confident in her capitulation. Maybe it was lack of quality sleep, or having been drugged and the knowledge that she had already slept with Johnny even if she didn't remember it, but she didn't feel nervous. She didn't feel tense or awkward.

She felt aroused, eager, languid. It was a glorious feeling, and as his hands wandered over her flesh, she explored his as well, admiring the muscles in his chest, his shoulders, his biceps. There was evidence in the muscular strength of his mortal days spent in the boxing ring, and she tried to imagine him sweaty and intense, bouncing on his feet. Never would she have imagined she would be attracted by that thought, but she was, and she had been intrigued when she'd read his history in the VA dossier. Running down his arms, she gripped the belt loops of his jeans as he slipped his tongue inside her mouth to mate with hers. The thrust and retreat made the warm ache between her thighs grow more urgent, and she shifted restlessly, well aware of her lack of panties. There was no protective barrier between her desires and the cool rush of air-conditioned air.

Johnny seemed to pick up on her subtle nonverbal cue, because suddenly his hand was strolling up her leg beneath her skirt as he kissed her, and she instinctively turned her knee out to give him access. It was forward for her, but she never even hesitated. If she were going to have sex with a case subject in an apartment he was not allowed access to, she was damn well going to make the most of that decision. That way, when she removed herself from the case, she would at least have gotten the pleasure for the pain of stepping down.

"Is this okay?" he asked, his hand pausing on her inner thigh, charming her with the thoughtfulness of his question.

He clearly wanted to make sure they stopped before the point of no return if she wasn't sure, and she appreciated that. But she had no intention of denying herself at this point.

"Yes, please continue." Lizette tilted her head back, then gave a little moan when he simultaneously cupped her sex while nipping at her ear. It wasn't a bite to draw blood. It was a questing, teasing gesture, possibly to test her tolerance, or maybe just because he wanted to play. Whatever the reason, Lizette enjoyed the foreplay, her body humming with anticipation, moisture deep within her spreading over Johnny's finger as he stroked inside her.

"I don't mourn the loss of your panties at all," Johnny murmured into her ear.

"At the moment, I don't either," she said, her voice sounding breathless to her. His forearm pressed against her, trapped between them, and Lizette found herself moving her hips, matching his strokes with a rhythmic rocking, so she increased the impact. It wasn't something she normally would have done, but it felt so obvious, so natural, that she just went with it.

"That's it," he said, his tongue trailing down her neck and finding the slight swell of her breast above her bra.

Then he bit her, without warning, sinking his fangs right into the plump flesh, causing her to cry out in ecstasy.

"Oh, *mon cher!*" she said, without thought, the endearment slipping out purely meant as appreciation for the way he made her feel. "That feels wonderful."

No man had bit her before during sex. It wasn't entirely proper, as vampires didn't feed off of each other, but she had heard it was a highly erotic experience that many indulged in. But Jean-Baptiste had thought it crass, common, and since his death, there had been no man she had trusted enough or let go enough with to allow such a thing.

She hadn't allowed Johnny so much as he had just taken, but she couldn't believe what the sensation of his fangs puncturing her skin had done to her. It was like having an orgasm, only better. It made perfect sense to her why vampires indulged in biting each other, because it was like he was drawing pleasure up out of her on a pulley, each suck dragging from every inch of her body a tense, wiry ecstasy. She felt it everywhere.

Because he was drawing on her blood, sucking with enough intensity for her to feel the tug and pull, but not enough to cause pain, he didn't reply. Instead, his thumb moved over her clitoris and stroked the swollen nub. The stimulation both above and below the waist had her clinging to him, her body tight and hot and ready to explode. An orgasm was imminent if she didn't stop him, and she did not want to come. Not yet.

"Please." She grabbed his wrist and tried to move her hips away.

For a second he didn't respond, but then he stepped back, breathing hard, his hand still on her thigh, his mouth red with her blood, a trickle running down his lower lip onto his chin.

"What's wrong?" he asked. Even as he spoke, his eyes drifted closed. "Did I hurt you?" His tongue came out to stroke from one corner of his lower lip to the other, lapping up her blood.

He looked so aroused, so intense, so clearly enjoying her taste, that Lizette forgot what she was going to say. She just watched him, goose bumps racing along her skin as she realized that it didn't matter that he had removed his finger from inside her. Her inner muscles were quivering, her hips rocking forward, her breast aching from his point of entry as she watched him taste the very essence of her. It was overwhelming, and she reached for him, wanting her own taste.

Lizette gave him a long, deep kiss, capturing his mouth roughly, plunging her tongue inside to taste her own blood mingled with the rum. His hands gripped her hard about the waist and he was making a deep, barely audible sound of approval in the back of his throat. When she broke the kiss, she tilted her head and smiled at him, her eyelids heavy, handcuff jangling.

Then she bit his neck, letting her fangs drop in like steel into butter, the skin giving way with ease. When the first drops of his blood flooded over her, she almost fell backwards from the pure intensity of pleasure. It was intoxicating, and she sucked harder, feeling him tense against her, his grip tightening, his moans rising in volume and frequency.

"Fuck, that feels good," he told her.

Afraid to stay too long, take too much, lose control, she pulled back. Her intention to lick the remaining sweet drops off her lips was thwarted by Johnny descending on her mouth with an urgency that sent her falling backwards into the kitchen counter. She grappled to hold on to his waist, then realized she was in the perfect position to undo his jeans. Yanking harder than was strictly necessary, she had them unbuttoned and the zipper down while they kissed, his hand popping her bra clasp on her back. Then he bit her other breast.

Oh dear. Lizette tried to hold on, tried to keep herself cognizant, but she was losing herself to some strange, desperate, urgent desire to have Johnny everywhere on her body, inside her and sucking her dry. When he pulled back, she shoved his jeans down and bent over, dropping her fangs into his hip, along that mysteriously sexy muscle that men had which seemed to act as a directional to where their erection was. His jeans were caught, but she could feel his bulge pressing against her shoulder and breast as she let the tangy sweetness of his blood rush past her.

Her body felt hot and hyperaware, her hand shaking a little as she further freed him of his jeans and his briefs. When she broke away this time, he lifted her up, completely off the ground, his vampiric strength in evidence.

As he held her there, eyes racing over her breasts, he said, "Take your skirt off so I can fuck you."

She wouldn't have expected such brazen words to do anything but make her either offended or uncomfortable, or both. But instead, they only served to make her more desperate to have him do just that. She tossed her hair out of her way, and reached back to unzip her skirt. One small shove at the hips and it fell to the floor. It felt perfectly bizarre and perfectly arousing to be a foot or two off the ground, naked save for a lace bra, which was sliding down off her shoulders, her moisture stroked to the forefront by his touch glistening on her thighs.

"What now?" she asked him, lifting her leg to wrap it around his hip. She repeated the process with the other leg.

"Now I do this." He shifted slightly, then suddenly he was thrusting deep inside her.

"*Merde alors!*" she swore, which should have embarrassed her, but didn't, because she was beyond caring about anything but how goddamn good he made her feel.

Digging her fingernails into his shoulders and holding on, she threw her head back and accepted his hard cock into her body.

There was no way he was suffering from any sort of Irish curse. She may not have been around the block more than once or twice, but she was informed enough to understand that he was in possession of that which would be the envy of many a man. She was certainly feeling most appreciative.

So much so, that she had an orgasm.

Johnny felt Lizette's muscles tightening around him, her head thrown back, hair tumbling freely into the air, and he pumped harder, enjoying the view of her pure pleasure.

He didn't think that he had ever been so turned on, so completely lost in the moment of sex with a woman. Her face was very expressive, her eyes doelike, her sounds unchecked and raw. He hadn't expected the elegant curtain to be pulled back quite so easily, yet all it had taken was one bite and she was gone, as far into the rush of lust as he was.

Now she was squeezing him everywhere, nails digging into his flesh, muscles clamping onto his cock in a way that had his mouth hot with saliva and his balls tight. She felt so fucking good and he was losing control.

Not wanting to come so soon himself, the minute she quieted down, he carried her a few feet to the area rug in his living room and laid her down on it. The bedroom was too far, but he didn't expect her to take it on the kitchen tiles. She gave a soft moan of protest when he pulled back out of her entirely. Like she thought he wasn't going to come back. The irony of course was that he couldn't leave her.

But he didn't want to think about that. He just wanted to think about sinking back inside the warmth of her body and making her come a second time. Three was his current record with her, according to his fictionalized version of what had happened, so he wanted to best himself. What guy wouldn't?

"Lizette, open your eyes," he commanded as he plunged into her again. He wanted to see those expressive inky pools, wanted to see how good he made her feel. It mattered to him.

She did, but it clearly took effort, her arms slack, thighs sinking farther apart. She was enjoying herself, but in a slower, slumberous way, and taking it nice and pretty was not what he had in mind at the moment. Since he had so thoroughly enjoying biting her and she had so obviously liked it, too, he dipped down and sank into her shoulder, enjoying the hiss of approval from her right along with the first taste of tangy fluid rushing past his lips.

But she surprised him by raising her head and biting him right back on the opposite shoulder.

Holy shit. Johnny paused to close his eyes and just enjoy the ecstasy, the connection, the intimate and primal joining. It felt base and elevated all at the same time. Lizette bit him harder, her heels kicking into the backs of his thighs like she wanted him harder, deeper.

Still with his teeth in her skin, Johnny rolled her so she was on top, and while he'd intended her to stop there, she continued to roll until they were across the room, crashing into the coffee table with his hip and shoulder. They were both on their sides, him still thrusting inside her, Lizette pulling her fangs out to give a satisfied cry as she exploded in another orgasm. Her chin, her chest, her teeth, were all saturated with both of their blood, and he licked his lip, gritting his teeth. It was the hottest thing he'd ever seen, all that red against the pale, smooth white of her vampire flesh, her normally red lips stained even darker, a gruesome eroticism that only a vampire would understand. Biting was more intense than oral sex for mortals, and looking down at her, his puncture marks in her shoulder, her cries of anguished passion, he couldn't resist his own body anymore.

Leaning down and taking her mouth, blending her blood with his, her tongue with his, her body with his, Johnny exploded in the most intense orgasm he'd ever had.

Stunned, they both lay there intertwined for a good two minutes, blinking at each other. Finally Johnny reached out and wiped some of the blood off her lip and licked it. "That. Was. Amazing." There were actually no words to describe how off-the-charts awesome that had been.

"Indeed."

It was such an understated, typical-Lizette response, he gave a choked laugh. "I think I found the most authentically French thing in the Quarter," he told her.

"What? Me?" She brushed her hair back off her forehead, her breasts still rising rapidly from their vigorous encounter.

"Your vagina." He grinned and waited for the reaction.

It was immediate.

"Ah!" She gasped in indignation and smacked him on the shoulder. "How dare you!"

"Or as I like to call it 'La Pussy.'"

"I like to call you 'L'Asshole.' Note the liaison due to the vowel sound."

That made Johnny laugh even harder and he shifted, pulling out of her. "You're killing me."

"No, I am going to kill *you*. You are outrageous and inappropriate."

"So you keep telling me. But I actually think you kind of like that about me." He winked at her. He did think she liked it. It was like he said all the things she might think in her head but didn't allow herself to say out loud.

"I think you are arrogant and insufferable." Then she gave a smile. "But you are also right. I cannot exactly explain why I like you, but I do."

"It's a good thing I don't suffer from low self-esteem." Johnny stroked her arm lightly and reveled in her smile. This felt good. "Maybe you like me for my stellar penis."

"It is adequate."

That was a ringing endorsement from Lizette. He'd take it. This felt amazing, all of it. The sex, the teasing, the comfortableness of lying next to her.

If it had been like this last night, no wonder he had handcuffed himself to her.

She was the bomb in bed. Or in this case, on the floor.

"Do you want to take a shower?" he asked, because they both looked like a crime scene. There was drying blood smeared all over.

"That would be wonderful."

Johnny sat up and waited for her to follow, then he stood. It was then she seemed to remember that they were handcuffed, which meant they would be showering together, because she said, "I would prefer to shower alone."

"Why?" he asked, genuinely puzzled. "I've already seen you naked. In fact, you happen to be naked right now." He put his free hand on her smooth ass to further prove his point.

"I know, but sometimes a woman requires privacy."

He had no idea what she was talking about. "It's not like you're taking a crap, you're in the shower. With soap and water and a sponge. That is sexy. What's the big deal?"

Her tongue clucked. When her tongue clucked, Johnny was starting to realize there was no point in arguing with Lizette. She had made her mind up about some moral piece of whatever and she wasn't going to back down. But she didn't say anything. Maybe because she was realizing that it was a fortunate thing they were vampires, because neither one of them was ever going to need to use the toilet like a mortal would. Even he had to admit that would have been awkward.

And now he had officially killed the mood. Johnny mentally kicked himself. They'd been on such a sex high and he had fucked it up by pushing the point and mentioning *crap*. He was L'Asshole. So he lightly kissed her. "Never mind. Of course you can shower by yourself if you want. I'll just sit outside the shower curtain, okay? We can take turns."

"Really?"

"Of course." Even if it was completely stupid, in his opinion. But he was willing to do it for her.

Which was how he found himself sitting on the cold porcelain tub, freezing his ass off, chin in hand. While his other arm dangled behind him getting hit by the warm spray and flopping around at Lizette's will as she jerked him to and fro, washing her body. Washing her body. Damn. He really wanted to be a party to that process. He wanted to squeeze gel soap into his hands and slide them all over her, from head to toe. He wanted to lick between her thighs and listen to that catch in her breath she gave.

Now he was sitting naked on the edge of the cold tub with a boner.

Lame. That's what this was. And honestly, he was pretty damn sure he would have just ignored her protestations and jumped in anyway with any other woman because they had already had sex. That entitled him to shower sharing. But for whatever stupid reason he just perched like a naked bird feeling bitter while his arm went numb from hanging there in the cuffs.

"Finished. May I have a towel?" She popped her head out from behind the curtain.

Damn it, she was beautiful. It was making him grouchy. But he stood up without hesitation and grabbed her a towel. "Need help drying off?"

"No, thank you."

Of course she didn't. Because that would be fun for him. "I'm coming in," he told her, the dried blood on his shoulder and neck starting to pull at his skin. He was just about out of patience.

But she was quick, emerging from the shower wrapped in the towel. "It's all yours."

They traded positions, and she managed to avoid any contact with him whatsoever in the transition.

Funny how when he was the one standing in there, his arm was still stretched to capacity and he was hunched over. She had half of his arm out of the shower as she toweled her hair dry, while he felt like a chimpanzee trying to learn to use tools. He was all bent over and bouncing around on the balls of his feet trying to get some shampoo onto his head one-handed.

What the fuck.

Her French pussy had clearly whipped him.

Because he wasn't complaining. He was just one-handed washing while his arm went completely numb and water slapped him in the face.

Lizette didn't offer to dry him off. Not that he expected her to, but it would have been a nice gesture.

"Our clothes are in the kitchen," she told him, still burrito-wrapped in her towel, her damp hair falling over her shoulders in waves.

"Your clothes are trashed. How about I find something of mine for you to wear." Not bothering with a towel, because well, he liked to be naked, and she couldn't stop him, he went over to his dresser.

Rifling through his T-shirt drawer, he found a Union Jack shirt. "Oh, look, here's one for you."

"Ha-ha. Aside from the subject matter, I cannot wear a T-shirt with these handcuffs."

She was right. She would need a sweatshirt or something, which was ridiculous because it was ten million degrees outside. "You're going to have to wear a T-shirt. It's too hot for anything else." He found one that was loose, and just a plain gray cotton. "Here, try this."

Lizette turned her back slightly, which was ridiculous, but she did, and edged her towel to her waist to put the shirt on. Of course, her left arm fit in normally but the right one couldn't, so her flank was completely exposed. But Johnny could fix that. He rifled through his dresser and found a stapler.

"What are you doing?" she asked, sounding alarmed.

"Trust me." He stapled the shirt together, closing the gap from waist to arm pit. It looked weird, but she was in, and it was clean, even though the shoulder was bunching.

"But . . ."

"What?"

"I don't have my bra on."

He hated to tell her that no one would ever notice. She wasn't exactly a busty chick. But he just told her quite honestly, "You can't tell. I swear."

"Are you sure?"

"Yes. The shirt's really baggy, there is no way you can tell."

"I feel ridiculous. I wish I had panties."

He wasn't sure what the one statement had to do with the

other, but he could at least fix the second problem. "Do you want to borrow a pair of my underwear?"

"No! Of course not. That would be . . ."

"Inappropriate?" he asked, pulling a pair out of his drawer for himself. He bent over and stepped into them. Of course, the motion caused her to have to bend over, too, putting her face in very close proximity to his cock.

This had potential.

"I know precisely what you are thinking."

"Yeah?" Good, then he wouldn't even have to ask or suggest.

"It is not going to happen."

Damn. "You're sure? Because I would return the favor."

"No. That is not something I have ever done."

Was she kidding? She'd never blown a guy? Wow. "Because you think it's gross or because it's just never happened?"

He wasn't sure how anyone could go several hundred years and never at least have the option of sucking cock presented to her, but then again, they didn't move in the same circles. Maybe Paris was dead these days. His unintended pun made him want to grin, but he controlled himself and just stood in his underwear waiting for her response.

"I have limited experience with men, as I mentioned. Jean-Baptiste, he considered that particular action reserved for a mistress, not a lady."

Jean-Baptiste sounded like a pretentious prick. "So wait a minute, you're telling me he'd let a prostitute blow him, but not you? That he wasn't even faithful to you?"

She swallowed visibly. Her words were defensive, but her tone was soft, maybe even sad. "Yes. But that was the way of our world. I never expected him to be satisfied with me alone."

That was fucked-up. "But let me guess . . . you were expected to be faithful to him."

"Of course." She looked like that was a ludicrous question. "I never wanted to be with another man. I was in love with him."

Johnny wanted to ask why, but he kept his mouth shut. He didn't know the guy, and she was right, times had been different. So he concentrated on what that meant. "So you never have, but have you ever wanted to?"

"Certainly. It has crossed my mind on more than one occasion that I would like to have the experience. I would like to know if I am capable of creating that sort of a response from a man."

She had never given oral sex to any other man, yet she was open to the idea. That was the hottest thing he'd ever heard in his entire life. He could be the first man she put her mouth around and sucked to oblivion. An erection sprang to life, and he wondered if there was a casual way to ask to her to reconsider dropping to her knees.

"When I am ready, I will let you know," she said.

For some reason, that did something really weird to the interior of his chest cavity. Johnny brushed her hair back off her cheek and looked into her deep brown eyes. "I really like you, Lizette." It was a completely cornball, lame-ass thing to say, but it was how he felt.

She smiled. "That's not going to make me change my mind."

The ironic thing was, for once he didn't have an angle, nor was he joking around. He didn't even bother to explain that to her. He just found himself saying earnestly, "I wish you didn't have to go back to France. I wish we had more time to spend together."

The smile fell off her face and she tilted her head, studying him. "What do you mean?"

"I mean I want more time to get to know you, both in bed and out. I don't want you to leave yet." He took her hand and held it a little more aggressively than romantically. But he had a point to make.

Her expression softened. "I don't think that I want to leave yet either."

"Then maybe it's a good thing you canceled your flight." He kissed the corner of her mouth because it looked delectable. She looked delectable.

"Perhaps it is." She sighed. "But I only have a room at the hotel through tomorrow."

"You can stay with me," he said, because he was crazy. Crazy about her and just plain crazy. Because never once, in his entire life, had he offered for a woman to stay with him. Not even his sister.

So the fact that he had just suggested to Lizette that she shack up with him for an undetermined amount of time meant that he had completely lost it. Her body had numbed his brain. There was no other explanation.

Of course, there was another explanation, but he refused to consider it.

Which was why he suddenly found himself hustling her out of the bedroom after he yanked on his jeans and grabbed a clean shirt to take with him. "You know, I just had a thought. There is a metal shop down on Rampart. I bet they can cut us out of these cuffs. Your skin is starting to chafe."

"I'm fine."

"Well, we have to get out of them sooner or later." He handed her a pair of basketball shorts from his dresser to wear.

"What is this?"

"Shorts for you. Unless you want to put your skirt back on. But the shorts might help with your concern over a lack of panties."

"Oh, that is true." She sat down and pulled them on. "Thank you, that is very sweet of you."

Feeling like he couldn't breathe all of a sudden, Johnny led her through the apartment and out the front door, feeling much better when the sultry night air hit his skin.

And since they were passing the bar with a vampire bartender on the way back to his place, he decided he needed a drink. Bad. Like a big gigantic drink that would make him forget that for a split second, he had felt pleased that Lizette had canceled her plane ticket and ordered lingerie sent to his apartment. He wanted to obliterate the idea that he might actually be happy living with a woman from here to forever. With Lizette. That she was *the* woman.

Holy crap.

Johnny yanked the door open to Fahy's and held it open for Lizette, anxiety crawling up and scratching him on the balls. "Do you mind if we stop for a second?" he asked, even though he'd already pulled open the door. If she said no, he wasn't sure what he was going to do, but it wasn't going to be pretty.

He had just freaked himself the fuck out.

And Lizette was going to be staying with him.

Chapter Twelve

IF THESE WALLS COULD TALK
(Thankfully the Bouncer Can)

DRAKE knew exactly what Josie Lynn was referring to, but maybe it was the residual effects of the drugs, or that fact that she was standing only inches away from him and he really, really dug how she looked in his shirt, but his brain just didn't seem to be working.

"Our kind?"

Josie Lynn nodded. "Yeah, she said, 'our kind must stick together.'"

"Oh, that." He started walking and she quickly fell into step beside him, casting glances at him, clearly awaiting an explanation.

"She was just referring to the fact that we—" he paused, then said quickly and rather proudly, "are performers. Because I'm in a band. So she considers us all, you know, contemporaries."

She considered his explanation. "So why wouldn't she consider the Chers contemporaries, too?"

"She's just jealous of all the changes and other female impersonators' success. Rivalry, I guess."

Josie Lynn nodded, seeming to accept his explanation. Thankfully. There was no way Drake was going to tell her that Madame Renee Chevalier had been a vampire even longer than he had. Vampirism was going to stay out of the topic of conversation completely. Because first, she'd think he was totally mad. And second, if she didn't, she'd be scared shitless. Neither a good option.

"So do we head to the nightclub on Royal?"

"I think we'd do better to see if I can get into my apartment," Drake said.

"What? Not willing to go into the nightclub dressed like that?"

He shot her a look, although truth be told, he would be glad to get into some pants that weren't squeezing his balls quite so much.

"I can't say these are the most comfortable clothes I've ever worn," he said, wriggling himself to adjust things a little, which didn't help. Everything was smooshed against the unforgiving plastic. "But mostly, I think we are probably going to need cash. And I also wanted to see if Cort, my roommate, you know, Katie's husband, is there."

Josie Lynn gave a nod, and he realized he was probably over-explaining.

"Anyway, I'm hoping he might know or remember something. Maybe he saw something odd before we all started tripping."

"Where's your apartment?" She said, looking around like she wanted to keep their mission moving. So much for actually becoming comfortable around him.

"This way," he pointed. "On Toulouse, on the block just across from The Dungeon. So maybe we should go to my place, hit

The Dungeon to see if we can get any info there, then to Queen Mary's."

They started down Bourbon, dodging groups of revelers, a few drunks who'd gone way beyond revelry and damn near into oblivion. Then a bunch of religious fanatics waving signs and telling everyone they were going to Hell. Just an average night on Bourbon.

"Hey, Legs." An obviously inebriated guy in his mid-twenties who, given his Saints jersey, appeared to be a local, grabbed Josie Lynn's arm as they walked past.

"I like the short little dress you got going on here," he slurred, his bleary eyes still managing to look focused enough on her. "Why don't you join me and my buddies?"

"No thank you," Josie Lynn said, her voice hard and annoyed. She jerked her arm out of the man's grasp, but he only reached for her again.

"Hey dude, leave her alone," Drake warned.

The guy gave him the once-over, then glanced at his two buddies before saying, "What are you going to do about it in your shiny, bright blue pants?"

Then he returned his attention to Josie Lynn.

"Come on," the drunk coaxed. "I'd love to have a chance to see what's under all those pretty ruffles."

Drake didn't wait for Josie Lynn's response. Instead he grabbed the arm of the man that held her and twisted it, so the rude drunk was not only no longer touching Josie Lynn, but also not even facing her.

"I said leave her alone." Drake jerked the man's arm upward just enough that the drunk cried out in pain. "Now are you and your friends going to move along and not bother this lady anymore?"

The man didn't answer right away, and Drake couldn't help jerking his arm again.

"Alright," the man shouted, the pain in his shoulder clearly making him more willing to answer promptly. Drake cast looks toward his two friends. Neither looked inclined to jump to their friend's defense. In fact, they both kept glancing around them as if they hoped no one was even noticing the tussle. Yeah, they were no threat.

Drake jerked his arm one last time, then released the drunk. "Just get out of here. And try to remember your manners, will you?"

The jerk shot him an angry look but said nothing more. His buddy urged him to just come on, and the guy did, staggering off into the crowds.

Drake turned back to Josie Lynn. "Are you okay?"

Josie Lynn answered with a furious glare, then she started walking in the direction of his apartment.

Drake stood there, stunned, then jogged to catch up with her brisk, determined pace.

"Cupcake? Why are you mad at me?"

She stopped so suddenly and spun toward him so fast that he almost mowed her over. Instead he caught her shoulders, both to balance her and to stop himself.

"Can you please stop calling me that?"

"Okay," he agreed readily. It was an honest mistake anyway.

"I could have handled that," she said, her tone not angry or irritated, but rather flat and resolute.

Drake frowned, confused. Okay, just a moment ago she had clearly been angry with him, and now she seemed guarded, pulling up a wall of strength. It made no sense.

"I have no doubt you could have handled it. I saw the gator deal. But I was just trying to help."

"Well, don't."

She started walking again, and again he followed, although this time he didn't rush to catch up with her. He couldn't figure her out. In Madame Renee's she had willingly accepted his protective touch when that letch Donald had been giving her a look like he'd like to eat her whole. Yet, he stepped in when some drunk dude was actually getting physical and she was pissed. Women were confusing at best. This one was utterly mind-boggling.

He started to hasten his pace to catch up with her, especially since she was going to walk right past Toulouse, when another man approached her. This man was tall and barrel-chested. Far more intimidating than the silly drunk.

What the hell? All this male attention was getting to him. She was definitely cute—well, beautiful if you asked him, but damn there were plenty of pretty women on Bourbon. Why did men feel the need to approach his lady?

His lady? Okay, where had that come from? And he needed to stop that kind of thought right away. Josie Lynn wasn't even close to *his lady*. She could barely stand him.

Still he felt his protectiveness—and possessiveness, if he was being honest, rise up again like hackles on a feral dog.

"Hey Josie Lynn, how are you feeling tonight?"

Some of Drake's protective concern tamped down as he realized the man knew her. Then he looked at Josie Lynn and realized from her puzzled expression that she had no idea who this man was.

Even though she'd just informed him she was perfectly capable of taking care of herself, he moved to stand close beside her.

"Drake," the man greeted, extending a beefy hand toward him.

Drake accepted in, knowing for a fact he'd never met this man before.

"I bet you're feeling even rougher than this little one," the man said, jerking his head toward Josie Lynn. "You two were pretty wrecked. And wild."

The big guy smiled, but Drake didn't sense any lasciviousness or even judgment in his grin. He'd genuinely found them amusing.

"Yeah, we were," Drake agreed, really hating that he had no idea what he was referring to.

"Come have a drink with me before I start my shift," the giant said jovially.

Drake looked at Josie Lynn, who shrugged. It probably made sense to do so, since clearly this guy remembered them from last night. And from his familiarity must have talked to them for quite some time.

"Sure," Drake said and waited for the man to lead the way.

It shouldn't have surprised Drake, but it did, as the man led them straight to The Dungeon.

They entered the dark entryway that seemed to be set up more like a novelty haunted attraction than a bar. The man led them through a few hallways to a back bar that was mostly empty, although the hard rock still pounded off the walls and made it hard to hear.

"What can I get you?" the man asked.

Drake ordered his usual whiskey, neat. Josie Lynn hesitated, then after an uneasy look around the place, asked for a glass of wine.

"So dude, you two had a pretty kick-ass night last night," the man grinned with approval. He turned to Josie Lynn. "You are pretty damn feisty."

Even in the shadowy light, Drake could see her blush.

"I don't think I've ever seen anyone get the better of Obsidian. Woman or man."

Well that answered two suspicions of Drake's. Yes, Josie Lynn's run-in had been with Obsidian. And he'd been right to avoid that chick. She was scary.

He glanced at Josie Lynn, who looked embarrassed and bemused all at once. But she did seem to find her voice, having to practically shout over the music.

"Why did I fight with her?"

The man gave her a somewhat surprised look himself. Apparently he hadn't caught on to the fact that they had no clue what had happened. For the entire night.

"She was trying to make moves on your man here." He tilted his head in Drake's direction. Then he frowned, his gaze moving over Drake. "Interesting outfit, buddy."

"Yeah, I know. Thanks." This guy clearly wasn't terribly quick, if he had just noticed Drake's look.

The man frowned at him a moment longer, then turned back to Josie Lynn. "You definitely put her in her place."

"Then what happened?" she asked, her words coming out stiltedly as if she really didn't want to know, but knew she needed to.

The burly guy grinned again. "Well, let's just say a good fight seems to turn you both on."

Josie Lynn reached for her glass of wine and downed half of it. Drake personally wanted to ask for more details, but he was pretty sure Josie Lynn would have turned her Cajun fighting skills on him.

Instead he settled for saying, "We didn't cause too much of a scene, did we?"

"Nah," the man said. "Nothing that hasn't happened here before."

Drake wasn't sure what that meant exactly. He was pretty certain a lot of things had happened here before.

"And you two got interrupted by Zelda, before you got too hot and heavy."

"Did we leave with her?"

The man nodded, gulping down his Jägerbomb.

"She said she needed to find her wedding dress. And her groom." The guy chuckled, his laugh deep even over the pounding bass of Nine Inch Nails reverberating in the room. "In that order."

Drake smiled, not finding that information as amusing as this guy did. Where had they gone after that? Zelda's sex room? Or somewhere else before they ended up there? And how hot and heavy had he and Cupcake really gotten? Damn, he wished he remembered. Especially that last part.

"Oh shit," the man suddenly said. "Looks like your nemesis is back."

Both Drake and Josie Lynn turned to see Obsidian walk into the room. Tonight she wore even more black eyeliner than last night, obviously trying to mask a pretty impressive shiner. But it did little to hide the injury, especially since tonight she wore a purple corset that just seemed to bring out the black-and-purple bruise all the more.

She paused when she saw them at the bar, but strode into the room anyway.

"She must be a masochist as well as a sadist," the giant said, shaking his head and pretty much voicing Drake's own thoughts.

She walked over to the bar, taking a seat just one down from Drake. The bartender, whom Drake didn't recall either, shot all of them a rather wary look before going to take Obsidian's drink order. Clearly she remembered them, too.

"Maybe we should just go," Josie Lynn said, making her voice loud to be heard over the music. But the song ended midsentence so everyone could hear her, crystal-clear.

"Yes, maybe you should," Obsidian said wryly, but then she smiled invitingly at Drake. "You can of course stay. Surely you are bored with the company of some uncouth, backwoods Cajun by now. Only good for one night. And only good for one thing."

She gave Josie Lynn a withering look. "If you're even good for that."

Drake stared at the woman. Maybe the reason he instantly had found her so unnerving at the wedding wasn't because she was a whip-wielding domme, but actually because she was nuts. What the hell was she thinking when Josie Lynn had already kicked her butt once? Masochistic was right.

Drake then shot Josie Lynn a look, because he sensed her shifting beside him. This was going to get ugly. Josie Lynn had already been annoyed when she'd walked in here, and he suspected Obsidian's goading was not going to improve that mood.

And Drake was right. Josie Lynn now stood. There was going to be another brawl, and frankly he didn't think Obsidian was going to just luck out with a black eye. But instead of pushing out her barstool, and going over to the clearly non-too-bright domme, Josie Lynn pushed the stool aside and stepped closer to him. In fact, she didn't just step closer, she placed her hands on Drake's knees to get him to swivel toward her, then she stepped in between his spread thighs.

Drake had no idea what she was doing, but he sure as shit wasn't going to stop her. She then placed a hand on either side of his face, leaned in and kissed him utterly senseless.

So senseless that it took him a moment to react, but when it registered that Josie Lynn's full, soft lips were moving over his, he groaned hungrily and caught the back of her head with his hand, taking control of the kiss.

She made a small noise and met his intensity without hesitation. Drake wasn't sure how long the kiss continued, but he knew it wasn't long enough, and he was reluctant to let her back away from their embrace. But he didn't miss the lust-hazed look in her sky-blue eyes, making them almost glitter in the dim light.

Satisfaction filled him. She was as attracted to him as he was to her. Of course, being a vampire, he could also sense her desire, smell it. It was unbelievably arousing, the best, most heady scent he could recall ever encountering. Even more so than blood. Or maybe it was because the intense fragrance was a part of her blood, an essence unique to Josie Lynn alone. And just for him.

His fangs descended, like an inexperienced teen unable to control his bodily reactions. That hadn't happened to him since the very first years of his vampirism. He kept tight restraint over his vampiric desires. Not to mention, the last time he'd experienced a blackout, at Johnny's wake, which was a long story in itself, he'd ended up with an implanted fang. That fang just didn't descend down without conscious thought on his part. Yet there it was poking his inner lip.

And frankly, he didn't care that he was having such lack of control. He was too aroused. Too desperate to keep touching his Cupcake.

Just when he would have leaned in and kissed her again, Josie Lynn moved back from the lee of his thighs. Still dazed by his own desire, it took him a moment to realize that her attention was now on Obsidian. A smug smile curved those lips he'd just tasted.

"Hmm," Josie Lynn said with haughtiness that rivaled the self-assurance of any lady of the court that he'd grown up with, "does that look like boredom, darling?"

"Not to me," the big guy still seated with them said with a great measure of admiration.

"Not to me either," Drake said, pulling Josie Lynn back to him.

He had to kiss her again. And she allowed it readily. Fortunately he did have the expertise to kiss her without nicking the soft, fragile skin of her lips with his fangs.

Oh, he wanted to. He wanted to taste her. He wanted to strip her naked and fill her completely. With his cock. With his fangs. He hadn't wanted to bite a human for decades, always knowing what a slippery slope feeding from a mortal was. At the beginning of his life as vampire, he'd been insatiable. Biting anyone, everyone. He'd been dangerous. Much to his shame, he'd been deadly. But he'd gotten control of that until feeding from humans didn't even tempt him.

Until now.

But this wasn't just a desire to feed. This was a desire to feed from Josie Lynn. Only Josie Lynn. This was about a hunger that had nothing to do with satisfying his need for blood. This was about satisfying his need for this woman.

It was overwhelming. And this time he broke the kiss, afraid for the first time in probably a hundred years that he couldn't keep his lust in check.

Josie Lynn swayed slightly in his hold, her lips parted and glistening from their kiss.

It was Drake's turn to feel smug. Oh yeah, Miss Josie Lynn was definitely affected by him. Very affected.

"Please just get a damn room," Obsidian said, picking up her martini and leaving the room.

"You really rub that one the wrong way," the big guy said. "But then she never handles not getting what she wants very well."

Drake tried to sort out his scrambled, desirous thoughts. Not easy with Josie Lynn still positioned between his legs. She seemed to be having the same difficulty, because she blinked a few times, then moved back to her barstool.

With a little distance between them, his thoughts cleared a little. "What—what does she do if she doesn't get her way?"

"Oh, she's a mean one," the man stated, all humor gone. "Zelda is a dominatrix because she finds pleasure in it, and she wants her partner to find pleasure, too. Obsidian is a domme because she likes to hurt."

Drake glanced at Josie Lynn, who was already looking at him, and he could tell she was thinking the same thing. Maybe Obsidian was somehow involved in the events of last night.

"You probably don't have anything to really worry about. Hell, she knows you can definitely get the best of her," the man said, offering Josie Lynn a smile of respect. "But I do think she could be a dirty fighter. So just be aware."

He stood then. "And you know if you ever need my help you got it. And you can always find me at the door. Speaking of which, I better clock in."

Drake realized the man was a bouncer here. He knew the guy looked familiar. Drake had probably seen him dozens of times. After all, Drake had been working on Bourbon for years. That was oddly comforting to know a bouncer had had an eye on them last night. They'd at least been safe here. Well, Obsidian hadn't been safe, but this guy seemed to think she'd had it coming anyway.

"Thanks." Drake offered the man his hand. "Sorry, I don't remember your name."

"Marcus. And you're with that band that plays right over at the Old Opera House, right? The Impalers?"

Drake nodded. "That's me."

"Dude, you are a kick-ass guitarist."

"Thanks, Marcus. We appreciate you looking out for us last night."

Marcus chuckled. "I didn't need to look out for you guys. You had your own little bouncer right here." He nodded toward Josie Lynn.

Josie Lynn smiled, but Drake could see that she wasn't comfortable with everything that had happened. Last night or just earlier.

"Okay, have a good night." Marcus left them.

After Marcus left, Drake glanced at Josie Lynn, who appeared very focused on her glass of wine. Yeah, she wasn't going to want to discuss their kiss, or how fabulous it had been. In fact, he suspected she was going to attempt to act like it never happened.

As if just to validate his thoughts, she said, without looking away from her infinitely fascinating wineglass, "So maybe Obsidian is the one who put the drugs in the punch."

Drake nodded. "She seems like she could be a likely candidate, but we should keep looking for the Chers. There's definitely something suspicious about them. And as we discussed, it seems like they would have needed an inside person to drug the guests."

She polished off her wine like it was shot of tequila. "Let's keep moving then."

Oh, she was absolutely not discussing the kiss. No way, no how.

"Okay," he said.

KEEP MOVING. THAT was Josie Lynn's first instinct, just like it always was. She wanted to forge ahead and get the answers they needed. She certainly didn't want to be making out with a Bourbon Street band guy. Talk about the king of all bad boys.

No, she had to amend that, she *did* want to be making out with a Bourbon Street band guy, and that was why she had to keep moving. Get this mystery solved and get away from him ASAP.

Hadn't her last bad-boy boyfriend taught her enough of a lesson about why this type of man was exactly the type of man she needed to avoid? Sure, this guy would be fun for a while. But then things would go horribly wrong. He'd want to "borrow" money. He'd want a place to crash for "just a couple days." Or he'd be seeing other women on the side. Or all of the above. Josie Lynn had experienced it all. And she wasn't going there again. Ever.

"So should we head to your place?" she asked as she stood, reaching for a pocket she realized she didn't have—not that it mattered, since she didn't have any cash either. Shit, this no-money thing was a real pain in the ass.

"Don't worry," the bartender, a pierced and tattooed woman in her early twenties said as she brushed a shock of fuchsia hair out of her eyes. "Marcus picked up the tab on these for you."

"That was nice," Drake said, clearly relieved, too.

"Well you did buy all the rounds last night," the woman said, giving them a look that stated it had been *a lot* of rounds.

"Oh right," Drake said, not sounding nearly as worried as Josie Lynn felt. How much money had they spent last night? And did that mean they'd had their wallets—and clothes—at that point last night? *And exactly how much money did we spend,* she thought again. She didn't have money to spare.

She didn't have any money at all, it would appear.

Drake thanked the bartender again, then waited for Josie Lynn to lead the way.

"You first," she said. She had no idea how they'd gotten to this back room, and frankly the combination of loud, thumping metal music, dim lighting, and winding hallways was too much for her to deal with.

And it definitely wasn't the fact that she was so shaken by Drake's kiss. No, not at all.

She followed him through the hallways that just seemed to lead from one bar or nook to another. The Dungeon didn't seem like an appropriate name for this place. The Creepy, Really Loud Maze seemed like a better name to her.

The operative word being *creepy*. A cold shiver snaked up her spine, and she found herself looking behind her. She expected to see another patron—after all, it was a bar and club, but the hallway was empty.

Drake made another turn only to end up in another hallway. They passed another strange little alcove and again, Josie Lynn felt that weird shivery feeling at the back of her neck.

She looked behind her again just in time to see a flash of purple and red and black slip into the nook they'd just passed.

Obsidian.

Was she following them? The idea unnerved Josie Lynn. A lot. Marcus made it sound like the woman had a reputation for being more than a little strange. And they'd just considered the idea that she was nutty enough to drug a whole wedding party.

Josie Lynn touched Drake's arm, and he immediately stopped.

"I think Obsidian just stepped into that alcove," Josie Lynn said leaning close so he could hear her over the thundering industrial music. "I think she might be following us."

"She is," he said with full certainty.

"Did you see her, too?"

Drake shook his head, which suddenly turned to a nod. "Yeah, I did."

Josie Lynn frowned. She hadn't seen him looking back at any time. But maybe he had at the same time she did.

"What do we do?" she asked, truly disturbed by this weird chick.

"Ignore her. She's no threat."

She looked behind her again to be sure Obsidian wasn't coming. "But Marcus made her sound pretty much like a wackadoo."

Drake smiled. "She may be a wackadoo, but you are definitely safe with me. No worries."

He took her hand and continued down the hallway. Josie Lynn glanced back over her shoulder. She wasn't sure if she was really safe with Drake, but his strong hand around hers did make her feel better.

And once they were out of the tangle of shadowy hallways and back onto the crowded, garishly lit streets of the French Quarter, she decided she had a new appreciation for Bourbon Street. All the people made her feel safer. Although she had to admit, Drake was making her feel safe, too, and she definitely wasn't willing to release his hand.

There was no way around it. Obsidian was weird.

"Now you understand why I was avoiding her. She's not right," Drake said as if he was reading Josie Lynn's mind, and she had to admit she did understand why. She just wished she didn't always react so strongly to his method of avoiding.

Damn, he was a good kisser.

And those thoughts, my friend, will get you neck deep into all sorts of trouble. Trouble with a naughty smile, an amazing kiss, a killer body, and sexual skills she was willing to bet would leave her a heap of cum-soaked Jell-O.

Okay, that image was kind of gross . . . but she suspected very accurate.

And one she had to forget about. But what other things could he do with that mouth?

"Are you okay?"

She frowned up at him, wondering if she'd actually said some of her thoughts aloud or something.

Oh dear God, please tell me I didn't say that Jell-O thing aloud.

"You're squeezing my hand," he explained, clearly seeing she had no idea why he'd asked.

She instantly released his hand. "Yeah—yeah, I'm fine. I just wish we could figure out what happened last night."

He looked down at his now-empty hand, then back at her as if he didn't believe her, but he said nothing more, leading her across Bourbon to the other side of the street. They walked past a bar that she recognized as the one Marcus had mentioned they played at. Instead of walking into the bar door, he took a small side one.

"You live over the bar where you work?" she said as soon as they were in the somewhat quieter stairwell.

"Crazy, huh?" he said. "But I'm rarely late for work."

They went up a rickety flight of stairs to a door covered in peeling red paint.

"Here's hoping Cort is here." He turned the doorknob and the door opened, but instead of looking relieved, he stared down at the knob.

"What's wrong?" She tried to see what had him looking so concerned.

"The door was jimmied open." He cautiously pushed the door open and poked his head inside. He remained still.

Listening, Josie Lynn guessed, although something about his utterly motionless stance seemed like he was doing something beyond listening. Sensing seemed like a better word, even though she knew that couldn't really be what he was doing.

"The apartment is empty," he said after a moment.

"How can you tell?" She hadn't heard anything either, but that didn't mean someone wasn't hiding inside. Hell, for all they knew, there were five Chers lying in wait. Truthfully, that didn't sound too scary, but at this point Josie Lynn wasn't trusting anyone.

"Well, I'm not totally sure," Drake said, sounding almost . . . guilty like he'd been caught in a lie or something. Maybe he was just trying to sound certain to comfort her. "But I think it's safe. I'll go in first though."

"I certainly hope so," she said wryly. "It's your apartment. I know I fought a gator for you, but this one is all yours."

He smiled. "If there's a gator in here, I'm deferring back to you. Sorry."

She smiled, too. "Okay. Fair enough. But everything else is yours."

"Deal." Drake pushed open the door without hesitation and strolled in the door. The entrance led directly into a small but tidy kitchen. The lights were on and everything looked normal.

Again, Drake walked into the hallway without any signs of hesitation. He really did seem pretty confident the place was empty.

Brave? Or foolish? Josie Lynn couldn't decide.

The hallway was flanked by a few sets of doors, three were closed and one was open and dark. The room at the end of the hallway, which Josie Lynn could already tell was the living room even from this distance, was lit as well.

Drake headed directly toward that room, not acknowledging the other doors as he passed them. Josie Lynn was no cop or detective. She wasn't even that good at Clue, but she was pretty sure they should be checking every room just in case. She didn't want to get it with the candlestick in the conservatory by Bob Mackie Cher.

"Aren't you even going to check the other rooms?" she whispered.

Chapter Thirteen

BENNY AND CHER

LIZETTE severely resented the fact that men claimed women were complicated. They were the ones who changed their minds with no warning or logic and who seemed terrified of just speaking the truth.

Five minutes earlier Johnny had been slowly and skillfully kissing her, and sounding very sincere in saying that he liked her, and wanted her to stay with him for a few days. She had been flattered and intrigued by the idea of spending time with him, and so she'd said yes. Then his mood had immediately changed, and he had just about dragged her out of the apartment, insisting they get the cuffs cut off, with an urgency previously unseen. She had actually thought he'd been somewhat enjoying their enforced togetherness. But not so now.

He was bouncing on the balls of his feet, and had practically begged to stop for a drink without any warning whatsoever. How could he go from purring contentment to skittish without any apparent trigger? It was a mystery to her, and she instantly lost a bit

of the contented mood that she had been feeling. Was that what
he had done? Changed his mind? Regretted his suggestion for her
to stay with him?

Had he just been hoping for oral sex after all?

Now she wanted a drink as well. Bastard. She had never felt
particularly concerned about her attractiveness or her lovemaking
skills, and yet for some reason Johnny made her doubt herself.
Made her want to please him, including taking him into her
mouth. The very idea made her blush, as she had been so trained
to think of it as crass, but she had thought he would like it. She
had trusted him with the truth, but now she was feeling uncertain. Which was frustrating in the extreme, and she vowed not to
let it get the best of her. She was not insecure, and she was not
going to let some fickle vampire who faked his own death make
her feel inadequate in any way.

She realized it was the same bar they had met in the other
evening when she had been showing him the list. Funny how
then she had been so sure of herself and her professionalism. Now
she had just made love to him on the floor and she still wasn't
wearing underwear. But oddly, she didn't feel particularly upset
about it. Well, she wasn't entirely comfortable not wearing panties, but that had nothing to do with Johnny. She had reconciled
herself to the fact that she must have slept with him because she
liked him, and that was perfectly acceptable. She was owed vacation time, so there was no reason she couldn't resign from this
case and spend a few days with Johnny.

After canceling the lingerie and vibrator orders. Speaking of
which, she should do that soon. They sat down at the bar, the
same bartender from the other night waving to them. Lizette ordered a glass of wine and crossed her legs while Johnny looked

everywhere but at her, his fingers drumming on the ancient wooden bar.

"Is that Cher?" she asked him, eyeing a woman bent over with a pool stick. Her legs were a mile long, her skirt extremely short. Her companion was a muscular young guy wearing a very prominent cross on his chest.

"You know who Cher is?" Johnny asked her.

"Everyone knows who Cher is." She suspected every woman secretly wished that when she turned sixty she would magically morph into Cher. That wasn't Lizette's desire, as she would never have the kind of showmanship that Cher displayed, nor did she aspire to that, but she did admire her ability to ignore everyone else's opinions of her. "I believe that is her Bob Mackie look, given the headdress she's wearing."

"Sweetheart, that's not Cher. It's not even a woman."

"What?" Lizette stared a little harder. "That's a man?" It didn't look like a man. There was no . . . hair. Well, there was plenty of hair on her/his head but not on her silky-smooth legs.

"I think he was at the wedding last night." Johnny stood up. "Wait, is that Benny? Nigel," he called to the bartender. "Is that Benny with Cher over there?"

"The one and only. Benny, not Cher. There is definitely more than one of her running around this town."

Feeling like there was an inside joke she was not privy to, Lizette studied the duo at the pool table. "Who is Benny?" Lizette asked.

"He's a stripper who works at the gay club, and he's friends with my sister. I should say hi. Come on, I'll introduce you."

Suddenly aware of the fact that she was wearing Johnny's T-shirt stapled closed and Johnny's oversized nylon sports shorts,

Lizette rose with Johnny and tossed her hair back. She really wished she hadn't lost her Louboutins . . . she'd prefer to be wearing them if she were going to be introduced to a well-dressed transvestite. He was bound to be up on fashion and Louboutins were like style armor—no one could touch you if you were wearing them.

"Benny! What's up, bud?" Johnny shook his right hand, the free one, with the broad-shouldered pool player. "Who's your friend? I think I saw you at Zelda and Saxon's wedding last night, right?"

"Totally. That wedding was full of fabulous people. I loved it, even if Zelda is a bit of a bitch." Bob Mackie Cher stuck her/his hand out. "I'm Richard." He grinned. "And yes, you can call me Dick. In fact, I prefer it."

Lizette marveled that his voice was so deep, in sharp contrast to his very feminine appearance. His cheeks were as smooth as a baby's bottom, and she wondered how much the laser hair removal had set him back.

"Who is this little precious?" he asked, smiling at her, false eyelashes fluttering, feathered headpiece bobbing slightly.

"This is Lizette, my friend in town from Paris. We got a little drunk last night and uh, found ourselves a bit tied up." Johnny lifted their handcuffed hands.

Did he have to mention that? It was possible no one would have even noticed if he hadn't brought it up. Now she had Dick and Benny grinning at her.

"Nice to meet you," Dick said. "I guess the cuffs explain the interesting ensemble." He gestured to her shirt.

"Pleasure," she said with a nod, though she wasn't really sure it was.

"I'm Benny."

The other man stuck his hand out. She shook it with Johnny's limp hand dangling below hers, because she couldn't exactly shake with her left hand. "*Enchanté.*"

"I'm straight," he told her, which seemed a little unexpected. "I just dance at the gay strip club because the money is good."

"That's nice," she told him, unsure of what a proper response was.

"If you were a gay man, he'd tell you he's gay," Dick said, rolling his eyes. "Benny likes to get whatever he can. Which I can't say I have a problem with, but just so you know the score."

"Thank you, but I am not interested either way," Lizette said, trying to be polite. She really couldn't imagine herself feeling amorous toward the bulky Benny, even if she hadn't just been sexually intimate with Johnny.

"She's with me, bonehead," Johnny said dryly. "Can't you see we're handcuffed together?"

"Well, how do I know why you're handcuffed? Maybe it was a social experiment. Maybe it's some kind of weirdo ritual you guys do, I don't know." Benny waved his hands around. "Hey, is Stella still dating that bass player?"

"Yes, she is," Johnny said. "So no go for you."

"Damn. You know I want to bag your sister. I'm sorry, maybe that's tacky, but it's true. She's like my first—"

Johnny cut him off. "Have you seen Saxon?"

Benny's jaw shut. Dick shook his head. "No. Not since Zelda got her wig in a wad and threw us out of the reception last night."

"What time was that?"

"Two."

"Hmm."

"Were we still there then?" Lizette asked Dick. "Did you notice?"

Dick eyed her shrewdly. "You don't remember?"

"Not exactly, no. I cannot say I was paying attention to the time." She had no intention of admitting the entire night was a complete black hole.

"I didn't notice," Dick said, in a dismissive way, not looking her in the eye.

For some reason, Lizette didn't believe him. There was just something about his posture that seemed stiff. He sounded friendly, but she had the sense he was not a friend to them.

"Hey, if you want those cuffs taken off, I have a friend who is fabulous at picking the lock. I can give him a call."

Johnny glanced at her. He didn't look suspicious of Cher at all. "Sure, that would be great. I'm sure Lizette would appreciate just a little bit of space."

What did that mean? Two hours ago she would have thought it was thoughtful, but now she felt like there was a hidden meaning behind his words. Maybe she did need a bit of privacy to collect her thoughts. Johnny had offered for her to stay with him and she had said yes automatically, without even stopping to weigh the consequences. She was not normally impulsive, but it had felt right.

She was falling for him. She could not help herself.

But now she had the feeling that something was simply . . . off.

"I saw Saxon," Benny said.

"What? When?" she asked, because Johnny was conferring with Dick and didn't seem to have heard him.

Benny reminded Lizette of a puppy—he was quite eager to please and possibly would lick you if you let him.

"About an hour ago. We were having a drink to celebrate his marriage."

"An hour ago?" she asked in surprise. "How long were you together?"

"Couple hours. I ran in to him here after my day shift at the club. So I guess it was probably around ten." But then he looked around and patted the pockets on his tight jeans. "But wait, what time is it now?"

"It is two."

"Then I'm not really sure. But it was tonight. That I can tell you for sure." He gave her a friendly smile.

That was interesting. Not Benny's smile. The fact that Saxon had been with him after waking up for the night. Did that mean he'd been with them in the dungeon until he'd woken up? But surely he would have roused Zelda as well if that had been the case, at the very least to make sure she was all right. "Did he mention not remembering his wedding night?"

Benny gave her a blank stare. "Who doesn't remember their wedding night? I mean, come on. It's kind of noteworthy."

"That's true." Lizette glanced over at Johnny and Dick, who were now busy looking at the screen of Dick's phone. "Care for a drink, Benny? Let's sit at the bar, shall we? Johnny, Dick, can we sit at the bar?"

Johnny gave her a distracted nod, but he didn't protest when she started dragging him the three feet to the barstools. He held out a stool for her, then continued his conversation with Dick, which seemed to have left the field of handcuffs and ventured into the territory of online gaming. There was a lot of weaponry discussion and strategizing going on.

"Okay, thanks." Benny followed her as well, pool stick in tow. "I'll have a Heineken," he told Nigel.

"Riesling, please," she ordered, crossing her legs after she climbed onto the stool. While the bartender moved to get their drinks, she turned back to Benny. "When I meant memory loss, I was thinking more along the lines of when someone drinks to excess, or perhaps has something slipped in their drink that makes them lose their memory of the night."

"Oh, gotcha." Benny nodded. "I totally understand. I had that happen to me once, you know. The night of Johnny's wake. I totally didn't know any of these guys until that night."

"Really?" she asked politely, though she wasn't particularly interested. Her focus was on the night prior, not what antics Benny had gotten into in the past. "So Saxon didn't mention anything like that about last night?"

"Nope. He said the wedding was a blast and Zelda tore him up in bed. He was smiling and looking good." Benny grinned.

Now that was odd. So Saxon remembered the night, but no one else did? How had that happened? "Did he say where he was going when he left here?"

"Nope. So the night of Johnny's wake, did he ever tell you about that?"

"Not specifically." Which was the truth. He had told her why he had faked his own death, but he hadn't described the outcome or how quickly he had come clean with his friends and family. Obviously not before they'd had a wake for him. That must have been awkward, and Lizette found herself in sympathy with Stella. It must have been horrific for her to plan her brother's funeral.

"So it's really a funny story." Benny thanked Nigel and took his drink from him. "So like I said, I had never met any of these guys in my life, and I just went to work as usual, except it was Tarts and Vicars night at the club so I was dressed like a priest, crucifix and all. I forgot to bring a change of clothes, so it was either walk home in a Speedo or the costume, so I left the robe on. Then I don't remember a damn thing until I woke up the next night in a bathtub three blocks off Bourbon with a chick screaming and a bunch of hungover dudes all arguing with each other. Then a bat bit me. I mean, just swooped down out of nowhere and bit the shit out of me, and while she's biting me, she just turns into a hot babe. Like bam! There she is—hot babe sucking on my neck and I thought, 'Whoa. These people are vampires. Could anything be any fucking hotter?'"

Lizette almost fell off her stool in a dead faint, her panic growing with each and every word he spoke. "What do you mean?" she managed, a strange buzzing sounding in her ears.

"I mean it was like my fantasy come to life, man. Stella is smokin'. I've been trying to get her to bite me again ever since, you know what I'm saying?" He winked. But then he sighed. "But she's all into that Wyatt guy. It sucks. Where am I going to find another vampire chick like her? She's my Dark Angel."

Lizette felt hot, her fingers gripping the edge of the bar. She forced herself to take a sip of her wine to collect her thoughts, though the sweet liquid almost made her gag. "So are there a lot of women who pretend to be vampires in New Orleans?"

"Sure. But this isn't pretend. Stella is the real deal. So are Johnny and all those guys I hung out with that night."

This was a disaster. An absolute complete and utter disaster. It was a breach in security of epic proportions. This man was just casually mentioning to her that vampires existed. He was mentioning names. To her, whom he didn't know at all. If he was willing to disclose such information to a total stranger, how many people had he told thus far?

It was catastrophic.

She didn't dare look at Johnny. She felt like if she did, the entire truth of who they were would be written all over her face, and there would be no way out of this situation. She would find herself tied up in a laboratory like Jean-Baptiste had, being dissected alive. Johnny and Dick seemed to still be stuck on gaming, so she didn't think he had heard her conversation with Benny.

Suddenly it also occurred to her that it was a rather alarming coincidence that on two separate occasions where a large group of vampires had gathered, multiple people had been drugged to the point of no memory.

That terrified her. Was it a conspiracy? Were the mortals out to kill vampires? Vampires out to expose and eliminate other vampires?

She did not know what any of this meant.

"I cannot believe this," she whispered.

"Wait a minute."

Her head snapped up. She realized Benny was staring at her. "You're one too, aren't you? Of course you are! God, I'm so stupid." Then he put his hand over his mouth. "Sorry, am I not supposed to say the *G* word? Ever since I gave Saxon that crucifix burn on his forehead I'm always worried I'm like causing you pain or whatever."

"I am not . . . a vampire," she managed to say, though the words stuck in her throat. Her entire life had been spent hiding the truth, to the point that no one had ever suspected what she was. In two hundred years she had never once been accused of being a vampire, and she found the direct question overwhelming and frightening to the point of paralysis.

"You don't have to deny it. I should have guessed it before. You're pale and you're from Paris."

What did that have to do with immortality? "I am just French. I wish I were immortal," she said, with an attempt at deflection. "Then I wouldn't have to worry about watching my weight." It seemed like something a mortal woman would say, but Benny seemed to immediately dismiss her words with a wave of his hand.

"Whatever. Your secret is safe with me." His eyes lit up in a way that only deepened Lizette's fear. "You can bite me if you want. Drink my blood. I'm down with that."

That snapped her out of her stupor. "Don't be ridiculous!" she said to him. "No one is going to be biting anyone." Of course, that had not been the case ninety minutes earlier, when she and Johnny had been sinking their fangs into each other. But this was why their identity needed to be a secret, why the VA was so important. Benny was most likely harmless, albeit a nuisance, but for every Benny, there would be a mortal who could present a real danger to their very existence.

It infuriated her that Johnny and others were so casual about letting mortals know the truth.

"That sucks." Then Benny burst out laughing. "Ha-ha. Sucks."

Lizette wasn't one to normally roll her eyes, as she saved her irritation with others for her private thoughts, but she could not restrain the impolite gesture now. She was not in any mood for manners. "Call Saxon and tell him he needs to meet us here. *Now.*"

Benny's laughter cut off and his lips jutted out in a pout. "You don't have to be mean. Geez."

Knowing that she was about to lose her shit entirely if something didn't happen in the next sixty seconds, Lizette took a deep breath. "Will you please call Saxon and ask him to meet Johnny and me here? It's extremely important."

"Sure. Are you sure you aren't interested in biting me?"

Before she could respond, Johnny finally seemed to have pulled his head out of his imaginary computer screen game playing and heard what they were discussing.

"Hey," he told Benny. "Don't be talking to her like that. I just told you she was with me."

Yet, that wasn't the kind of assistance she was looking for from him. "Johnny, may I speak with you outside? Benny saw Saxon earlier tonight and he is going to call him on our behalf and ask him to meet us here."

Johnny wasn't even looking at her, she noted with total frustration. Did he not understand the importance of what was happening? They had been *outed*.

"Can it wait a second, babe? Dick's friend Brian just walked in."

"It really cannot wait!" she said shrilly.

JOHNNY WASN'T SURE why Lizette suddenly had a bug up her butt. Here he was trying to get them out of handcuffs and she was shrieking at him. Though he supposed he had been acting weird for the last hour. He wasn't exactly stellar at hiding his awkwardness, and his sudden and unexpected feelings for Lizette made him feel hugely awkward. Going-through-puberty awkward. So maybe she was just picking up on the vibe he had created. Which was why it made even more sense that they get out of the cuffs.

"Brian has a lock pick," he told her. "Dick says he can spring us in two minutes flat."

She didn't say anything, but her foot was tapping furiously on the rung of her stool and her fingers were drumming on her purse, which she had slapped onto the bar. With more attitude than grace, she dug into her bag one-handed and pulled out a wad of singles. One by one she started counting them out and Johnny had to admit he was mystified as to what the hell she was doing.

"Are you a dancer too?" Benny asked.

Oh, bad question. Johnny winced.

"No." Her response was almost a growl.

Johnny shifted on his seat, suddenly fearful for his testicles. She looked enraged and he had no clue why. Fortunately, he was spared from having to confront the issue by Brian approaching Dick, and introductions were made all around. Lizette ignored them, even as Brian pulled on the cuffs to examine them, forcing her hand to dangle over the bar.

"This is a double lock. Little harder but nothing I can't handle. It will just take me a minute or two." Brian wasn't as tall as Dick, but he had a similar build, long and lean, and he had straight black hair and a strong nose. Between his features and the necklace and vest he was wearing, Johnny had the impression he was of Native American descent.

"Thanks, man, I appreciate you doing this."

"Sounds like a crazy night." Brian was quiet, calm, pulling a pick out of his pocket and studying the lock on the cuffs with intense concentration. "So who should I spring first?"

"Lizette," Johnny said without hesitation. She clearly needed something, maybe being free of her titanium restraint would improve her mood. Funny how an hour ago he had been panicking at the thought of Lizette staying with him, now he was panicking at the thought that she might not want to stay with him. Stupid. Completely and totally stupid.

"*Merci*," she said coldly and formally, which was not at all reassuring. Then she said something to him in French that he suspected was her explanation of why she was so pissed. Only he of course couldn't understand a freaking word she was saying.

"I know," he told her, because really what else was he supposed to say? They had a skinny guy with Cher hair in between them jamming a pick into their cuffs.

Wait a minute. Brian looked like Cher, too, now that he thought about it, though he was dressed like a man and wasn't wearing mascara. But there was something familiar about him. Johnny swung his gaze back and forth between Dick and Brian and felt a niggling of a memory. "Were you both at the wedding last night?"

Dick grinned. "Maybe. Don't you remember?"

Brian had been Half-Breed Cher. He was sure of it. "I'm starting to think that all we need is a Turn Back Time Cher and we'll have Cher through the decades." God, that was weird. If a flash mob of Cher impersonators broke into "I Got You, Babe" all around him, he was out of there.

"First lock undone," Brian murmured, hair sliding over Johnny's arm as he worked in concentration.

Lizette said something in French.

"Absolutely," Johnny said.

"Dude," Benny said.

"You're a little slow on the uptake," Dick said. "Of course we are."

What? "You mean you are Cher through the decades?"

"Duh. Every tranny gang needs a theme of sorts."

Tranny gang? Did such a thing exist? And if so, why? It wasn't like he and the other guys were a vampire gang. They were just a group of friends who hung out. They were a band, which was a legitimate reason to call themselves a group. "What makes you a gang?"

But Dick clucked his tongue. "Never mind."

"Got it." Brian clicked open the ring around Lizette's wrist and let her free, then closed it again.

Lizette's eyes lit up and she bent her arm and clutched her now-free hand to her chest. "Oh, thank you. I cannot tell you how much I appreciate this!"

Wow. That sounded like eager relief to be rid of her attachment to him. Johnny felt a little bitter.

"Oh, shit, we're late!" Dick glanced at his phone. "Benny, we have to blow. Brian, let's go."

"I never said I would blow you," Benny said.

Dick rolled his eyes, his fake eyelashes fluttering. Glittery eye shadow floated down to land on his flawless cheeks. "Trust me, I wouldn't want you to. It would be like—"

Johnny cut him off because truthfully, he didn't want to know where that statement was going. "Brian, can't I at least buy you a drink for your help?"

But Brian shook his head. "Sorry, Richard is right. We need to take off. Since I only got your friend free, don't worry about it."

Hold up. "You're not going to get me out of the cuffs?"

"Sorry, got to run." Brian started to move away from the bar. Dick was already almost at the door.

"Can't you at least leave me the pick?" he asked.

"No, this is custom-made. Look, I'll catch up with you in an hour or so, okay? See ya."

Then they were gone and Johnny was left staring at the door as it swung shut behind them. So he was no longer attached to Lizette, but he still had a metal bracelet on. He sighed.

Benny hung up his phone and said, "Saxon isn't picking up."

Johnny could have told him that. He'd been calling the guy all night and he hadn't picked up. Lizette said something in French. Johnny was getting a headache. It was like his hangover was reappearing.

Maybe it was time to come clean. "Lizette, I have to tell you the truth. I don't really speak French. I have no fucking idea what you're saying. Or have been saying."

It wasn't that big of a deal, right? Just a minor fact he had forgotten to share with her.

"Uh!" She gasped in indignation. Then she threw her glass of wine in his face.

The cool liquid hit him before he could react, and Johnny blinked, droplets on his eyelashes blurring his vision. He licked his lips and found her taste in wine was too sweet for his liking.

"How dare you!"

Johnny wished he had a counter to keep track of how many times she had said that to him in the last eight hours. It would make a fun drinking game, if he were in the mood for fun. Which he wasn't.

"Pretending to understand me all this time! I feel humiliated."

"Yeah, a whole whopping eight hours. The breadth of my deception is enormous." And yes, that was sarcasm. "At least you're out of the handcuffs now."

He wiped his face with his hand and flung wine onto his jeans. That had not been a drink-in-the-face offense, he had to say.

"Which is excellent news because it means I can walk away from you." She rose from her stool, head held high, slapping down a pile of ones to pay for her drink.

She was leaving? Where was she going? Johnny stood up, the loose end of the cuffs dangling and hitting him in the thigh. "Is everything okay?" he asked, because it seemed like a safe enough question to ask. If you asked a woman what was wrong, she either said she was fine or she jumped your shit for thinking something was wrong. This way, it sounded more polite.

Which did not explain why Lizette, the most by-the-book woman he had ever met, flipped him off as she strode out of the bar in her stapled T-shirt, expensive handbag firmly on her shoulder, his shorts sagging on her narrow hips.

Flipped him off.

What was that?

Chapter Fourteen

GIVE ME ALL YOUR LOVIN'

DRAKE cast Josie Lynn an almost confused look over his shoulder, but then nodded. "Oh right. Sure."

He paused at the first door, gently placing a hand on the doorknob. He hesitated for a second, then whipped it open and flipped the wall switch. The room illuminated to reveal a roomful of guitars and other music equipment, but no signs of anyone.

"Everything looks fine here," he said, and Josie Lynn immediately pressed a finger to her lips. If anyone was there, they probably already knew someone had entered the apartment, but she didn't want Drake to make it so easy for the intruder to know exactly where they were.

He looked puzzled for a moment, then whispered, "Right. Better to keep it down."

Exactly, she thought. Why wasn't he worried?

He went to the next door, this one open but dark. He reached around to the light switch. The light turned on and revealed a white-tiled bathroom. Drake stepped inside, glanced around, then shook his head.

"The shower," Josie Lynn mouthed, pointing to the closed shower curtain.

He made an *oh right* sort of expression and took a quiet step toward the curtain, covered with different depictions of Elvis Presley. Elvis through the decades, apropos for Chers through the decades to hide behind, Josie Lynn thought.

Again, she noticed he didn't hesitate to rip back the curtain, as if he knew beyond a shadow of a doubt there was no one hiding in the tub. And he was right. Aside from several bottles of shampoo and conditioner, a bar of soap, and a razor, the shower was empty.

She stepped back from the bathroom door to let him out. She didn't even look over her shoulder. He seemed so certain the place was empty that she was starting to think she might be overreacting, too.

But as if to appease her, he moved past her to the next door. He turned the doorknob and pushed the door open, but before he could even reach for the light switch, something swooped out of the room.

The only impression Josie Lynn got was the shadowy image of something flying close to her head and the whoosh of wings.

"What the hell?" Drake said, voicing her very own thought.

But she didn't stop to answer. Instead she grabbed his arm and tugged him into the dark room, slamming the door behind them. She fell back against the door and pulled him back against her, using both of their bodies to block the door.

They stood still, only their breathing audible in the blackness of the room.

"What—what was that?" she finally whispered after a few moments.

Drake didn't answer right away, then he muttered as if with dawning realization. "Saxon."

"Saxon?" What on earth was he talking about? That was a bird or some other flying creature. She shivered. God, she hated things that flew.

"I—I mean that was probably Saxon's pet," Drake said, although even without being able to see his expression, she didn't quite believe his explanation.

"Saxon's pet? What is it? And why would it be at your apartment?"

"He must have left it here because of the wedding."

Okay, not sure why he'd do that, but whatever.

"What the heck is it?"

"A—a bat."

WHY THE HELL had he told her that? Drake mentally kicked himself. Who had a pet bat?

"Who has a pet bat?" she asked, obviously coming to the very same conclusion.

"The same guy who has a pet alligator," Drake said, rather proud of that quick connection.

"Oh."

She seemed to buy it, even though it wasn't the truth. He suspected whatever had flown past them was actually Saxon. This happened the last time they'd all blacked out due to being drugged.

The last time they'd all blacked out due to being drugged. Wow, who really got to say that twice in a lifetime? Even as long as all of his friends had all lived, it still seemed like a weird thing to say. But last time, Stella had been the one who got stuck in bat form. This time he was willing to bet it was Saxon. That would explain why he'd gone missing on his wedding night.

Josie Lynn shivered, her whole body vibrating against his. The subtle movement was enough to make him groan.

"Are you okay?" he murmured, moving his face closer to hers. He could feel the warmth of her breath and the sweet scent of the wine she'd drank on her lips.

"I'm—I'm fine." But she shuddered again.

He could now smell her arousal and he couldn't stop himself. His hands found her hips and pulled her even closer. She gasped, and for just the briefest moment, he thought she was going to surrender and allow her body to stay pressed tightly to his. That she might even kiss him. Or let him kiss her.

But instead, she pushed at his chest with a strength that surprised him, although he wasn't sure why. She was a tough cookie. He knew that.

"What's wrong?" he asked, trying to ignore his disappointment, because he knew she wasn't telling the truth about being okay. He could smell fear on her, too, though that was harder to focus on than her desire.

He moved away from her, even though he really didn't want to, and flipped on the light. They both blinked as their eyes adjusted to the sudden brightness.

She remained against the door, her back tight against it and her arms crossed around her, like she was cold. Or truly freaked-out.

"What's wrong?" he repeated.

She still didn't answer for a moment, though he could also see that she was notably pale. She was really shaken, although in what he'd already learned was Josie Lynn fashion, she was trying to hide it.

"I hate things with wings, okay? Birds, bats, big flying bugs." She wrapped her arms tighter around herself, but her expression clearly stated she hated admitting that fear.

Any fear, he suspected.

"Well, we all have things that freak us out."

She shot him a skeptical look. "And what freaks you out?"

He didn't even have to hesitate. "I hate enclosed spaces. And being constrained in any way."

She dropped her arms, immediately distracted from her fears by the admission of his. "Really?"

He nodded.

"But you seemed okay with being in that sex swing thing earlier."

"I was faking. I was absolutely freaking out."

"Good acting," she said, sounding truly impressed.

"Thanks."

Since they were talking candidly, he decided to keep the confessional going.

"Can I ask you a question?"

Some of her reserve returned, and she crossed her arms back over her chest. Always protecting herself. Always acting strong. Even when she was unnerved—like right now.

She nodded, even though he knew she didn't really want to answer any questions.

"Why did you kiss me at The Dungeon?"

"To irritate Obsidian," she said in a way that stated that she clearly hoped that was answer enough and this would be the end of Twenty Questions.

Too bad. She wasn't going to be that lucky.

"You were affected by our kiss. I could feel it. And you already know I'm very, very attracted to you."

He expected her to deny his claim, but instead she just nodded. "I am attracted to you."

Shit, that wasn't even an enthusiastic admission and he was as hard as tempered steel.

"You confuse me," he admitted. "One minute, I feel like we are actually communicating, and you're almost comfortable with me. Then the next you shut down and are distant."

She gave him a helpless look, like she had no idea what he wanted her to say.

"For example, why did you seem fine with my being protective of you when that creepy Donald was talking to us at Madame Renee's, yet when I stepped in with that drunken jerk on Bourbon, you were angry with me?"

She looked away from him, and for a moment, he just assumed she would tell him she didn't know. Or that she didn't need to explain herself, but then her vivid blue eyes found his.

"Because I liked you protecting me too much."

He hadn't expected that.

"Why? I wanted to protect you. I like protecting you." He liked it a lot. Probably he liked it too much, if truth be told, especially given she was a woman he barely knew. And human to boot.

"Because I find it's just a lot better if I take care of myself."

Suddenly he realized why she could go from soft and aroused to prickly in seconds flat.

She'd been hurt. Badly hurt from the looks of it. She didn't trust him—or any man, he was willing to bet.

Why hadn't he realized that earlier? Wasn't that why he tended to keep himself distant from women and relationships, too?

"I can understand that," he said softly. "Believe me, I can. But we all need help sometimes. And we all have to trust someone once in a while, too, even if it's hard."

She laughed then, the sound hard and bitter. "That's kind of rich coming from you. You are telling me to trust you, but you think I'm a thief and a liar."

Drake could easily understand her incredulity with him. He stepped closer to her, but left a few inches of space between them, not wanting her to feel cornered. That was the last thing a woman who didn't trust men—or maybe anyone—needed.

"I stopped thinking you were involved in the drugging and robbery basically before we even left Zelda and Saxon's."

"Why's that?" she said, her tone no softer, no less filled with sarcastic mistrust.

"Because you could have run at any point tonight. Hell, you could have darted and left me to fight a gator if you wanted, but you didn't. I know you want answers just as much as I do."

She stared at him for a moment, and then her arms dropped back to her sides. Her guard was coming down a little, but she clearly didn't know what to say.

He didn't want her to say any more. He just wanted to touch her. Reassure her that she could trust him. He wanted to continue to protect her. He wanted to make love to her.

He shifted closer, and her eyes met his. Again, he expected to see caution and doubt in her eyes, but instead he saw something almost like tentative hope in her unblinking gaze.

He risked moving closer still and slowly reached out to touch her cheek.

"I know you still don't trust me, but I honestly don't want to hurt you. I'm going to be totally honest with you. I really want to kiss you."

She managed to surprise him again. "I really want to kiss you, too."

JOSIE LYNN COULDN'T believe she had told him that, or that she was leaning in to meet his lips. A part of her kept repeating this was a terrible, terrible idea and she was bound to get hurt. But another part, which at the moment was being much louder and making much more sense, kept telling her to take a risk, go with it, enjoy this moment.

She liked the second voice's advice better.

And when Drake's lips captured her, she liked it even more. Damn, this man could kiss.

His mouth molded to hers like it had been made just for her. She couldn't remember a kiss quite like his, so perfect, so earth-shattering, so . . .

Dangerous, the party-pooper voice stated.

Then Drake's tongue slipped over her lips, tasting her. Then deeper. Then she didn't care if this was dangerous, she just wanted the moment to continue. Her tongue found his, and he moaned, pinning her against the door. His hands moved to her hips, pulling her tightly against him, his muscular body hard and heavy and delicious against hers. Her arms looped around his neck and she could feel the brush of his hair against her fingers.

"Damn, you make me crazy," he murmured against her lips.

Crazy, that was exactly what this was. But she didn't want to stop, and clearly, neither did he as his hand slid down her hip to hike up the hem of his shirt. His fingers, rough from playing guitar, she supposed, stroked over her bare upper thigh. The sensation was thrilling, those roughened fingertips strong and masculine, just like the rest of him.

"I want to go slow," he whispered, but even in her haze of desire, she knew *want* was the operative word. Slow wasn't going to happen for either of them. It was as if they'd finally admitted this enormous attraction and nothing was going to stop them from being together. Not even the luxury of exploring each other's bodies. They'd take the luxury next time.

Next time. Was she even sure there would be a next time?

Stop thinking, the lust-driven side of her brain told her. Just feel. Just fuck.

Drake's brain seemed to be telling him the same thing, because his hand slipped between her thighs, nudging her tiny lace panties aside to rub the already-wet flesh underneath. She gasped, arching against him. He growled, finding her swollen clit, circling it with his thumb as a finger slid inside her. Then another finger.

She dug her fingers into the muscles of his shoulders, angling her hips upward to afford him better access, deeper access.

"You are so hot and wet. I have to taste you," he said, his already-raspy voice a low rumble. She made a dismayed noise as his fingers left her throbbing sex.

He smiled at the sound, that naughty grin of his making her ache even more.

"Don't worry, love, I'll be right back down there. Believe me."

His talented fingers then moved to the buttons of his shirt, flicking each one open until he reached the belt she wore. It only took him moments for that to hit the floor with a muffled thud. Then he parted the shirt, exposing her to his hungry eyes.

Josie Lynn was not a thin girl. She had full, heavy breasts, a slight curve to her belly, and flared hips. And Drake looked like he wanted to gobble up every part of her.

"You are absolutely perfect," he said, his voice, husky and worshipping.

God, she loved the look in his dark, intense eyes. She felt perfect.

He ducked his head, capturing one of her rosy nipples between his lips. He sucked and swirled his tongue around it, until again she was arching her back, demanding more. Her fingers tangled in his hair, pulling him closer.

But he still managed to shift away to lavish attention on her other breast as his hand returned to stroke between her thighs. She cried out as her orgasm hit her, sudden and fierce like a wild summer thunderstorm. Powerful, electric. She sagged against the door, weak from the intensity of it. But Drake wasn't about to allow her respite.

She watched in a daze of ecstasy as he slowly dropped to his knees. She registered the creak of Zelda's plastic pants as he did so. At another time that might have made her laugh, but right now, all she could think about was that his face was level with her wet pussy.

He leaned close and breathed in as if he was savoring the scent of her juices, the action so erotic that even with her forceful release, she was instantly aroused again.

He smiled up at her as if he could instantly tell when she became ready for him again.

Then, his eyes still locked with hers, he leaned in and ran the tip of his tongue up the slit of her moist, swollen lips. Josie Lynn made a noise deep in her throat. Nothing had ever been so sensual, so utterly sexy as watching him taste her like that. He did it again, penetrating her lips deeper and again deeper still until he found her aching clit. Then all attention remained there.

Again she sank her hands into his hair, this time to steady herself, really to support herself, because her legs felt like Jell-O. He lapped and sucked until she came. Then came again.

"Oh God," she moaned mindlessly, pinned to the door with his weight against her legs and his mouth between her thighs.

"Please," she begged, not totally sure what she was begging for. He was already giving her more pleasure than she'd even thought possible. Yet she continued to beg. "Please."

But he seemed to understand what she wanted, even if she didn't, because after one final parting lick over her, he rose.

She watched again, helpless to do anything else as he stripped off his T-shirt to reveal his muscled chest smattered with just enough dark hair to make him look ridiculously manly. Then he shucked off the turquoise pants, kicking them aside.

Josie Lynn had already seen his cock, although she hadn't allowed herself the chance to truly admire it. Now she did. He was large and thick, jutting up against his lower belly.

Even as spent as she should have been, she wanted that inside her. She wanted him to stretch and fill her.

He smiled again as if he had this amazing ability to read her thoughts. He caught one of her legs, lifting it up around his hips so he could situate himself between her thighs again. This time with his body. Then he caught her other leg and picked her up.

She gasped, startled by the action and his strength. She was petite, but not light, yet he didn't even seem to be straining to hold her. Then he angled their hips until she could feel the head of his penis entering her.

Slowly, oh so slowly, he eased her down onto his full, hard length. Her body struggled to accommodate him, but even that was a delicious fight. Finally he was buried deep inside her and she nearly came again just from that feeling of having this gorgeous man a part of her. Filling her so completely.

He didn't move right away, letting her grow comfortable with his girth, but then he began to lift her up and down, the unhurried friction exquisite.

"That's it," he soothed, "just ride me. I want to feel you tight and hot and wet all around me."

She was helpless to do anything other than what he wanted. And she wanted it, too.

His movements became more rapid, his thrusts deeper, and soon she was crying out again. But this orgasm was the most intense of all, because Drake came at the same time, shouting out his release.

She curled around him, her head on his shoulder, her arms around his neck, her legs around his back. And she felt totally safe, totally relaxed in his strong hold. She didn't even realize they'd moved until he eased her off himself and onto the bed.

He followed her down, but then rolled them both so she was on top, straddling him.

He looked up at her, those intense eyes of his seeming to look deep inside her, trying to understand everything about her. No man had ever looked at her that way. Like she was the most fascinating thing in the world.

She felt her heart thump in her chest and knew she could so easily get into trouble with this man. But she didn't care. Not right now anyway. Not with him looking at her like that.

She didn't feel any insecurities sitting above him, exposed to him, her breasts still heavy and her nipples taut from their lovemaking. She'd always been shy about her size, her build, but with him, she simply felt sexy. Desirable in every way.

He brushed a lock of hair from her cheek, the touch so tender, her breath caught.

"Why don't you trust men?" he asked, his voice raspy and soft at the same time.

She knew she shouldn't tell him. It was too soon to open herself up that way, but she found herself looking into those eyes of his, so dark brown they were almost black, and answering.

"I was recently involved with a man who told me he loved me. Told me he wanted us to build a life together. To get married. Then he made off with all the money I'd saved waitressing and bartending to start my catering company, which meant I had to take a loan I really can't afford to get things up and running. And believe it or not, he isn't the worst guy I've dated." She smiled self-deprecatingly.

"Wow," Drake said, stroking a hand down her shoulder and arm. "I can see why you'd be a little wary of guys."

She nodded. "What about you? Why the fear of confined spaces? Of being restrained?"

Drake's hand stilled on her arm.

"You don't have to answer that if you don't want to."

His fingertips, so much like his voice, both raspy and gentle, began to caress her skin again. "I, too, was involved in a few very bad relationships. Of course, several of them I brought on myself. But one—let's just say Obsidian probably couldn't hold a candle to her. Pain was very much her pleasure."

Josie Lynn studied him, trying to imagine what he was implying. Had this strong, virile man been abused by a woman? Physically abused? The idea stunned and disturbed her.

"You must have loved her very much to tolerate something you didn't like that way."

That was the only reason she could think of as to why he'd allow any woman to apparently torture him.

He sighed. "Well, that was long ago, Cupcake." He instantly made a face. "Sorry, I know you hate when I call you that."

She smiled slightly, then leaned forward, her lips just millimeters from his. Her full breasts pressed against his hard chest. "Want to know a little secret?"

"Yes," his response was a breathy growl.

"I actually like it. A lot."

She kissed him.

DRAKE GROANED, LOVING her sweet lips and the weight of her full, round breasts flattened against him.

Goddamn, she was the sexiest woman he could remember ever being with. Every single thing drove him mad. Her sky-blue eyes. Her sassy smile. Those amazing breasts that he wanted to kiss and suck some more. The taste of her—everywhere, which he also wanted some more of. Her ass, her legs, but most of all, her strength and determination.

Josie Lynn was no pampered woman like those he'd dallied with when he was human. Spoiled and coddled. Nor was she like the vindictive, cruel bitch who'd made him a vampire. Giselle's strength had come from being a vampire and it had made her a bully. She was determined, but only to torture and torment others. And he'd been her focus for a long time. But that was decades ago. And now he was lying with a sweet, giving, voluptuous woman who he knew was strong and determined because she had to be. And he wanted to help her. To take away some of that need to be so strong. He got the feeling she could use someone else to shoulder a little of her burden.

As she continued to kiss him, her lips soft and teasing, her tongue hot and wet, his cock reacted, prodding at the juncture of her spread thighs.

She lifted her head, giving him a surprised smile. "Again? Already?"

He smiled back, too. "I could make love to you all night."

She ground her hips against him, rubbing his erection against her damp, soft core.

"I can feel that."

She stroked against him again.

He moaned and so did she.

"Cupcake, I can go all night, but what about you? Are you sore?"

She shook her head. "I'm Cajun, baby."

He didn't know what that meant, but it made him chuckle, and his chuckle turned to another long moan as she slid his full length deep inside her.

Then she started to ride him, her hands on his chest, her thigh squeezing his hips, her vagina massaging him like she'd been made only for him.

"Damn," he muttered, amazed at how she felt.

She pivoted her hips up and down, stroking his length, her gorgeous breasts bobbing with each bounce. Holy shit.

Then she stopped.

"Do you hear that?"

He frowned, dazed and disappointed she'd stopped riding him. "Hear what?"

Then he heard it, the muffled, distant sound of someone singing. How had he not heard that while she had? He was a vampire, his hearing was, well, supernatural, yet he'd been so wrapped up in enjoying Josie Lynn that he hadn't been aware of anything else. She was like his kryptonite.

"Do you hear it?" she asked again, her hand still braced on his chest, her head tilted as she listened.

Again, singing filtered in from the other room. But it was strange, almost mechanical sounding. But gradually he recognized the song.

"Is someone singing Barry White?" Josie Lynn asked, giving him a bemused look.

He nodded. "Can't Get Enough of Your Love, Babe."

"That's what I thought. Is it coming from inside the apartment?"

It was, but he didn't want to startle her. "I'm not sure." Then he heard something else besides the weird, dissonant singing. He heard footsteps coming down the hallway even though they were nearly silent.

Someone was coming.

He quickly pulled Josie Lynn down against him and then snagged the edge of the comforter, tugging it over them just as the door opened. Josie Lynn made a startled noise, but kept her face buried against his neck.

"I knew it," Cort said. "When the stupid parrot starts singing Barry White, I know exactly what it means."

"Hey," Drake said trying to sound casual. "What's up?"

Cort gave him a pointed look. "The question is what's up with you? And why are you up to it in my and Katie's bed?"

"Would you believe things just—sort of happened?" Drake asked.

"Absolutely," Cort said.

"Whoa," Wyatt said, popping his head in the doorway over Cort's shoulder. "Looks like you've been busy. Clearly not finding Saxon, but busy."

Josie Lynn made a small noise and buried her face deeper into the curve of his neck and shoulder.

"You know what guys, why don't you give me a minute here," Drake said, tightening his arms around Josie Lynn in a silent effort to comfort her. She pressed even tighter against him as if she wanted to just disappear into his body. Unfortunately, the more embarrassed she got, and the tighter she pressed against him and her muscles strained, the more turned-on he got. He was still buried deep inside her, and it was taking every inch of his willpower to hold his hips still. But damn, he wanted to be pumping in and out of her soft body.

"Oh right," Cort said, turning to leave, shooing Wyatt as he went.

The door clicked shut, and Drake hugged Josie Lynn again. "It's okay. They're gone."

She lifted her head out from under the blanket and groaned with embarrassment. "I can't believe they walked in on us."

"Well, we are in Cort and Katie's room," he pointed out. "Which technically isn't our fault. We were sort of trapped here by the bird."

She sat up more, bracing her hands on either side of his head, her beautiful breasts so close to his lips. "That was a bird? I thought you said it was a bat."

"Well, apparently it was a bird. A real asshole of a parrot," he explained almost absently, his attention on her nipples, which were so pink and deliciously puckered.

"Is the parrot Saxon's too?"

He shook his head, then caught one of her nipples in his mouth, unable to stop himself.

Josie Lynn gasped and arched her back, pressing her nipple tighter to his lips.

"Sh—shouldn't we stop? This isn't your room."

"We're already here," he said, tracing his tongue around her distended nipple. "And Cort already knows we're here. So . . ."

He drew her nipple deeper into his mouth.

She made a whimpering noise and began to move her hips.

"You are so evil," she breathed, bobbing up and down on him, taking him hard and deep.

He smiled, even as his own breathing came in short, pleased gasps. "Not evil at all. I just know what I want. And I want you more than I've ever wanted anyone."

Her motion slowed, and her blue eyes held his, and he could tell instantly even through his own ecstasy, she was trying to gauge if she could trust his words.

He curled a hand around the back of her head and drew her head down to his, kissing her deeply, passionately.

"Trust me," he said against her lips, then kissed her again. "Please trust me."

She rose up again, then nodded, just the slight movement of her head, but he knew she meant the tentative agreement, and his heart seemed to swell in his chest.

He caught her hips and increased their speed until both of them were crying out their climax. She fell limply onto him, her body so soft and warm and his.

Drake Hanover hadn't felt this way about a woman in centuries, and he didn't plan to let her go. She'd learn to trust him. She'd fall for him like he was already falling for her.

Chapter Fifteen

WANTED: DEAD OR ALIVE

IZETTE wasn't sure where she was going. To her hotel, she supposed, if she knew which direction that was. She was turned around. Looking right and left, she tried to figure out which way was Bourbon Street. If she found Bourbon, she could make her way back to her hotel, where she could pack and get the hell out of this crazy city. Blind panic was causing her to lose the ability to think or focus, and she realized after changing directions twice that her phone would guide her to the hotel with its navigation app.

Digging into her handbag, she scrambled for it, making a sound of distress the second she realized Johnny had followed her out of the bar. She knew she needed to deal with him, unfortunately. She needed to question him on his knowledge of local conspiracies and dangers, and she needed to lecture him about the inappropriateness of sharing their identity with mortals. She was going to need to report that fact back to the VA.

"Lizette! Wait! Where are you going?"

She thought about unleashing her anger on him in French, the

English-speaking cad, but then she realized she wanted him to be able to understand everything she was saying. "I am going to my hotel and then I am leaving. I'll be back in Paris by tomorrow night if I can arrange it."

"I thought you were going to stay with me." Johnny looked confused, which either made him an idiot of epic proportions or deliberately obtuse. She was starting to think it was the former.

"I am afraid that is not possible now that I know the truth!"

"What, that I can't speak French? I'm sorry, I should have told you sooner, but at first I kind of nodded when you used it and you took it as understanding, and then I felt totally stupid telling you the truth."

That sounded very much like the thought process he would follow. While she did appreciate his honesty—although it was rather late—that sort of behavior was at the crux of the problem, and the reason why she was feeling like she wanted to run away and hide in the forest for a decade. He spoke before he thought. He acted impulsively.

Now that attitude had the entire race of vampires at risk.

So she told him that. "It's not about speaking French, though it doesn't thrill me that you would lie about something so silly and unimportant." She glanced around, checking to see if anyone was in hearing distance. "This is about the fact that Benny seems to think we're vampires."

Understanding dawned in his eyes and he rubbed his jaw, the handcuffs a vivid reminder of the last eight hours and all the ways she had compromised herself. She had allowed him entrance to his apartment. She had slept with a man on the Dead List. She had compromised the investigation. And she had lost her panties. All while being ridiculous enough to think that she could fall in love with such a man, given a little time and a few more orgasms.

Enough. She was putting an end to this madness right here and now.

"Oh. Well, that's just because of the night of my wake Stella and Wyatt and the rest of the band were drugged, and Stella got stuck in bat form and she needed some blood to morph back and Benny was passed out in the bathtub, so she just took a nip, just enough to change back. I don't think he really believes we're vampires though."

"Of course he does!" she hissed, aware of a mime crossing the street. He may not speak, but he could certainly hear. "He was discussing it as if it were of no consequence. As pure fact. You know as well as I do that live feeding is not permitted."

"It's not *illegal*. We don't have a government. It's just not recommended. But in this case it was necessary." He looked stubborn. Mystified. Maybe even slightly annoyed with her stance. "It's no big deal."

"No big deal? It puts every one of us in jeopardy. We could be killed."

"You keep saying that, yet I don't see anyone wanting to kill us." Johnny held his arms up and out. "I'm still alive, despite what the list says, and Benny wouldn't slap a serial killer. He is not going to hurt us in any way, nor could he hurt us." Johnny grinned. "Have you noticed we're stronger than them?"

A profound sense of disappointment fell over Lizette. If he mocked the VA, in essence, he mocked her. "I am sorry, I cannot be so cavalier about it. I have seen what can happen to a vampire, despite his strength." No one should have to suffer what her lover had suffered before she had finally managed to sneak in and end his life. She would not watch another man she cared about endure such pain.

Johnny cupped her cheeks. "I think you're overreacting," he said softly. "Shit happens. Benny and maybe a few others know, but nobody believes fringe-society gossip. Good people though they may be, no one takes a stripper seriously. It's the way it is. And this is a live-and-let-live kind of town. No one gets in your business. So we're perfectly safe, I promise."

"Hey!" The sudden sharp voice startled Lizette and she glanced to the left. A man was running toward them. Not a man. A vampire. She recognized her kind and his lack of a blood scent.

"Raven?" Johnny asked. "What does he want?"

Lizette didn't stick around to find out. She started walking.

"I'm going to kill you, Malone! I'm going to cut your fucking head off and roll it from Canal to Frenchmen, hitting every rock I can along the way."

That did not sound promising.

Especially when Johnny suddenly grabbed her hand and told her, "Run!"

As she ran, grateful she'd lost her Louboutins after all, she felt remorse for flipping Johnny off. That had been childish. Now she was going to die, and she would not have even told him how she felt about him. Other than the fact that he annoyed her, that is.

"I'm sorry," she said, lungs bursting.

"For what?" Johnny took a sharp right and she stumbled, trying to keep up with him.

"For giving you my middle finger. That was rude."

"No problem. I'm sorry I'm such an idiot and I pissed you off." Johnny stopped at a wall and cupped his hands. "Jump up and over."

"What?" Was he serious? She couldn't scale a wall. "I work in an office. I can't do that!"

"Yes, you can. Put your foot in my hands and hold on to my shoulders. I'll boost you over."

Oh God. She wrung her hands for a second, glancing behind her. The man with the shaved head was barreling full force down the street toward them, looking very angry. "Okay." Closing her eyes, she gripped his shoulders and stepped into his hands. When she wobbled, she popped her eyes back open and made a sound of distress. "Johnny."

"Yeah? You can do it."

"Even though we can never date and I'm very angry with you right now, if I die in the next five minutes, I want you to know that it's entirely possible I could fall in love with you."

His eyes widened as he stared up at her. Then he cursed and threw her in the air in the general direction of the wall.

Lizette shrieked and flung her hands out for some kind of purchase. Fortunately, if you chose to look at it as fortunate in any way, Johnny's substantial strength had sent her over the top of the wall, and she landed half on it, half over it. Her fingernails dug into bricks as she started to slowly slide down, his shorts riding up around her waist. "Damn." She was going down.

She landed on her rump in a courtyard with a loud, "Oomph." It was not glamorous. It was not attractive. It was not even comfortable. But she was alive and she had not broken any bones. Though there was a killer still after them. He had clearly reached the wall on the street side, cursing and yelling as Johnny dropped to the ground softly. On his feet, of course, not his rear end.

"I'm coming over," the man said.

"This is private property," Johnny told him.

"Like you have any respect for private property. You ran naked through every room in my house."

Um. Okay. Lizette let Johnny pull her through the door at the back of the house and into a bedroom. It was then that she realized they must be at Wyatt and Stella's place. But that wasn't nearly as interesting as what the guy had just said. She resisted being tugged and turned back to see his face popping over the wall, a prominent tattoo on his face.

"Who is that, Johnny?"

"Raven. He's a douchebag."

"Why does he want to kill you?" She had a sinking feeling about all of this. The good news was that she didn't think she was really in any danger after all. The bad news was that Johnny had humiliated her once again.

Maybe she was wrong.

"Because I slept with his girlfriend."

She wasn't wrong.

Anger rose in her, like volcanic lava erupting. "Excuse me?"

"I didn't know it was his girlfriend!" Johnny shut the door and locked it. "She said she was single. It wasn't until a week later that I figured out what was what. I can handle Raven but I really don't want to get into a fistfight in front of you."

"So flinging me over a wall is better?"

He shrugged. "Maybe not. I just reacted. *Overreacted*, I guess, more accurately."

Which was all he ever did. Lizette made a sound of disgust. She couldn't believe she had told him she cared about him. Or that he had let her believe she was in genuine danger. "You need to learn to face your mistakes and responsibilities instead of running away." Given her own reaction with her middle finger, maybe she had no right to call him out on his behavior, but that only proved they clearly were not a positive influence on each other.

"What, you want me to fight Raven?"

"If that is what is necessary, yes. Or perhaps you should just face him man to man and apologize."

"Fine. You're right." He shot her a look she couldn't decipher and opened the door.

Of course she didn't want him to actually physically fight with anyone, but she wanted him to at least face the situation he had created, intentional or otherwise. She already knew that it would be impossible for them to have a relationship even if she did live in New Orleans, but somehow in her heart she needed to see that she wasn't wrong about him—he was a good man, with a kind heart. She wanted to know that she was right to trust herself, and that sometimes emotions weren't logical, but they were valid.

She wanted to believe in something as romantic as passion and love at first sight, even if it could not be acted upon.

JOHNNY KNEW IN his gut that Lizette was right, which was really damn embarrassing. She had a way of making him feel like he was a little kid who had pissed in his pants. But he knew that she had a point, one that Stella had been trying to drive home for years—he needed to grow up. He'd been feeling that very sentiment himself since his wake.

So he told her, "By the way, I feel the same way about you. I could fall in love with you, too, Lizette. Easily."

He would have expounded on the fact, except that Raven punched him in the face. His head cracked back. Damn it. He'd been sucker-punched.

That was unacceptable.

Ignoring the blood in his mouth from biting his tongue, he raised his fists into position and tried to reason with Raven. He did not want to hit Raven. He really didn't. He took no satisfaction in knocking someone to the ground, unless it was an arranged fight for sport. "Dude, come on. I'm sorry. I had no idea you were dating her."

"She has a name."

Oh, Christ. "Yes, she does. Melissa. Again, I'm sorry. I didn't know. Could we maybe do this another night, when I'm not hungover?" When Lizette wasn't standing in the doorway watching. It made him feel like a total douchebag. He was not the type of guy to poach on someone else's girl, and he didn't want Lizette to think for a minute that he did.

Okay, so he wasn't exactly Mr. Commitment. But he had always made sure women knew he was looking for casual. He had never cheated, never deceived, never gone after someone else's girlfriend or wife. He may be immature, but he had ethics. Standards, for Christsake.

"I'll buy you a drink, Raven, and we can talk it over, rationally."

Raven swung at him, but it was wide. Johnny easily dodged it. "Dude, I don't want to fight with you."

"That's because you're a slimy wimp who sneaks around in the dark seducing women."

Wow. That made him sound far more ambitious than he really was. "Hardly."

"Is that how you scored your French whore?"

Hey, now. That was crossing a line, big time. He glanced back at Lizette. Her face was frozen in mortification. "Should I hit him?" he asked her.

She shook her head no.

Damn. "Okay, baby." If she didn't want him to punch on her behalf, he wouldn't. Even if it was hard as hell.

"Raven, you need to apologize to Lizette right now," he said, trying to stay calm. He didn't yell. His voice was steely, eerily calm. Forcing his shoulders to relax, he told him, "This is between you and me. Don't insult her to get to me. That's not cool."

How mature was that?

Raven had finally dropped his own hands. "I'm not going to apologize to someone who isn't here. Not that I was going to anyway."

"What?" Johnny looked behind him. Lizette was gone. "Fuck! Thanks a lot, dickhead!"

Sprinting through the bedroom, he went through the shotgun cottage and out the front door. Down the street, he saw Lizette stepping into a cab. He ran, but there was no way he was going to catch her. She was around the corner and gone before he could go more than a block. "Shit!"

Pulling out his phone, he tried to call her, but she didn't pick up. Slowing to a stop, he stood on the corner and called his sister. "Hey."

"Hey, where are you?"

"I'm at your house."

"My house? Why are you at my house?"

"It's a long story. By the way, you and Wyatt should lock your bedroom door. I came right over the courtyard wall and I was in. That's not very safe."

"If we locked it, then how would you get in?" she asked wryly.

Good point. He wasn't always known for using the front door. "Have you heard from Saxon?"

"No."

"Where is the little freak? Benny said he saw him a couple of hours ago and he was fine, but I don't think he's going to be fine when Zelda finds out he's just been running around without her on his first night as a married man." The thought made Johnny wince. He pictured a lot of whipping in Saxon's future.

"Geez. You're probably right. Where did you see Benny?"

"Fahy's. He asked about you, of course. Then he went and freaking told Lizette we're vampires, and she freaked out and left and I don't even know what hotel she's staying in." Johnny started walking back down the street, realizing he probably shouldn't have left Raven alone in Stella and Wyatt's place. Given their unexplained long-standing tension with the guitar player who played in a rival band to The Impalers, he wouldn't put it past Raven to steal something. Like a bass guitar or an amp. Or Stella's pants. The guy was known for wearing girls' jeans. Gross. Johnny didn't hate the guy, but he didn't love him either. Sort of like his feelings on Benny.

"Oh, crap. Of course he did," Stella moaned. "I wish I could take back that bite on Benny, but what's done is done. Lizette will get over it, right? I mean, she's not going to narc on us or anything."

"I wouldn't count on her keeping quiet. She's a stickler." Along with a few other sexier things he didn't want to mention to Stella. "The thing is, she has a point. It's probably not smart for us to be telling everyone we meet the truth. All it takes is one obsessive person and we have problems."

"Wow. You don't usually think about stuff like that."

Well, maybe he was going to now. There had been a number of things during the course of the night that made him think maybe he needed to reevaluate his priorities. But he didn't really want to discuss that with Stella over the phone. "Are you coming home?"

"Yeah, why?"

"I don't know. I just need to talk." Now that sounded manly. Not.

"Okay." Stella sounded mystified. "Be there in a minute."

Johnny sighed and went back into the house that he had left wide open. "Raven?" he called. But when he got to the courtyard there was no sign of him, or in the house. "Whatever."

He was sinking on the couch and flicking on the TV when Stella came in the front door. "Hey."

"Hey. Where's Wyatt?"

"He's with Drake. So what's going on with you? Two nights ago you were acting like Lizette was just some annoying person sent from Paris to mess with you." Stella dropped her messenger bag on the coffee table, and then sat down next to it. "Then at the wedding you were dancing up a storm with her, and now you're acting like your life is over because she left. That's what you wanted, wasn't it? To get her out of your hair?"

She made it sound like he was a tool. "It's not that simple. I mean, of course I wanted her to go away initially. She froze my bank account and wouldn't let me in my apartment. But then we got drunk and woke up handcuffed together, and I don't know, we had a good time together." Both in clothes and out.

"So what's the problem?"

"The problem is she left!"

"No, that is the consequence of the problem. Why did she leave?"

Johnny shifted uncomfortably on the couch. "Because she thinks I'm an immature commitment-phobe."

"She said that?" Stella asked in astonishment. "I mean, it's true, but it was kind of rude to just throw it out there like that."

"No, she didn't put it like that. She said that I don't know how to follow the rules or take things seriously, that I don't take responsibility for my actions. She's pissed about Benny knowing the truth about us." He put his feet on the coffee table and sulked.

"Well, what is it you want?"

That was easy. "I want to get to know her better, but it scares me. I'll never be good enough for her and I can't promise that I can handle eternity without fucking it up."

His sister stared at him so long he wanted to throw a pillow at her. "What?"

"I'm just trying to reconcile the fact that you clearly dig this woman enough to want to attempt a genuine relationship. After one night. I don't think that's ever happened to you before."

Yeah, well. Maybe because it *sucked*.

"I guess it had to happen sooner or later."

"The thing is, Johnny, why do you always look at every woman and think it has to be either a hookup or eternity? Why can't there be an in-between?"

That was a good question. One he had honestly never asked himself. "I don't know. I guess because it seems like, being a vampire, a relationship is going to go on for a really long time. That's intense."

"There is such a thing as just dating, getting to know each other. Having fun, being monogamous, but not getting married."

"I suppose some people do that." But it seemed like for most people it was hard to stay content in that middle ground. "But Lizette was with some guy for a hundred years. That's only a couple of years less than I've been alive. She can commit the shit out of a relationship. How can I compete with that?"

"You're assuming that she wants another few centuries with someone. Maybe she would like to just ease into it this time around."

"Yeah, I suppose you're right." He felt more mature already. Look at how easily he had admitted his sister could be right. "But none of it really matters. She's going back to Oh La La Land and that will be the end of it."

"So that's it? You're just going to give up?" Her expression was one of clear disapproval.

"What am I supposed to do? Chase her down? Tackle her?" His handcuffs rattled as he asked the question, waving his hand around.

"You could start by getting your name taken off the Dead List. Do everything she wanted you to without prompting from her. Find out what really happened last night. I have a feeling she's the kind of woman who will appreciate the truth, even if it's unpleasant."

"You're right." Stella was right. There it was again. He tried to shake the feeling of melancholy. "Man, this is hard work. It was easier to fake my death."

"Keep that up and I'll arrange for your real death."

He didn't believe her for one second.

He did, however, believe that if he wasn't careful, Lizette might decide to keep him on the Dead List after all.

In fact, she just might put the whole lot of them on the list.

Then none of them would exist.

Which would be a problem.

Chapter Sixteen

PARTY OF FIVE

JOSIE Lynn knew she should have been totally mortified to walk out of a bedroom where she'd just made love to a man she barely knew in the bed of a couple she knew even less, but aside from being a little sheepish, she simply felt good.

Okay, *good* was an understatement. She felt amazing, giddy, like she was walking on air. She knew that by all appearances she'd just found herself involved with a man who was the stereotype of all things she'd sworn to herself she'd avoid. Sexy, too charming for his own good, wicked in bed, and a Bourbon Street guitarist to boot. But she found herself trusting him.

Her—trusting a man. She never thought she'd say that. Or at least not for a good long time. But something about Drake made her believe.

She followed Drake out of his roommates' room and across the hallway to his room. They'd been so close to making love in the right room, she smiled to herself at the ludicrousness of what they'd just done. The liberating wildness and excitement of what they'd done. She hadn't felt this free and happy in months—honestly, maybe not for years.

"Are you okay?" Drake asked as he crossed his room, which now that she was in, she could tell was his. It was as rakish as he was, with a huge burgundy velvet canopied bed covered in black silk sheets and tons of pillows. A guitar lay on the bed. And he had two armoires that looked expensive and antique. Like the bed.

"I'm great," she assured him, stepping farther into the room as he went straight to one of the armoires. While he looked for clothes, she wandered around, running her hands over his finely made furniture, torn between admiring that and Drake's finely made rear end.

"All of this furniture looks old," she said.

He gave the room a cursory glance, then returned to rummaging through his clothing. "It is. Most of it has been in my family for years."

She touched the velvet of the bed's canopy. There was an almost otherworldliness to the pieces. Like it all came from another time, which of course it had. But she was also reminded of how Drake could have moments where he seemed like he came from another time, too. There was a gallantness to him. And a strangely proper way of talking. And even when they'd been having sex up against a door, she sensed something almost proper—or elegant—or something, about him.

Maybe she'd just never met anyone like him before. She glanced over at him, standing there totally naked, still managing to look regal.

No, she'd definitely never met anyone like him before. Katie and Stella said he'd come from a privileged background. For a moment, a rush of insecurity filled her. What did she know about privilege? Nothing. She was just a bayou girl trying to make something of herself. And failing thus far.

"You are looking far too serious to be feeling great," Drake said, pulling her out of her reverie.

She smiled, although some of her giddiness tamped down a bit. "I was just thinking about finding out what happened last night."

That was sort of true.

"Right," he agreed, pulling out a pair of jeans and a black shirt. "We need to get back to work finding those Chers." He tossed his clothes on the bed, eyeing it. "Or we could just stay here a little longer."

Josie Lynn genuinely laughed at the naughty glint in his dark eyes. "I think we'd better behave for just a little while."

He walked over to her and pulled her into his arms. "Okay, super sleuth, but promise me you'll come back here with me after we are done. Because, my love, I am not done with you."

She smiled, but her heart seemed to beat both with joy and pain. She didn't want him to ever be done with her. But it was far too soon to make admissions like that. She did know enough about men to know talking commitment too soon was a surefire way to send them running for the hills. Or in her experience, another woman.

"I'd love to come back," she said, keeping her tone light and flirty. Even as that bittersweet pain filled her chest again.

Drake kissed her, then returned to getting dressed.

"I'm going to use the bathroom," she told him, pointing to the door, feeling the need to get herself together a little. She was sure she looked like—well, like she'd just had the best sex of her life, which was great for her mood, but probably not so great for her hair and clothing.

"Beware the bird."

She shuddered. "That's not even funny." She poked her head out the door to make sure the coast was clear.

"You'll take on a gator, but a parrot scares you." Drake chuckled.

She made a face at him, then stepped into the hallway. She could hear Cort and Wyatt in the living room. They seemed to be discussing where to find the person who owned the parrot, or at least that's what she thought.

She started to head toward the bathroom but changed her mind. Between the two glasses of wine and crazed lovemaking, she was beyond parched, and the refrigerator stood out like a beacon. Cold water. Yeah, that's what she needed.

She tiptoed to the kitchen, mainly to avoid the attention of the bird rather than Drake's bandmates. She opened the fridge to find it empty except for a six-pack of beer, a bottle of vodka and large blue Tupperware pitcher. Water? Juice? At this point, she didn't care, she just wanted something cold.

She pulled out the pitcher and set it on the counter, then she opened the first cupboard next to the fridge. It was empty.

That's weird. It seemed as if Drake and Cort and Katie had lived here for quite some time. Although she didn't exactly recall Drake saying that. She guessed she'd just assumed they had from the way Katie and Drake had been teasing each other about his frequent nudity. That seemed like the kind of joke old roommates would share.

She moved to the next cupboard, which was also empty. Finally, at the last cupboard, she found glasses. And only glasses. Regular drinking glasses, wine goblets, beer mugs.

Okay, these guys must definitely eat out a lot.

She reached for a plain juice glass and returned to the pitcher. Just as she lifted it, to start pouring a drink, she heard the loud flap of wings and a high-pitched caw.

"Jack and coke. Jack and coke."

She instantly jumped and screamed, both the pitcher and the glass crashing to the floor.

She spun to see where the parrot was, terrified it was near her. She located the red bird perched on the top of the refrigerator, regarding her with unblinking, beady eyes. Evil eyes.

"Are you okay?"

Josie Lynn looked away from the bird to find both Cort and Wyatt in the kitchen doorway.

"I'm—I'm fine," she managed, casting another wary look toward the bird. "The bird startled me. And—and I kind of made a mess."

She looked down, then blinked. The drinking glass had broken, and whatever had been in the pitcher had splattered all over her bare legs and the floor. And it definitely wasn't water, and it didn't look like juice either. Whatever it was looked dark red and viscous. Like blood.

"That fuckin' bird," Cort muttered, walking farther into the room. He held out his arm, and Josie Lynn flinched as the bird spread its wings—huge wings, as far as she was concerned—and flew down to land on Cort's upper arm.

"He is pretty much a drunken jerk," Cort told her, "but overall, he's harmless."

The bird waddled up Cort's arm and proceeded to bite his ear.

"Ouch, damn it! Okay, let me amend that," Cort said, still wincing from the bite. "He's mostly harmless to everyone else, but for some reason, he has a love/hate thing going on with me."

"I can see that," Josie Lynn said, though now her attention had gone from the bird to the stuff spilled all around her. What the hell was that?

"Here," Wyatt said, hurrying over to her. "Let me clean that up. Don't you even worry about it."

He placed a hand on her back and arm to usher her away from the mess. She kept looking down. That wasn't juice. It beaded down her bare legs, reminding her of times she'd cut herself shaving.

You are standing in blood, she thought. Even the way her footprints looked on the floor pooled and congealed like bloody imprints.

But it can't be blood. Why would they have blood? In a pitcher? In their fridge?

"What happened?" Drake came rushing into the room, his jeans on, but unbuttoned, and his shirt in his hand. He looked down at the floor and at Josie Lynn, and she could have sworn he saw a flash of dread before he masked it behind a look of concern.

"Are you okay?"

Josie Lynn nodded, even though she felt more confused than okay.

"I'm going to clean this up," Wyatt repeated. "Why don't you take her to the bathroom so she can wash up?"

Drake nodded, placing an arm around her and leading her down the hall. Again she had the feeling they all just wanted to get her away from whatever was splattered everywhere.

"You didn't get cut, did you?" Drake asked as he led her into the bathroom and turned on the faucet in the tub.

"I don't think so." But how would she know? Her legs and feet looked like Carrie at the prom.

He urged her over to the tub and had her sit down on the edge, then he tested the water.

"It feels warm enough. Go ahead and put your legs in." He turned to grab her a washcloth from the rack by the sink.

She did as he said, as if in a daze.

He sat down beside her and began mopping the sticky redness from her pale skin.

"What is this stuff?" she asked, her voice quiet, not sure she really wanted to know.

Drake shook his head, giving her a bewildered look of his own. "Some gross protein shake that Cort drinks. I think it's whey and pomegranate or acai berry or whatever is hip with health nuts at the moment. It's disgusting. I think he bought it through Amway."

Josie Lynn stared down at her legs as the redness rinsed away, turning the water pink, then swirled down the drain.

A protein drink. Pomegranate. That certainly made more sense than blood.

"You finish washing off, and I'll grab you something to wear."

She nodded, accepting the washcloth.

He stood and headed out of the room. Josie Lynn rewetted the washcloth and swiped it down her leg, most of the mess already gone. A glob of the stuff still clung to her inner thigh, and for a moment, she considered dabbing her finger in it and tasting it. But instead she wiped the spot away with the damp cloth.

She finished up and reached for a dry towel. After she patted all the water from her legs, she hung the towels over the shower rod and headed toward Drake's room.

"Damn, that was close," she heard Wyatt say from the kitchen.

"Yeah, that could have been bad," Cort said.

"Jack and coke. Jack and coke."

"Okay, I hear you, Winston. Man, this bird has a serious problem."

What did they mean *that was close?* And it *could have been bad?* Then she decided she was clearly making far too much of nothing. Cort and Wyatt could be referring to anything. After all, they were also talking about what appeared to be an alcoholic bird.

"Hey," Drake greeted her from his doorway. "I found a shirt for you. You'll probably have to make it into a dress again. But you seem to have a knack for that."

She smiled at him, deciding to let the past fifteen minutes go. What did she know about Amway protein drinks? They probably all looked like blood for all she knew.

She went into his room and quickly dressed using Zelda's belt to cinch this shirt, a sort-of-retro paisley shirt in greens and blues.

"Wow," Drake said, when she walked into the kitchen, which was now spotless. "I gotta say, I like this look even more than the pirate shirt."

"I think the pirate shirt might be ruined," she admitted. "I think pomegranate stains."

"Thank God," Drake said.

She laughed, knowing he truly hated that shirt, at least on himself. "I have to admit you look a lot better, too." She admired the way his jeans clung to his narrow hips and his black shirt fit his broad shoulders.

"Are you saying plastic turquoise isn't me?"

"You were actually sort of rocking them," she said with a teasing smile.

He chuckled. She loved his husky, rich laugh.

"Ready to go find some Chers?"

She nodded and was pleased when he took her hand. Damn, this night had really gone far differently than she imagined it was going to.

"Where did Cort and Wyatt go?" she asked as they left the apartment.

"They went to meet up with Stella and Katie and to get that damn bird a drink before it pecked Cort's eyes out."

Of course, she thought wryly. What a night indeed.

"They are going to meet us at Queen Mary's. I figured if we're going to confront a gang of Chers, we better have the numbers going in."

"Good call," Josie Lynn agreed, and they shared a smile.

It was funny. She still needed to find out what happened to save her business reputation and to make sure that Zelda and Saxon didn't somehow blame her for the bizarre outcome of their wedding, but she didn't feel nearly so stressed about the whole thing. Maybe because she now knew Drake believed she wasn't involved.

"Thank you," she said to him as they walked down Toulouse toward Royal.

"For what?" He gave her a cutely puzzled look.

"For believing me."

She didn't need to explain any further. He squeezed her hand.

"And you can always trust me."

And amazingly, she believed him.

"ARE YOU JUST going to pretend that nothing happened?" Dieter said.

Lizette carefully studied her magazine on the plane and didn't look at her assistant, who had been studying her far too intently for the last several hours. "Yes."

"That's not emotionally healthy, you know."

She paused on a Chanel ad, wishing beyond anything that Dieter would just drop it. "I wasn't aware you are a therapist."

"How about I am just your friend?"

That guilted her into looking up. She sighed. "I appreciate that, thank you. But the last few nights have been challenging for me. It's very disturbing to wake up and not remember what you did or where you went. I never want that to happen again."

Especially not now that she was flying over the Atlantic, panties on, suit nicely pressed, hair wound up in a tight bun, feet encased in a pair of pumps. Not her lost Louboutins, but classic, black, quality heels that made her feel in control.

"I can understand that. But that doesn't mean you just sweep it under the rug and run away."

That made her feel defensive. "I am not running away. I had to return to Paris, yes? It's where I live."

"You have some unfinished business with Johnny Malone."

There was a definite pang in her heart that she chose to ignore. "The case will be reassigned, but I think it should be fairly open-and-shut. I do not believe he is lying about his identity."

"I agree, but that's not what I was talking about." Dieter was a big guy, and he looked stuffed even in the seat in first class where they were sitting. If they were in coach, he would be eating his knees.

It was a seven-hour flight from New York to Charles de Gaulle in Paris, and Lizette envied the other passengers who were all snoring away on the nighttime flight. This was her day and she was spending it wide-awake with a magazine, replaying every minute of her single night with Johnny.

"I know. I am just choosing to feign ignorance." When she was miserable, which she was, she didn't want to discuss it.

"What does that accomplish, precisely?"

"It makes it easier to ignore my feelings entirely." Because if she allowed herself to consider those, she might agree with Dieter that she had run away. That for all her frustration with Johnny's behavior, she had not behaved with excessive amounts of maturity herself. In fact, she had been childish. She had run away.

And she had never disclosed why the VA and secrecy were so important to her to Johnny. She hadn't told him the truth about Jean-Baptiste and his torture. She was so used to steering clear of those emotions that she hadn't trusted Johnny with the truth when it probably would have gone a long way to helping him understand her dedication. Her paranoia. She sighed and slapped her magazine closed. "Dieter, have you ever met someone who shook your whole view of the world?"

"The woman who turned me into a vampire certainly changed my view of the world." He smiled at her.

It occurred to Lizette that she didn't even know how Dieter had died in his mortal life. "Good point. I suppose we all have that in common." But it also made her realize that in keeping her life so secretive, in working so hard to ensure the secrecy of others, she may have denied herself deep, meaningful relationships.

And what was the point of being alive if she had no one to share her life with?

QUEEN MARY'S WAS nothing like Madame Renee's, and Josie Lynn could see why Madame Renee was threatened. This burlesque club was lavishly decorated with lush overstuffed sofas in burgundies and golds. Huge crystal chandeliers hung from the ceiling, and the stage looked like something from the set of Moulin Rouge. It made Madame Renee's look even more pathetic.

Even the clientele seemed more upscale; businessmen, women

out for a fun ladies' night, and tourists with money to spend seemed to be the crowd here.

As they approached the dark wood and gold-accented bar, Josie Lynn saw that Wyatt and Cort were already there. With the parrot. Josie Lynn made sure all the men were between her and the bird as she took a seat, although the icky winged creature seemed far more interested in his drink than anything else.

"So any sign of the Chers?" Drake asked.

"Not yet." Wyatt said. "But a helluva Lady Gaga impersonator just finished."

Cort leaned forward to look down the bar at them. "Did you happen to see the Dancing Vagrant?"

Drake shook his head. "Sorry. You're stuck with the bird for a while longer."

Cort sighed. "Well at least this time the damn thing didn't rob anyone."

No sooner had he said that than a Cher impersonator, this one dressed as Moonstruck Cher, approached them.

"There you are," she said to Cort. "Do you know that damn bird of yours stole one of my earrings last night? And it was an exact replica of the ones Cher wore to the Oscars in 1988."

"Of course he did," Josie Lynn heard Cort mutter and reach for his wallet.

Josie Lynn studied the Cher, then leaned in to whisper to Drake. "He's one of the five. He was dressed as Believe Cher last night."

"Are you sure?"

Josie Lynn nodded.

Drake stood up and walked over to the Cher.

"You were at the wedding last night. You crashed it."

Moonstruck Cher gave Drake a slightly offended look. "Crashed? I don't think so. We were a gift to the bride."

As if they realized one of their own was being confronted, the four other Chers appeared from backstage, making a very impressive beeline toward them.

"Great," Wyatt muttered, "we're going to end up in a tranny brawl."

"Well hello, wild ones," Half-Breed Cher greeted them, hardly looking ready to fight.

Josie Lynn then realized she was talking to her and Drake.

"Wild ones?" Drake said.

If You Could Turn Back Time Cher clucked her tongue. "You two were naughty, naughty, naughty."

"But so much fun," Sixties Cher said.

Josie Lynn exchanged looks with Drake. This wasn't going at all like they thought it was going to go.

"We hung out with you all last night?" Drake asked.

"Obviously," Cort muttered, handing Moonstruck Cher a wad of cash. "Damn bird."

"Yes," Bob Mackie Cher said, "But clearly none of you remember it either."

"Either?" Wyatt said.

"Brian and I here," Bob Mackie Cher said pointing to Half-Breed Cher, "ran into a couple of your friends. The ones handcuffed together. And it was clear they didn't remember partying with us either."

"So you didn't drug and rob us?" Josie Lynn said, thoroughly confused.

All five Chers looked appalled.

"Would Cher rob anyone? Please," said Bob Mackie Cher.

"She is a goddess," If I Could Turn Back Time Cher stated adamantly. "Not a common criminal."

Josie Lynn supposed that was reasonable logic.

"Plus, we really are friends of Zelda's," Sixties Cher said.

"So who the hell drugged and robbed us?" Drake asked.

"Oh, we can tell you that," came a voice from behind them.

They all turned to see Johnny, Zelda, and Saxon—and behind them were two people wearing black leather masks with zippers over their mouths and cuffs on their wrists as they were being dragged along by dog collars and leashes. One of the leashes was the one Josie Lynn had used on Waldo, which meant the gator was probably on the loose again.

"Saxon figured out who drugged and robbed us," Zelda said proudly, and clearly fully recovered.

"Who?"

Saxon peeled back one of the masks on the bound couple, while Johnny pulled off the other.

"Eric," Josie Lynn said, not totally surprised. But her jaw dropped when she looked to the other culprit. "And Ashley?"

"**WHAT THE HELL** is going on?" Believe Cher asked. "Isn't that Madame Renee's daughter?"

Johnny wanted to laugh. He wanted to sit down in a chair and laugh his fucking head off at the sheer ridiculousness of this night, and his life in general. Here he was, standing in a burlesque club with five men dressed as Cher while Saxon revealed the culprits in the Great Wedding Dress and Drug the Vampires Caper. It felt like he'd fallen into an episode of Scooby Doo and he was the dog going, "Ruh?"

When Saxon had called him for backup after Lizette had taken off, he had shown up at Zelda's and found her with her new husband in the Dungeon, trussing up a couple of college kids like they were Christmas geese. Or worse. Now he was being told that this blond girl, Ashley, who had looked so sweet passing out crab cakes at the wedding, but was hissing defiantly now, was a transgender vampire's daughter?

Johnny didn't need his acute senses to smell bullshit.

"You're Madame Renee's daughter?" Josie Lynn gasped, standing close to Drake. "But he's so . . . old. And so fond of sequins."

"Doesn't mean he doesn't like to boom-boom with a young thing in his room," Bob Mackie Cher said.

Gross.

"So who drugged the punch?" Drake asked. "Was it these two?"

Neither Ashley nor Eric said a word, but it was clear from their silence that they were guilty as sin. Johnny's urge to laugh disappeared completely. Not only had Lizette disappeared on him tonight, probably on the first flight back to France, but now he also found out that a kid with daddy issues had drugged a whole roomful of vampires? It was mortifying.

"I saw her do it," Saxon said. "But since she was the catering assistant, I thought, like, she was supposed to add stuff to the sherbet. But when I thought about it, I realized you probably don't add pills to punch."

Johnny looked at Saxon, whose crimped hair was going limp in the humidity, and wanted to slap him upside the head. But he restrained himself. "So why didn't you black out like the rest of us?" he asked him.

"I didn't drink the punch. Dude, I don't do rainbow sherbet. I'm a purist. Orange only. I should have been more specific with Josie Lynn when we ordered it."

"Poor baby," Zelda cooed to him. "I'm sorry you didn't get your special sherbet. We can get some later and I'll feed it to you."

Johnny gagged a little in his mouth. Zelda had her foot on Eric's back to hold him in place after the kid, looking more bored than terrified, had sat down on the floor and was holding his head up with his palm. Johnny couldn't say he approved of the whole masks-and-leashes approach to the situation, nor was he okay with the image of Zelda feeding Saxon orange goop. He wanted to go home, desperately.

So he decided to take charge of the situation. "Okay, look. Eric and Ashley. You're fired, obviously. But that's the least of your problems. We can press charges for drugging us, but we'll go easy on you and let the whole damn thing drop if you tell us exactly what went down and then promise to never show your face in the Quarter again. Where do you live, by the way?"

"Mid-City," Eric murmured sullenly.

"So do we have a deal?"

"What do you want to know?" Ashley asked, flipping her hair back and meeting his gaze head-on.

"Is Renee your biological father?" Johnny was just too damn curious about that not to ask.

"Yes. He's not gay, he just likes to cross-dress."

Huh. He knew that Renee hadn't been a vampire for very long, and had wondered why the man had waited so long to cross over. Who wanted to be an old vampire for all eternity? But apparently Renee had been committed to being a dad and had put that before immortality. He had to say he admired the man's commitment to his daughter, even if she had grown up to be a conniving criminal with poor planning skills.

"So why did you drug us?"

"To rob you and frame the Chers for it."

Turn Back Time Cher gasped. "What! How dare you?"

Oh my God. Johnny looked to Drake for help, but Drake was too busy undressing Josie Lynn with his eyes to be of any assistance. How come Johnny was the one with the broken heart *and* the one dealing with divas and morons? This was not his usual role, being the responsible one, and he wasn't really digging it.

Fortunately, Wyatt stepped in and helped him out on this one. "Ashley, why would you do that?"

"Because my father's club is going to go bankrupt. It's not fair. I just wanted to get rid of some of his competition."

It was twisted and stupid and guaranteed to fail, but Johnny appreciated her loyalty to her family. He personally would do a lot for Stella. "What about the wedding dress?"

"I didn't take the wedding dress!"

Bob Mackie Cher looked a little guilty. "Okay, that one is on me, I admit it. Zelda and I were in the ladies room powdering our noses and we had a girl moment where we traded clothes. Only I may have slipped out of the reception before we could trade back, because, honey, that leather bustier was the tits." He held his hands out dramatically. "Eve presented me with the apple and I bit, I am sorry. I couldn't resist. I'll dry-clean the damn thing and return it." He sighed forlornly. "Though it may kill me."

Zelda cracked a whip in Bob Mackie Cher's direction, looking furious. He squealed and ran behind Sixties Cher for protection. Johnny felt a headache coming on, one no acetaminophen was going to fix.

"So where does Eric fit into this?" Josie Lynn asked, frowning at her former employee. "Why would you do this to me?"

"I just wanted to hook up with Ashley," Eric mumbled, rubbing his eyebrows. "I might have, like, a thing for her."

"Well, I think it's safe to say Eric has learned his lesson." Katie reached over and undid his restraints. "Go home, and next time think with your head, not your heart."

"Babe, I don't think it was his heart he was thinking with, but another body part," Cort told his wife with a grin.

"Your sweetness is my weakness," the parrot squawked.

Stella let out a laugh. "Is the parrot quoting Barry White again?"

Johnny felt like sighing. His heart was broken. Did no one notice that? Or were they all just blinded by bedazzled men and hoodwinking juvenile criminals? It wasn't every day Johnny found himself in love with a woman, and yet no one seemed to notice.

Once freed, Eric made a break for the front door, abandoning Ashley. So at least Johnny wouldn't be the only one not getting laid that night.

"Are we all done here?" he asked, waving his arms around. "Has every question been given a stupid answer?"

"I think we need to march Miss Ma'am here on down to her daddy," Believe Cher said, taking Ashley by the arm. "And have a little chat about what is ladylike behavior and what isn't."

As long as it didn't involve him, he was cool with it.

JOSIE LYNN DREADED talking to Zelda and Saxon. She couldn't have known what Ashley and Eric had planned. But she knew she had to say something. It had been her employees that had ruined their special day.

"Zelda," Josie Lynn touched the Amazonian woman's arm. "I'm so sorry this happened, and on your wedding day."

To Josie Lynn's surprise, Zelda just smiled.

"Honey, this is New Orleans. I never expected to have a normal wedding."

"Right," Josie Lynn agreed, because she wasn't quite sure what else to say.

"Just like I didn't expect to find myself married to a real vampire," Zelda said, smiling at Saxon. "Isn't that right, baby?"

Saxon put his arm around his wife, looking almost tiny beside her. "She didn't even believe me until today."

Josie Lynn frowned, casting a baffled look between the two of them. Vampires? Okay, maybe her employees weren't the only ones who were nutso.

Zelda gave Josie Lynn a conspiratorial look. "Well who actually expects to marry a vampire? But then again, it appears you are also involved with a vampire, so you understand."

Josie Lynn stopped gaping at Zelda to stare at Drake. He stood beside the bar, talking to Johnny. A vampire.

Then all the things she'd seen and heard came back to her in full clarity. The way Katie and Stella talked about Drake's past. Those moments when he seemed from another time. The talk of *their kind*. The mentions of bats. The blood—it had been blood in the fridge. Even his furniture.

Could it be true?

She looked at him again. She'd fallen for a vampire. And even if it wasn't true, she'd fallen for a man who very likely thought he was a vampire. She looked back to Zelda and Saxon. They all thought they were vampires.

Oh my God. She had to get out of here. She'd promised herself not to ever have feelings for a bad boy again.

Well, she should have told herself not to fall for madmen either.

"YOU HANDLED THAT well, my friend," Drake said, clapping Johnny on the back. "I felt like I was watching Perry Mason at work. Questions answered. Mystery solved. Even if it was the worst plan for a crime that I've ever heard. Framing a tranny gang of Chers. Only in New Orleans."

"Yeah, only in New Orleans," Johnny agreed, only half hearing his friend, his thoughts back on Lizette. How could she just leave without letting him explain? Apologize? Beg?

"So I see you got free from the uptight little Frenchie," Drake said.

"Don't call her that," Johnny snapped.

Drake raised his hands. "No offense meant." He looked around. "Where is she anyway? I'd have thought she'd want answers, too."

"She's gone."

Drake didn't speak for a moment. "You fell for her, didn't you?"

"Yeah," Johnny wasn't even going to deny it. Or play it down. He had fallen for her. Hard.

"And she just took off?" Drake said, his expression of sympathy making Johnny feel even worse.

"Fucking took off, man," he said, shaking his head. "Just gone. Goddamn Raven. She wouldn't even let me explain."

"Raven? Figures that asshole is involved. Sorry, man."

DRAKE COULDN'T RECALL ever seeing his friend look so upset. Johnny was all about a good time, all the time. He was also about keeping things light. No heavy emotions. No getting too invested. No falling in love.

Drake understood that philosophy. He'd always been the same way. He'd been burned way too many times. But just like Johnny, he'd let that rule fly out the window tonight. He was thoroughly smitten with Josie Lynn and he was well on his way to truly being head over heels.

"Damn," was all he could say to Johnny, because he understood how the guy must feel. He'd be devastated if Josie Lynn just walked out on him.

He looked toward where she'd just been talking to Zelda and Saxon, but she wasn't there. And the newlyweds were headed toward the bar. He frowned, looking around to see where she went, but he didn't see her amidst the opulent furniture and patrons.

"Hey, where's Josie Lynn?" he asked Saxon when his friend reached his side.

"She left."

"What?"

Saxon shrugged. "She just suddenly got all weirded out and said she had to go."

"Go? Where? Why did she get weirded out?"

Saxon looked confused by the barrage of questions. "I don't know where she went. We were just talking about the wedding and she suddenly said she had to go."

Why would talking about the wedding make her suddenly leave? Had she headed back to the reception venue to gather her stuff? But why wouldn't she tell him? Why wouldn't she think he'd want to go with her?

"What did you say about the wedding?" he asked. This just wasn't adding up.

"Just that she didn't need to apologize for her employees. No one expects a New Orleans wedding to go normally."

Drake frowned. Why would that upset her? That should have eased her mind.

"I mean, Zelda just married a vampire. Who's in a vampire band."

Drake gaped at his flaky friend. "Did you actually say that?"

Saxon thought for a moment. "Yeah, something like that."

Drake grabbed his friend's upper arms and shook him. "You told her we're vampires?!"

"Dude," Saxon said, looking down at where Drake held him. "You need to work on your Zen, man."

Work on his Zen. How the hell was he ever going to be Zen again? The first woman he honestly believed he could love with for all eternity had just run off, either thinking he was insane, or thinking he was really a vampire. Or both.

Behind him, he heard Johnny give a bark of bitter laughter. "And just like that. Gone. Dude, we're going to be a couple of old single creepy vampires living in some duplex together, aren't we?"

Drake shuddered. He liked Johnny, but yeah, there was no comparison between eternity with him and Josie Lynn.

Chapter Seventeen

CRUEL SUMMER

JOHNNY removed his sunglasses, as instructed by the French version of TSA, and tucked them into his sweatshirt pocket. That had been the longest flight of his life. Literally. When he'd come over from Europe to the States he had taken a boat. He had to admit flying was more convenient, but it had still felt like half his life. The whole time he had been wondering if he was going to get to Paris and Lizette was going to slam a door in his face. Or worse, if he was walking right into a VA trap.

But he'd had to come here. He had to make it right. He'd been sitting around surly for a week and he'd decided the only way to fix the situation was to get his sorry ass on a plane and make things right with the VA. And hopefully right with Lizette. She hadn't returned his calls, and at the very least he wanted to let her know what Saxon had told him about the infamous night of the wedding.

"Is your suitcase locked?" the customs official asked him. She was a petite woman in her **forties,** yet she looked like she wouldn't hesitate to billy-club him.

"No." Johnny tried not to look illegal or vampiric. This whole process made him nervous. Everyone scrutinizing his passport and giving him beady-eyed stares. He had a little better understanding of Lizette's fears after having just made his way through three airports. The world at large was much more suspicious than the average person in the French Quarter.

"I'm going to open it and look inside."

Great. "Okay." Johnny shifted on his feet, already knowing what the woman was going to find.

Yep. There it was.

As her gloved hands peeled back a pair of jeans, the vibrator Lizette had ordered was revealed. He had taken it out of the box to save space.

Her eyebrows shot up and she gave him a look.

He remained stoically silent. Let her think what she wanted. Everybody had their thing, and he wasn't going to be embarrassed. Much.

Then she found the six pairs of sheer panties and the crotchless one-piece teddy. The corner of her mouth twitched. Damn it. When more digging revealed the heels Lizette had ordered, she was clearly biting back a grin. She also was studying all of it with way more attention than any of it deserved. He started to lose patience.

"Those are gifts for my girlfriend," he told her, because *girlfriend* was a better explanation than his one-time lover who had ordered all of this under the influence, then had ditched him to go home to France. This customs chick was already being judgmental. He didn't want to add fuel to her fire.

"Uh-huh. You have good taste."

"*She* has good taste since she's the one who ordered them. But

I guess I have good taste for loving her." Now that he thought about it, he realized that was true. Maybe he wasn't so unworthy of her after all. "And even if these were for me, what of it? I happen to have transgender friends and your attitude is offensive." So there. Having his done his part to promote equality, he took his passport back while she closed up his suitcase.

She made a face at him. "Welcome to Paris, Mr. Malone."

"Thank you. *Merci*." He took his suitcase and got the hell out of there before someone changed her mind. He had an appointment he did not want to be late for.

LIZETTE WAITED FOR the elevator, looking forward to heading back to her apartment and stripping off her work clothes. The office had been quiet tonight, just her and two other employees, plus the janitor, who was used to their nocturnal work habits. The front for the VA was technical support, so it wouldn't seem unusual to their landlord that there were employees there during the night shift. The day shift was manned by mortals who had no idea who they really worked for, primarily doing accounting and payroll for the vampire VA employees.

She still felt jet-lagged, even though she had been home for a week. A solid eight hours of sleep sounded delicious, even if it was only 4:00 a.m.

The elevator door opened and she started to step on. Then immediately stopped. Johnny was on the elevator. He was just standing there in jeans and a T-shirt, like she had conjured him up out of some jet-lagged hallucination. The door started to close, hitting her on the shoulder.

"Careful." He reached out and pulled her forward by the hand. "You okay?"

She nodded, struck dumb.

He smiled. "Hey."

"Hello."

"Lobby?"

"What?" Lizette shook her head slightly, clutching her attaché case. "What are you doing here, Johnny?"

"Are you going to the lobby?" He gestured to the buttons on the wall. "And I'm here for two reasons. To clear my name through the proper channels of the VA. And to see you."

"Oh. I see." Heat flooded her cheeks, but at least her brain no longer felt completely frozen. "Yes, the lobby, thank you so much." When caught off guard, she always fell back on proper manners. "Are you leaving as well?"

"Yep. I just finished with my appointment. I think we'll have the red tape wrapped up in a few days, and I'll be off that damn list, hopefully forever, if not at least for a few centuries."

"That's excellent news. I wasn't aware you had a hearing now that I am no longer on the case." She was actually quite irritated with her co-workers. Someone could have at least warned her. Then she would have touched up her lipstick at the very least. She probably looked as exhausted as she felt, and she would much prefer impressing Johnny with her beauty, not making him re-lieved that she had left New Orleans.

The elevator door opened on the first floor and Johnny ges-tured for her to move out into the lobby first. He said, "I didn't have to come here for the hearing. But I wanted to make sure it got cleared up as soon as possible. I do respect what the VA is doing. I know that I've made mistakes."

Lizette stopped in the lobby and turned to look at him, her heart suddenly crawling up her throat. She had missed him. He was so handsome, so rugged, so different from other men in her life, both past and present. "Oh," she said eloquently. God, she wanted him to touch her. She found herself even leaning toward him slightly, just to catch a whiff of his scent of soap and something else she had never quite been able to define.

"Are you busy?" he asked. "Can we go somewhere and talk?"

Then, he did touch her. He reached out and brushed the back of his hand down her cheek. "I've missed you, Lizette."

Whatever walls she had erected around her heart came crumbling down without warning. "I have missed you as well. Would you like to come to my apartment? Most cafés are closed for the night."

"That would be awesome."

Lizette headed to the door and pushed it open. June in Paris was different from New Orleans. It was greener, not as hot. "How was your flight?" she asked politely, then hated herself for doing that. Manners were as much an armor as metal, and she wanted to learn how to be more open, more honest about her emotions. "I am sorry for leaving the way I did. That was not fair to you."

They strolled down the sidewalk together. "That's okay," he said. "I know I was being an ass, and I'm sorry for that. I was thinking, you know, that maybe we could sort of put that behind us. Start fresh." But then he seemed to doubt her response because before she could answer, he starting speaking again. "I wasn't sure what to expect, but this is a cool neighborhood. I like it. It suits you."

"It has been home for a long time." She lived in the fashionable 18th district, where the river and the Eiffel Tower dominated the landscape, along with cafes and shops. It was primarily residential, though offices such as her own were tucked here and there. "I do love it here."

"I brought the stuff you ordered with me. You know, your shoes and the other . . . things."

Oh dear. She remembered precisely what that other stuff meant. She had tried to cancel her orders when she'd gotten home, but it had been too late. She had written the purchases off as lost, and she realized she had underestimated Johnny yet again. He wasn't going to let a thousand dollars of her drunken purchases languish on his doorstep. That wasn't him. "Thank you, I appreciate that very much. I do love those shoes."

"What about the sexy panties? You love those?" he asked with a grin as she stopped in front of her building. "Because I have to say, I kind of was digging them when I opened the box to pack them in my suitcase."

"I don't know. I haven't seen them yet."

"By the way," he added, as she used her key on the front door. "I talked to Saxon about the wedding night. He actually remembers everything. It turns out he didn't drink the punch. He said that we were never alone. After the reception we were hanging in the group with everyone just having fun, and that the only reason we were in the dungeon was because you insisted such a thing couldn't exist."

That did sound like her, expressing skepticism over a sexual fetish. "So what does that mean?" Good God, she hoped they hadn't had sex in front of other people.

"No funny business. Saxon said it was all good clean fun. We were in handcuffs because he wanted to show us a magic trick with them, only he couldn't remember it and he couldn't find the key."

She didn't even care about the handcuffs. She was just relieved that they hadn't had exhibitionistic sex. Though she found herself oddly somewhat disappointed that they hadn't had the private, intimate night of wild and unbridled passion she had been envisioning. Of course, they had the next night, but there had been something romantic about the idea. "So where did my panties go? And why did I feel so . . . aware down there?" That seemed a rather puzzling mystery to her.

But Johnny didn't seem to think anything of it. He gave her a big grin. "You rode the mechanical bull at the Bourbon Cowboy. I saw the pictures. I'm guessing that might have had some impact on your girl parts. I'm sorry, I can't account for your underwear."

"What? Bull riding?" Lizette started up the marble stairs, her shoes echoing loudly as she walked rapidly. Of course, she couldn't stomp her way past her actions. "I'll have to see that to believe it. So did you find out who drugged the punch? It was the punch, yes?"

He nodded, keeping up with her on the steps. In a minute they were in front of her apartment. "It wasn't the Chers, like Drake suspected. It was Ashley, Josie Lynn's catering help."

"Really? Well, I have to admit I'm glad to hear the cross-dressers weren't involved. They seemed so helpful in the bar, and I rather liked their style. But why on earth would she drug a punch at a wedding reception?"

"It turns out she is the daughter of another cross-dresser who has lost business to the Chers in the last few years, so her plan was to roll the wedding and frame the Chers to give her father a leg up. Though one of the Chers did make off with Zelda's wedding dress. So basically it was like an entire night lost because of a catfight over clothes and stage time. Totally insane."

That was insane. "I am speechless." Lizette led him into her apartment, which was a typical Parisian place, with a small living area and an even smaller bedroom. "Make yourself comfortable." She still felt nervous, like what happened in the next few minutes could determine the course of her immediate future.

"This is a nice place," he said, sitting down on her sofa. "Have you been here long?"

"Ten years. Probably in the foreseeable future I'll have to move. My neighbor has been here the whole time and she is starting to ask me how I keep my youthful appearance." Which was a shame. She loved this apartment. She sat down next to him because she wanted to be close enough to touch, to read his eyes.

"It looks like you. It feels elegant and cozy all at the same time."

"I have to confess something to you," she blurted. "There is a reason why I am so committed to the VA and to our secrecy as a species."

"Why is that?" He sounded genuinely curious. "What happened to you? Beyond your family being killed, that is. It seems like there's something you're not telling me."

Lizette swallowed hard and studied her manicure. This was important. She needed to share the whole truth. "I want to tell you about Jean-Baptiste."

HOLY FUCK, WAS she serious? He'd flown halfway around the world and she wanted to tell him about her dead boyfriend? He literally wanted to talk about anything but that dude. They could even not talk at all and that would be preferable. But he forced himself to remain nonchalant and just say, "Yeah?"

Lizette kicked off her heels and tucked her slim legs under her skirt in a move that he found wildly distracting and really sexy. Okay, she could talk about the dead guy.

"You see, we had a solid relationship, but as I said, we were not without our issues. But I was committed to him and assumed we would have a future. But during the late nineteenth century, when medical schools were getting so heavily into dissections, you know there was a lot of grave robbing and whatnot going on, yes?"

"I can't say I'm really familiar with the time period, since I was born at the end of the century, but I can see how that would happen." Just a little before his time.

"Due to advances in science and anatomy, the human body was considered essential to the study of young medical students, and they were willing to look the other way as to how bodies were acquired. It was a booming business. Jean-Baptiste was stolen from his coffin in the catacombs on the assumption that he was a corpse."

That was more than a little fucked-up.

"But of course what happened was that when they dissected him, he woke up. Since it was daytime, he was disoriented, I presume, and they were able to secure him to their operating table and watch as he healed. So they dissected again. Again he healed." Lizette swallowed hard. "I witnessed a good deal of this as I followed the carriage in the hopes of rescuing him."

Shit. That was why she was so afraid of being caught. She'd seen the consequences. Johnny felt like a complete jerk-off. He reached out and took her hand, which she had clenched into a fist on her knee.

"But they never left him, and I couldn't see how to get him out of the restraints and help him move when it would take all my strength to protect myself from getting caught. So I watched his torture. It went on for hours and hours and he was awake for the entirety." Lizette stared at him with glassy eyes. "I will hear his screams of agony forever."

"That's horrible," he said, because there were no words adequate enough to express his sympathy and disgust. "I'm so sorry."

"Finally, after they posed for photos with his bleeding body, skin peeled back from all his bones, head scalped, nails driven through his hands to see what the result would be, they went out for a pint to celebrate their real-live Frankenstein. It was my plan to release him then. But Jean-Baptiste begged me to merely kill him. He didn't think he would survive anyway, and I would only be slowed down and putting myself at risk." She shook her head. "I couldn't do it. How could I?"

"Holy shit, baby . . ." Johnny was speechless. She shouldn't have had to make that kind of choice.

"But then one of them came back because he had forgotten his hat, and I knocked him unconscious. I knew I had to kill Jean-Baptiste then, so . . ." Lizette took several deep breaths. "So I did."

Johnny took her hand and stroked her cool skin gently. He spoke softly, awed by her strength, her tenacity for the last several hundred years. "I'm so sorry. I can't imagine what that was like for you. I understand completely why you feel the way you do."

"Thank you. It is important to me that you understand, because I do care about it. I do wish to live a life that is more spontaneous, but without unnecessarily risking my own safety or that of those I care about." Tears glistened in her eyes, true vampire tears of blood and pain. "I do not want anything bad to happen to you."

"It won't," Johnny assured her, humbled and experiencing a deeper sense of admiration for her than any woman he had ever met. This was what Stella and Wyatt were talking about. There was no urge to run, no need to fear commitment, when you had such a deep, impenetrable respect for the person you were with. "I am going to lie low for a while, and fix things with Benny and

Raven. I've got some growing up to do, and if you're okay with it, I'd like to do that here, in Paris. With you."

That was throwing it all out there. She might laugh, reject him in two seconds flat, or feel sorry for him. But you know what? He had flown halfway across the world, so he might as well go for broke. He may be maturing, but he was always going to be a risk-taker.

"I think that perhaps I would enjoy that," she said.

Oh, so French. She wasn't about to gush on him or squeal with delight. But Johnny could see it there, in her eyes. She was both excited and relieved. Just like he was. "Is there room in your pint-sized Paris apartment for an Irish drummer or should I find myself a hotel?"

Lizette gave him a smile that reminded him, discreet or not, the French were the inventors of some of the world's greatest love acts, starting with kissing with tongue and ending with the ménage. It was in her blood, and he wanted a bite of her.

"Oh, there is definitely room here for you. Shall I model some of the garments you were so kind to bring for me? Or should I start with the oral sex I would like to give you?"

Um. The choices boggled the mind, but he'd be a fool not to go for broke. "I'll take door number two if you're down with it." He kissed her. "And thank you, by the way. For being so amazing, for being so you. I think we're going to have some serious fun over the next few months."

"I couldn't agree more." Lizette bent over and unzipped his jeans.

Then Johnny discovered what the meaning of eternity really was as her head descending at an agonizingly slow pace.

But it was worth the wait.

Chapter Eighteen

I DON'T WANT TO LOSE YOUR LOVE TONIGHT

DRAKE played the guitar solo of "Talk Dirty to Me" like he had exactly seventeen times since the night Josie Lynn had disappeared. He'd played "Sweet Home Alabama" fifteen times. "Long Train Running" fifteen, too. "Jessie's Girl" eighteen times, because they always got more than one request for that one in any given night. And he'd played "Your Love" nineteen times, because that one was also a fan favorite. Which never really made any sense to him, since the band had really only been a one-hit wonder, and if you asked anyone if they knew The Outfield, the band that originally performed it, most people would probably say no.

Until Cort started to sing that first line, "Josie's on a vacation far away . . ." and the crowd roared in recognition night after night.

Drake had tried to pretend that was all it was. Josie was gone on vacation and she'd be back any day now. And unlike the song, he had no interest in hooking up with some other woman in her absence. Truth be told, he didn't have much interest in anything.

The bar was pretty quiet tonight and even a Poison song couldn't pull the crowd in if there was no crowd. It was a Sunday and hot as hell. Most smart people were staying in places that had efficient air-conditioning, unlike this place. Of course, heat and cold didn't affect him. Because he was a freakin' vampire.

There had been plenty of times over the decades he'd wished he were still human. But none more so than now. He wished he could go find Josie Lynn as a simple man and tell her he loved her and he'd grow old with her. He knew that was all she wanted. A man she could trust and love.

Instead she'd met the ultimate bad boy. Her worst nightmare.

And what had he really been thinking anyway? That he'd eventually tell her and she'd just say, "Oh, you're a creature of the night. Groovy."

The band finished up the Poison song, and Cort announced they were going to take a short break.

"You were behind on that whole song," Cort said as he walked past him.

Drake yanked the plug out of his guitar and glared at his friend. "Maybe it wasn't me. Maybe it was that idiot on drums."

Cort raised his hands to show he didn't want to fight. "I'm not making an issue about it. I'm just letting you know, that's all. I know your head hasn't been in the music lately. And I get it. But don't blame Benny because your heart is in shreds. He may not exactly be a genius but he's adequate, and you know we needed to do something to guarantee he keeps quiet about our special blood-drinking habit. So don't piss him off."

Cort's words irritated Drake even more. It was bad enough his heart was in shreds, he didn't need everyone knowing it. He set his guitar on the stand with more force than necessary—honestly, with more force than he would have ever used before this funk. His guitars used to be his babies. They used to be enough.

Oh shit, he was turning into one of those musicians who thought of their guitars as women. Or compared them to women.

This sucked.

"Dude, you okay?"

Oh no. He couldn't take this again. What was coming now was even worse than Cort and the other band guys' sympathy.

"I'm really sorry, Drake. I should have thought before I spoke, man. But you know how I am." Saxon gave him one of his puppy-dog looks.

Saxon had tried to apologize at least a dozen times and in a dozen different ways since Josie Lynn had taken off, and while Drake appreciated that his friend regretted what happened, he couldn't take any more acts of contrition. He felt shitty enough without worrying about Saxon feeling shitty, too.

"Listen, Saxon, it is what it is. I'll get over it, but honestly I don't want to talk about it or her. It isn't helping."

Saxon nodded, then his eyes widened and he opened his mouth, and Drake knew more words of regret were coming, despite what Drake had just said.

"Seriously, Saxon, I can't take any more of your apologies. I know you are sorry. Enough said about it."

"But—"

"No," Drake said, shaking his head. "I don't want to hear it. Please."

"But really," Saxon said, the woeful puppy-dog look gone. Now he was grinning. From ear to ear. "You're gonna wanna hear this."

Drake stared at him, wondering why he was even questioning his odd little friend's behavior. Saxon was nothing if not odd.

"Really. You are going to want to hear what I have to say."

Drake sighed. Clearly he was going to have to suffer through another explanation so he could finally just go get a shot and hopefully numb himself a little.

"Josie Lynn is here."

Drake stared at Saxon, not understanding. How was this an apology? In fact, this was the worst—and perhaps cruelest—attempt to help yet.

"Alright, Saxon, thanks for trying to cheer me up. In your own weird way."

"No, man, for real." Saxon pointed past him.

Drake turned, still expecting this to be another of Saxon's cockamamie ways of trying to help. But then he froze.

Josie Lynn stood near the doorway, looking a little nervous. Looking absolutely gorgeous.

He blinked, sure he must be imagining her. It had been almost three weeks. He'd given up on the idea of seeing her ever again. But there she was.

Her gaze met his and even through in the hazy, dimly lit bar, he could see how amazingly blue her eyes were. Her hair was loose, framing her face in waves of golden honey.

He didn't realize he was walking down from the stage and going to her until he was only a foot away. Close enough to touch. To kiss.

"Hi," was all he could think to say. His brain mush.

"Hi," she said back.

"I—I've . . ."

What the hell did he say? He didn't know. He considered himself a pretty clever, articulate guy, but nothing came to him. Nothing that would be good enough to make her stay.

"So rumor has it you're a vampire. Is that true, or are you and your friends all nuts?"

He stared at her, then cleared his throat nervously. Neither answer was a good one. Neither answer was going to get her to stay. But he wasn't going to lie to her. Not like the other men she'd been with.

"I'm a vampire."

She nodded, not looking particularly surprised. Nor did she look like she planned to run.

"I thought that was probably the case."

Wow, she was taking this way too well.

"So why aren't you running in terror?"

She tilted her head, considering his question. "Because I've had time to think about it. And because you said I could trust you. And because I figured if you really wanted to hurt me, you had ample opportunity, both the night we blacked out and the night after."

"True."

She nodded, and he was afraid this was all she'd come for, to validate the truth, and he couldn't let her leave.

"I've—I've missed you." Okay, that sounded kind of lame, but it was out and he wasn't stopping. He wasn't giving her the opportunity to leave. Not yet. "I've thought about you every day—well, you know, every night. I've wanted to try to contact you."

"But you did contact me," she said, and reached into the purse and pulled out an envelope. He knew exactly what it was. He'd sent her an anonymous letter with cash in it. Because he knew she needed help with her business. Because he knew she wouldn't accept his help unless she didn't know it was from him.

But she did know.

"You figured out where I lived," she said. "You could have come to see me anytime, yet you didn't. Why?"

"Because I didn't want to scare you," he said simply.

She nodded again, and then to his utter shock, she stepped forward and kissed him. He wanted to pull her against him, he wanted to deepen the kiss and let her see all his longing for her. But he didn't dare.

"I've missed you, too," she said against his lips.

"Even though I'm a monster," he whispered.

She smiled up at him, shaking her head. "You are not a monster. You are the only man I've ever known that I could trust one hundred percent."

"How do you know that?" he asked, even though it was absolutely true.

"Because you believed me. You protected me." She lifted the envelope again. "You wanted to help me. You let me go because you knew I had to figure all this out. And most of all, because when I look in your eyes, I can see you love me."

He groaned. "God, I do. I love you."

He pulled her against him and kissed her hard this time. "Is it possible to love someone this much after just one night?"

She grinned up at him. "I don't know, you tell me. You've lived a lot longer than I have."

"All I know is in all those years, I've never felt this way about anyone."

"And I know I don't have as many years as you, but I've never felt this way about anyone either."

They gazed at each other a moment longer, then kissed like they were the only ones in the room. But alas they weren't, and soon Drake felt a thump on his back.

"Hey, it looks like we won't be forced to be ancient bachelors together after all, huh?" Johnny grinned at Drake, fresh off the plane from Paris. He loosely held Lizette's hand, happy to be back in his adopted hometown even if it was only for a week to pack up his apartment.

"Thank God for that," Drake said, smiling as he stuck out his hand to shake it. "Welcome home, bro."

"At least it didn't take a wake this time to spawn true love," Stella said joining them, giving her brother a pointed look.

"Well, it kind of did," Johnny said, giving Lizette an affectionate smile. She was wearing her hair down loose and he thought she was the most gorgeous woman on earth. "My fake death made this all happen."

"Don't say that with such pride," Lizette said in admonishment, laughing. "It was still a terrible thing to do."

"Yeah, that was like so rude," Saxon said appearing in the group. "Unlike my wedding, which was beautiful."

Yep. Saxon was still smoking the wacky weed if he thought that debacle could be classified as beautiful. But, Johnny couldn't argue that it had played a role in bringing him and Lizette, and certainly Drake and Josie Lynn, together.

The ever-sweet Katie said, "Maybe it was just meant to be." She leaned into Cort's side, smiling up at him. He kissed her.

"I think you are all wrong," said Benny, twirling his drumsticks like he was an overenthusiastic majorette. "I think it takes blacking out and getting one helluva hangover."

None of them could argue that.